DEAD MAN WALKING

DEAD MAN WALKING

Simon R. Green

This first world edition published 2016
in Great Britain and the USA by
SEVERN HOUSE PUBLISHERS LTD of
19 Cedar Road, Sutton, Surrey, England, SM2 5DA.
Trade paperback edition first published
in Great Britain and the USA 2016 by
SEVERN HOUSE PUBLISHERS LTD

Copyright © 2016 by Simon R. Green.

British Library Cataloguing in Publication Data
A CIP catalogue record for this title is available from the British Library.

ISBN-13: 978-0-7278-8623-1 (cased)
ISBN-13: 978-1-84751-725-8 (trade paper)
ISBN-13: 978-1-78010-786-8 (e-book)

All Severn House titles are printed on acid-free paper.

Severn House Publishers support the Forest Stewardship Council™ [FSC™],
the leading international forest certification organisation.
All our titles that are printed on FSC certified paper carry the FSC logo.

Typeset by Palimpsest Book Production Ltd.,
Falkirk, Stirlingshire, Scotland.
Printed and bound in Great Britain by
TJ International, Padstow, Cornwall.

*C*all me Ishmael. Ishmael Jones.

    I am the monster who hunts monsters. The man in the shadows that even the shadows are afraid of. The secret agent whose life is the greatest secret of all. And some of the cases I work on are trickier than others.

Even secret agents feel the need to raise their heads above the parapet sometimes. And so we emerge from the shadows just long enough to sniff the air, take a meeting, drop off information; or put the hard word on someone who's been showing too much interest in something they shouldn't. London has always been the favoured meeting place for spies of all kinds. Ever since Christopher Marlowe (who knew Faust personally) took his orders from Dr Dee (who spoke with angels on a regular basis) as part of Queen Elizabeth I's intelligence network, London has been both a sanctuary and a feeding ground for all those people who aren't supposed to exist. Drifting quietly down streets with no name, we slip discreetly into crowded bars or private back rooms, to discuss the matters and make the deals that shape the fate of nations. We come and we go and you never see us; because you don't need to know the kind of things we have to do, so you can sleep easily in your beds.

There is a world beneath the world; a hidden place of secrets and lies, deception and double-dealing, masquerade and murder. Where people you've never heard of work for departments that don't officially exist, doing things that no one will ever admit to. It can be a fascinating life if you don't weaken, but it's not for the faint of heart.

ONE
Food for Thought

I t was a surprisingly sunny day in mid-Autumn when I first heard that the prodigal son wanted to come in from the cold. I was sitting in a pizza parlour on Oxford Street, happily working my way through a deep-dish meat-feast that was supposed to serve two, while waiting for my contact to show up. All around me, the tables were crowded, the noise levels were satisfyingly high and, because it was after all the middle of London, I could make out half a dozen different languages adding to the protective babble. When the world thinks you don't exist, and you want to keep it that way, you learn to be very careful about where you show your face. Fast-food outlets are always a good place to hide in plain sight. Where people are always coming and going, and any number of conversations can take place without fear of being overheard. And as long as you don't tip too little or too big, even the waiter won't remember you.

I'd chosen a table at the rear, with my back to the wall; so I could be sure of getting a good look at everyone else. The price of freedom is eternal vigilance and a healthy dose of paranoia. My chair was set far enough back from the table that I could be sure of getting to my feet in a hurry without my legs getting trapped; and I'd already worked out six different ways to quietly disappear, should it prove necessary. One of the disadvantages of living in my world is that you can never relax when you're out in public. You always have to be prepared for enemy action.

The Colonel slipped in off the street with an easy grace and stood for a moment just inside the doors, so he could look the place over. Like a predator checking out the possibilities at a new watering hole. This haughty-looking individual was a new Colonel, the old one having been murdered last year. I caught his killer and avenged his death, but that didn't bring him back. The Colonel is the middleman, the go-between, the overseer and case officer for all his very special agents. I have no idea what his real name might be; but then he doesn't know mine.

If the Colonel is a mystery, the Organization we both work for is a myth, an urban legend of the hidden world; the people who move behind the scenery, making the decisions that really matter. I have no idea who or what they might be, but as long as they preserve my anonymity and provide me with work worth doing, I'm happy enough to go along.

The new Colonel was a tall and elegant presence in his mid-thirties, dressed in the finest three-piece business suit Savile Row had to offer. Which should have made him stand out in such an everyday setting; but he was wrapped in so much unselfconscious authority no one wanted to look at him for fear of attracting his attention. In his own way, he was as invisible as I was. Almost certainly ex-military, given his bearing, and handsome enough in a supercilious sort of way. He looked the pizza parlour over as though he'd never set foot in such an establishment before and now, having done so, was convinced he'd been right all along.

His stern gaze finally picked me out of the crowd, and he strode through the packed tables with a magnificent disdain for one and all. A waiter tried to distract him with a brandished menu, so he could direct the Colonel to a table in his area; only to wither and fall back under the Colonel's icy stare. The great man finally slammed to a halt in front of me, and I made a point of ignoring him as I concentrated on my pizza.

'Next time,' said the Colonel, in his best clipped and businesslike tones, 'I will chose the setting for our meeting.'

'No you won't,' I said, looking up to fix him with my best cold stare. 'You can call me any time and I'll answer, because that's the deal I made when I joined the Organization. But I decide when and where I appear in public. I wouldn't feel safe in any place you'd feel comfortable.'

The Colonel indulged himself with another small sigh. 'Did you lecture my predecessor like this?'

'I didn't need to,' I said. 'We respected each other. Tell me, why are you always the Colonel? Did I join the army and nobody told me?'

'I really couldn't say.'

'And people wonder why I have trust issues. Would you care to order something? So you won't look entirely out of place?'

'I think not,' said the Colonel. 'I shall be dining at my club later.'

'You won't get food like this there.'

'Exactly. Now let me explain why you're here.'

'Does it have something to do with Mummy and Daddy and a very special hug?'

'I understand the old Colonel was prepared to indulge your general impertinence and lack of respect,' he said heavily. 'I, on the other hand, am famous for my complete lack of a sense of humour when it comes to such things.'

I smiled at him, not entirely unkindly. 'Unclench, Colonel. You'll last longer. Trust me, I've been doing this a lot longer than you.'

'Since 1963, to be exact,' said the Colonel. 'You don't look your age, Mr Jones.'

'You don't know my age,' I said.

'I've read your file,' said the Colonel. 'It didn't take me long, because there isn't much in it. No personal details, no background, no photos . . . Just a list of the cases you've worked on, and their outcome. Who are you, Ishmael Jones?'

'Wrong question,' I said.

'What is the right question?'

'You see,' I said. 'You knew it all along.'

He studied me for a long moment, as though he believed he could see right through my defences if he just tried hard enough.

'All our agents are assured their anonymity, but you take your privacy to extremes. How are we to protect you from your enemies, if we don't know who and what we're protecting?'

'No questions,' I said. 'That was the deal I made when I joined.'

He sighed, just a little dramatically. 'In an organization that exists to deal with mysteries, you seem determined to be the biggest mystery of them all.'

'Is someone planning to deal with me?' I said.

'Not while you can still be useful. But if you continue to insist on keeping things from us . . .'

'I'm not the only one,' I said. 'Unless you're suddenly prepared to tell me your real name?'

'After you, Mr Jones.'

I didn't quite laugh in his face. 'I don't even know who it really is I'm working for.'

'Which is as it should be.'

'Do you know?'

'I doubt it,' said the Colonel.

'What do you want with me?' I said. 'What could be so important that I had to drop everything just to sit down with you? What could be so secret you couldn't even bring yourself to hint at it over the phone? A phone, I might remind you, that was given to me by the Organization. Along with a firm assurance that God herself would have a hard time listening in.'

'Frank Parker wants to come home,' said the Colonel.

And that stopped me dead in my tracks. I knew that name. Everyone in our line of business did. Parker used to be one of the Organization's most respected field agents. I never met the man; but it's inevitable that people like us will hang out with people like us. And over a drink or three it's inevitable that we will end up exchanging gossip, and trying to outdo each other with strange tales and weird adventures. Because only we can talk openly about the kind of things we do.

Frank Parker spent more than twenty years operating in the wilder areas of the hidden world. Taking down people, and things that only pretended to be people, to protect Humanity and keep the world safe. As a reward, he was given all the most important and dangerous cases. Because Parker was the Organization's blue-eyed boy; their foremost troubleshooter, destined for great things. Back in the day, you could frighten a whole room full of really bad people just by dropping his name.

And then he went rogue. Just dropped out of sight one day; and the next thing anyone knew, he was working for everyone except the Organization. Doing bad things for bad people, for really good money.

I sat back in my chair, ignoring my meal. I wasn't hungry any more.

'So Frank Parker has reappeared,' I said. 'What do you want me to do? Organize a whip-round for his coming-home party?'

'Hardly,' said the Colonel.

'Did he ever betray any of his fellow agents?' I said.

'No,' said the Colonel. 'He never did . . . Even though the pressure on him to do so must have been immense.'

'So he didn't leave because he was mad at the Organization,' I said. 'He just wanted out. Interesting . . .'

'Irrelevant,' said the Colonel.

'Not from where I'm sitting,' I said.

'After several years of working for the opposition, Parker disappeared again,' said the Colonel. 'No one could find him, even though some very highly motivated people spent a lot of time looking. Most of us thought he was dead and that we could all relax at last. But just twelve hours ago Parker reached out to us.'

I didn't ask how. The Colonel wouldn't tell me.

'Did he say where he'd been, all these years he's been missing?'

'No. Just that he wanted to come home, as soon as possible.'

'Does the Organization want him back?'

'He says he's ready to dish the dirt on everyone he ever worked for. Tell us everything he ever did for them. In return for having all his sins forgiven, and a new identity to retire behind.'

'And you couldn't afford to miss out on a deal like that,' I said.

'A chance to bury so many of our worst enemies, and put right some of the damage he did when he left? Oh yes, Mr Jones, we want to know everything Frank Parker knows.'

'Even if it does sound a little too good to be true?' I said carefully.

'Exactly,' said the Colonel. 'Always look a gift horse in the mouth, because it might have a small army tucked away inside it. Parker is currently installed at Ringstone Lodge.'

I didn't let anything show in my face. I'd heard of the Lodge, and not in a good way. An isolated and extremely secure interrogation centre; for defecting agents, suspected traitors, and anyone who knew things the Organization wanted to know. Ringstone Lodge, where the truth will out. One way or another.

'I love a good gossip as much as any other agent,' I said. 'But I have to ask, why are you telling me this, Colonel?'

'Because we need to be sure whether the man we have really is Frank Parker,' said the Colonel. 'Extensive and repeated plastic surgeries have made him unrecognizable. And since we have no physical records on file, it's hard to be sure just who it is we've got. And we need to be certain before we can trust any of the information he gives us.'

'What has this got to do with me?' I said. 'I never even met the man.'

'We're limiting the number of people with direct access,' said the Colonel. 'Because Parker, if he really is Parker, claims to have solid information about bad apples within the Organization. Not just from his time; but right now.'

I looked at him for a long moment. 'And you think that's possible?'

'People above me do. We need a field agent to join the interrogation team at Ringstone Lodge. Because only another agent would have the necessary experience to ask the right questions and evaluate the answers.'

'You need to know whether he's a ringer.'

'Exactly. So, off you go to Ringstone Lodge. Two very experienced interrogators are already in place; they'll do all the heavy lifting. Technically you'll be in charge, but don't push it.'

'Have there been any attempts to get to Parker since his return?' I said. 'To silence him, before he can name names?'

'Not so far. But if there are traitors within the Organization, we can't be sure how long his location will remain secret. The Lodge has first-rate security protections in place, but . . .'

'Yes,' I said. 'But . . . How long can you give me before I have to make a decision?'

'Forty-eight hours. After that, word will get out and the opposition will start taking steps to limit the damage his information could do.'

'So,' I said. 'No pressure, then.' I sat up straight in my chair as a thought struck me. 'I take it I do have the Organization's assurance that no one at the Lodge will start asking me awkward questions?'

The Colonel smiled briefly. 'I can understand how someone with your privacy issues, and such an inflated sense of your own importance, might well be reluctant to see the inside of Ringstone Lodge. But don't flatter yourself, Mr Jones, we're really not that interested in your no doubt murky background. Unless, of course, there's something you're not telling us . . .'

'More than you could possibly imagine,' I said.

'Only guilty people need to keep their lives secret,' said the Colonel.

'And that attitude is exactly why I take such pains to guard my privacy,' I said. 'I serve the Organization and in return they hide me from the world. That is the beginning and end of our relationship. The moment you do anything to threaten that, I am out the door and in the wind. And you can explain to your lords and masters how you lost them one of their best field agents.'

'You really think you can just disappear these days?' said the Colonel. 'Constant surveillance has made it a much smaller world. You have no idea how much effort goes into hiding you and your fellow agents.'

'Parker managed,' I said.

I looked expectantly at the Colonel. Normally, this would be when he handed over the briefing file for the mission. He looked steadily back at me.

'There is no file on this case,' the Colonel said carefully. 'And there isn't going to be one. No official record, nothing in writing, no paper trail. Because if there are traitors operating inside the Organization, they can't be allowed to know that Frank Parker is threatening to reveal their identities. There is no mission. I am not here talking to you. The only people who know about Frank Parker are those who've had direct contact with him, who are currently enjoying a nice holiday somewhere very secure in complete isolation; and those at the very top who give me my orders. And that's the way it's going to stay.'

'So the left hand doesn't know who the right hand's interrogating?' I said.

'Officially,' said the Colonel, 'no one knows Parker is being held at Ringstone Lodge. There are no records of his arrival in this country, and everyone at the Lodge has been brought in specially from outside the Organization just for this particular operation. All the security, interrogation and support staff have been sequestered from the Ministry of Defence. They don't know what we want their people for, and they know better than to ask.

'All of these individuals have worked with us before and have proper Organization clearance. They'll tell you everything you need to know, once you get to the Lodge. But let me be very clear: you are not to contact me until you have made a decision as to whether or not this potential gold mine really is Frank Parker. And whether the information he is offering is worth anything. I will take it from there. Parker will then be sent on somewhere else, the Lodge people will be dismissed, and you will be free to return to wherever you consider home.'

'Fair enough,' I said. I looked at him thoughtfully. 'You've made it clear you don't approve of me, or my methods. So why haven't you argued for one of your other agents to work this mission?'

'You were selected at the very highest level,' said the Colonel. 'Because you are our most secretive agent, who has always maintained the greatest distance between yourself and the rest of the Organization. You are therefore the least likely to be involved with any of our possible traitors.'

'And, of course, if anything should go wrong I will be the easiest to blame and throw to the wolves. Because absolutely no one is in my corner.'

'I knew you'd understand,' said the Colonel.

'Is that it?' I said.

'One last matter,' said the Colonel. 'We understand you prefer to work with a partner these days. Penny Belcourt.'

'Yes,' I said. 'The one person I can trust to watch my back and not stick a knife in it.'

'You are expected to ensure her silence on all relevant matters,' said the Colonel. 'Or we will.'

He rose to his feet. He took his time doing so, to make it clear leaving was entirely his idea. 'You have your assignment. I don't expect to hear from you again until you've decided about Parker. Now I really must be on my way. Civilized food and a decent wine list await.' He paused, to give me one last significant look. 'I will find out the truth about you, Ishmael Jones.'

'If you do, let me know,' I said. 'I've been wondering for years.'

He turned his back on me and strode out, waitresses scattering before him like startled birds. I felt under pressure to prove myself to this new Colonel; even though, with my experience and proven success rate, I shouldn't have needed to. But like everyone else in this world, the Organization runs on 'What have you done for us recently?'.

And I still couldn't shake off the uneasy feeling that this might all be some kind of trap, designed to lure me inside Ringstone Lodge and then lock the door behind me.

Penny came bustling over from the next table and dropped into the chair the Colonel had just vacated. She grinned cheerfully at me and I smiled back at her. A striking presence in her mid-twenties, Penny Belcourt had a pretty face with a strong bone structure and a mass of dark hair piled up on top of her head. Along with flashing eyes, dramatic make-up, a pleasantly trim figure, and enough nervous energy to run a funfair for a month. She nodded dismissively after the departing Colonel.

'Told you he'd never know I was here. He was so busy being important I could have danced the Time Warp on top of the table and he wouldn't have noticed. Are you going to eat all of that?'

She tore a slice off my pizza with one hand and crammed as much as she could into her mouth, rolling her eyes and making exaggerated noises of contentment.

'I wish you wouldn't do that,' I said. 'If you want something, just order from the menu. I'm good for it.'

'I only wanted a taste,' said Penny, indistinctly. 'It's a big pizza. You can spare some.'

'That's not the point,' I said.

'It's good to share,' Penny said firmly. 'Also, very human. You should have learned that by now.'

'I have been living among you since 1963,' I said.

'Among isn't the same as being,' she said crushingly. 'You're still an outsider in many ways. That's why you need me.'

'That's not the only reason I need you,' I said.

She smiled. 'You are a sweetie.'

Penny had been my unofficial partner since I saved her life from the unnatural thing that killed the rest of her family at Belcourt Manor. She'd inherited a small fortune, which meant she was free to help me out as and when. We loved each other, as much as two people can when one of them isn't entirely human. Penny helped to keep me grounded, and provide the human touch I still sometimes lack. I've been a part of human society for over fifty years, but I often think I'm no nearer understanding people. Penny assures me there are a lot of people who also feel the same way.

'Is this going to be a real case, at last?' said Penny.

'They're all real cases,' I said. 'Information gathering may not be sexy, but it's not always about monsters.'

'But the monsters are real, in your world.'

'Yes,' I said. 'They are.'

'Where are you staying now?' she asked artlessly.

'Just another small hotel,' I said. 'You wouldn't recognize the name if I told you.'

'I want to be with you.'

'I am with you as much as I dare. I have to keep moving; because I can't afford to be noticed, to make ripples on the surface of the world. There's a reason why I've survived all these years, in this very suspicious world.'

'I thought the Organization protected you!'

'They clean up after me, on the few occasions when I do get noticed. But I haven't stayed hidden this long by relying on the kindness of strange organizations.'

'I want to spend more time with you,' said Penny. 'Just the two of us. All this dodging around makes me feel I'm just visiting your world.'

'I spend as much time with you as I can,' I said. 'Any more could endanger you, as well as me.'

We held hands across the table, reaching out to each other across a divide greater than she could understand. Then Penny shrugged and changed the subject. She's always been good at that when she realizes she's losing an argument.

'This hidden world of yours is absolutely fascinating! I've been doing all kinds of research, and have dug up some amazing stories.'

'You can't trust everything you read on the Internet,' I said. 'A lot of it is put there by groups like the Organization, as disinformation. To steer people away from the really nasty stuff. For their own protection.'

'So how much of it is true?' said Penny.

'Everything you wish wasn't.'

'When are we going to get a proper case?' said Penny. 'I want to fight monsters and save the world. I can do it, I'm spy girl!'

'You could say this case has a monster in it,' I said. 'Frank Parker has more blood on his hands than any one man should have to account for.'

Penny frowned. 'I thought you said you never met him?'

'I know about him. Secret agents gossip like schoolgirls. Just because they know they shouldn't. Parker made his reputation by being able to break into anywhere, steal anything, and be gone before anyone even knew he was there. He also killed a lot of people who needed killing, to make the world a better place. But after he left the Organization he killed a great many more, just because someone put a price on their head. Of course, how much of this is reputation and how much is true is hard to tell. In our game, everybody lies.'

'How good was Parker when it came to the monsters?' said Penny.

'He killed his fair share,' I said.

'Why did Parker quit?' Penny asked. 'What could make him walk away from a job he was so good at? Did something happen? Something must have happened.'

'Presumably,' I said. 'But no one knows what. The only weird thing about Parker, that made him stand out from all the other agents, was that he was supposed to be unkillable. There are all kinds of stories about him surviving being shot at close range or thrown from a great height. He's walked away from plane crashes, explosions and impossible odds.'

'Could he be . . . different, like you?' said Penny.

'Not as far as I know,' I said. 'But if he was as good at hiding his true nature as I am and something happened to threaten that . . . No wonder he just abandoned his old life and ran. And only worked for money after that, to make sure no one would ever get close again.'

'There must be someone in the Organization he worked with who could identify him!'

'Field agents mostly work alone,' I said. 'It's safer that way. Our only contact with the Organization is through the Colonel. And the Colonel who gave Parker his orders has been dead for some time now.'

'Is it really going to be that difficult to decide whether or not it's actually him?'

'Parker's changed his face so many times, he could be anyone.'

'You never changed your face,' said Penny.

'I really should,' I said. 'But my face is one of the few things I have left from the old days.'

'Have you ever met anyone higher up than the Colonel?' asked Penny, wriggling excitedly on her seat as a thought struck her.

'No,' I said. 'And I don't want to. The last thing I need is the people in charge taking a special interest in me.'

'Then how can you be sure there actually is an Organization?' Penny said triumphantly. 'I mean, what if it's all just one big bluff?'

'I really don't care,' I said. 'They're powerful enough to hide me from the world's curious gaze. Nothing else matters.'

Penny sat back in her chair and studied me for a long moment. 'You really don't want to go to this Ringstone Lodge, do you? Is it really that bad a place?'

'It could be very bad for me.'

'But you're still going.'

'Of course. It's the job. And because if this is the real Frank Parker, I want to know why he quit. What he found out about the Organization . . . Perhaps when he tells me why he had to leave in such a hurry, I'll want to run too.'

'You are a very suspicious person, Ishmael.'

I looked at the remains of my pizza and pushed it away. I had no appetite left.

'I don't think you should go with me, Penny. This could turn out to be a very unpleasant case.'

She gave me a hard look. 'All the more reason to have someone there you know you can trust.'

'I did manage to survive without you for a great many years.'

'There's more to life than surviving,' said Penny. And she smiled dazzlingly at me, until I smiled back. 'How long before we have to set off for the Lodge? Is there time for dessert?'

'There's always time for dessert,' I said.

Penny clapped her hands together delightedly. 'You do know what to say to a girl!' She picked up the menu and studied it carefully. Before asking, quite casually, 'Is there anything unusual about Ringstone Lodge?'

'It has a reputation for being haunted.'

She stared at me over the top of the menu, her eyes big. 'Really?'

'So they say. The Lodge encourages such stories to help keep people away.'

'Do you think we'll get to see any spooks and spectres?'

'I doubt it. I don't believe in ghosts.'

Penny slammed the menu down on the table and stared at me accusingly.

'You? Of all people?'

'I may walk through the hidden world on a regular basis, but what I find there is still real,' I said. 'And solid enough for me to lay my hands on, when necessary. Just because some weird things are real, that doesn't mean all of them are.'

TWO
Questions, Questions

When some agents know they're heading into dangerous territory, they like to go loaded for bear. Heavily armed bears, wearing Kevlar. I prefer to avoid guns. Specific weapons can limit your responses and I like to leave myself room to improvise. And to be fair, I am nearly always going to be the most dangerous person in the room.

But none of the usual rules apply to Ringstone Lodge.

The Lodge can be found in the North Riding of Yorkshire. About as far north as you can go before you bang your head on Hadrian's Wall. Beautiful countryside, wild and free; easy on the eye, but hard on the heart. You have to work to make a living out of that cold ground. The North Country is old and heavy with history. And what secrets it has, it holds close to its chest.

Ringstone Lodge stands alone, miles from anywhere. So no one can hear you scream.

In the end, I decided to take the train. It would have been a really long drive, and I didn't want to arrive at the Lodge exhausted and running on fumes. I was pretty sure I'd need all my wits about me when I came face to face with the seekers after truth. I sent Penny home to pack while I stopped off at one of my safe houses to pick up a few essentials, and we met up an hour later at King's Cross Station. I like King's Cross, you can always be sure of any amount of noise and bustle to hide yourself in. I arrived with just a backpack, because I have always believed in travel light, travel fast. It's a battered old thing that's seen a lot of use, with colours so faded it's become as anonymous as me. Never carry anything you're not prepared to leave behind in an emergency. I once had to bolt down the backstairs of a well-known hotel wearing nothing but my socks, plus my backpack with a stolen laptop in it.

Penny had taken the time to dress in a whole new outfit: a dark blue jacket over a gleaming white blouse, a dark skirt over dark stockings, high heels and a really big hat. I looked her over thoughtfully, as she stood poised and smiling before me.

'Why?' I said finally.

'Because we're going to be meeting people, darling. Important people. Dress to impress, that's what I always say.'

'Well, if nothing else you should make a fine distraction,' I said.

She sniffed loudly. 'Your look never changes, basic and scruffy. I've seen better-dressed people selling the *Big Issue*.'

'I like to feel comfortable,' I said calmly. 'No one's going to look twice at someone who looks like me.'

'Once would be bad enough,' said Penny.

She'd brought a really large suitcase. It was also quite remarkably heavy, as I found out when I tried to carry it for her. I made some dramatic noises, indicating imminent back problems and popping knee joints, and looked at her reproachfully.

'We're only going to be at the Lodge two days, maximum. What have you got in here?'

'A girl likes to be prepared,' Penny said loftily.

'What for?' I said. 'Moving house?'

She smiled sweetly at me. 'You know I'm going to make you pay for that remark, darling. And anyway, what are you carrying in that dinky little backpack? Guns and explosives and secret spy devices?'

'Just a change of clothes,' I said. 'We won't need guns and explosives where we're going.'

Penny shot me a look. 'Are you sure about that?'

'If I wasn't, we wouldn't be going,' I said. 'And I've never had much faith in clever spy toys. In my experience they always let you down just when you need them most. I prefer to improvise, with whatever's around at the time. I have learned to depend on myself and my own abilities, because I've never let myself down.'

Penny sighed, and shook her head. 'James Bond would have had a fold-up helicopter in there.'

'In case you hadn't noticed,' I said, 'Bond gets beaten up on a regular basis. This way to the train, Penny Galore.'

I've always believed in travelling by train. You can pay in cash, leave no paper or electronic trail, and step on and off at as many platforms as you like if you want to check whether someone is following you.

Paranoid? Why do you want to know?

We travelled first class, in the designated quiet carriage, because Penny has been known to attack people who insist on talking loudly into their phones when she wants a bit of peace and quiet. You really don't want to know where she was going to stuff the phone belonging to one particularly obnoxious city trader. Fortunately it turned out he could run really fast, for a fat man. But such moments, enjoyable as they are, do tend to attract attention; so the quiet carriage it was. Penny stretched her long legs out into the aisle and happily worked her way through the latest issue of the *Fortean Times*, while I looked out the window at the passing scenery and thought of many things.

Starting with Frank Parker. We'd never worked together, never moved in the same circles. Never even been in the same city, as far as I knew. Parker left the weird side of things behind as he moved up in the Organization. From field agent to supervising officer, with responsibility for the more political operations. Because even the Organization has to deal with the realities of the world as well as all the weird things that threaten it. Parker worked all over the world, according to stories I'd been told in strict confidence. Slipping across borders and in and out of countries. Often talked about, but never seen.

The two of us must have started out in the Organization at much the same time. He'd risen a lot further, but then I never was ambitious. Because ambition gets you noticed. We'd be about the same age; but whereas I still looked like a man in his twenties, just as I had since I first appeared in 1963, Parker would look his age. Plastic surgery can do many things, but it can't make you look twenty again. We'd both seen the world change a lot; but it seemed the world had changed Parker a lot more than it had ever changed me.

Of course, Parker was only human.

I thought hard about what might be waiting for us at Ringstone Lodge. I try to plan for every eventuality, including the ones most people never think of because they're too extreme. When you work for the Organization, strange shit and weird menace come as standard. If you get caught off guard, you have no one to blame but yourself.

Proper preparation prevents having your soul stolen, or your aura left in tatters. Or being locked up and interrogated by your own people.

Some hours later, we arrived at the nearest station to Ringstone Lodge. Penny was fast asleep, not even stirring as the train slowed to a halt. I retrieved my backpack and her suitcase, and shook her shoulder firmly. She came awake with a jolt and looked at me with wide eyes, then sat bolt upright as she realized the train wasn't moving any more. She erupted out of her seat, crammed her hat on her head, grabbed her suitcase from me, and headed for the carriage door.

'You should have woken me before!' she said loudly, not looking back. 'Given me time to prepare . . .'

'You looked so peaceful,' I said, ambling unhurriedly after her. 'I didn't like to disturb you.'

'You know I hate waking up in a hurry! I'll be feeling disturbed and upset now for hours.'

'Probably the best frame of mind,' I said, 'when it comes to Ringstone Lodge.'

Evening was fast approaching, and the darkening sky pressed in around the platform's dull yellow lights. I made a point of volunteering to carry Penny's suitcase off the train, as well as my backpack, and she walked ahead of me with a satisfied smile on her face. I couldn't see it from behind, but I had no doubt it was there. She strode down the platform with her head held high, one hand holding her hat in place against the gusting breeze, her high heels clacking loudly in the quiet. I followed after, but thanks to years of long practice I didn't make a sound.

Ringstone Halt was just a small local station, consisting of two platforms with old-fashioned grey-stone buildings. The station sign looked to be decades old, and no one had attended to the overgrown flowerbeds for almost as long. No one else got on or off the train, which didn't hang around. It seemed positively eager to be on its way again, as though it had heard about Ringstone Lodge and wanted nothing to do with it.

I looked up and down the deserted platform. No sense of welcome, or even an acknowledgement of our presence. There was a complete absence of station staff, and the ticket office was locked up tight. A prominent sign made it almost offensively clear that the office was only open until twelve noon. Penny stopped at the single narrow gate that led to the outside and looked back at me. She wasn't smiling any more. She might not have my exalted senses, but she can pick up on a bad atmosphere as quickly as anyone. The station had everything short of a large flashing neon sign warning that this was somewhere you would not want to be once it got dark. I moved manfully forward, hauling Penny's suitcase along with me, and we went outside to see what was waiting for us.

Nothing particularly interesting, as it turned out. Pleasant if characterless countryside stretched away before us under the lowering dark-grey sky. Open fields and bare hardscrabble ground bounded by low stone walls. No one to meet us and no one around, not even a few grazing sheep or cattle. No birds sang, no insects buzzed, and there wasn't so much as a breath of moving air. A long narrow road, completely devoid of traffic, plunged off into the distance before disappearing over the brow of a low hill. The view was acceptable but uninvolving, like a really uninspired jigsaw puzzle.

I dropped Penny's suitcase down beside her and she immediately sat on it, while glaring at me like this was all my fault.

'How frightfully uninviting, darling. It looks like everyone in the vicinity heard tales of this marvellous new thing called civilization and went running off in search of it. Why can't we ever go anywhere nice?'

'We go where the job takes us,' I said. 'You know what they say about the spy game: if you can't take a joke, you shouldn't have joined.'

'Is that really what they say?'

'Sorry,' I said. 'That's classified.'

Penny sniffed loudly and glanced back over her shoulder. 'I'm surprised such a small station is still operating in this day and age.'

'Probably only kept open to serve the Lodge,' I said sagely. 'For people like us.'

'There are no people like us,' said Penny. She glowered about her. 'I can't help noticing a complete lack of taxis, and not even a hint of a bus service. Hell! I'd settle for a pony cart or a rickshaw.'

'Someone from the Lodge will turn up,' I said.

Penny gave me a hard look. 'Did the Colonel tell you that? Did you get it in writing?'

'No. It's just standard procedure.'

Penny shook her head. 'You have faith in the most unlikely things, darling.'

We waited quietly outside the station, and then we waited some more. The day slowly shut itself down, the shadows lengthening while the air grew uncomfortably cool. Nothing moved, no matter where I looked. It was like the end of the world had sneaked up on us while we weren't looking. I hate it when that happens. I kept a careful eye on the only road, but no traffic interrupted the grim foreboding of the road to Ringstone Lodge.

'If no one turns up, we could be in for a hell of a long walk,' said Penny. 'And I'm not wearing walking shoes. If I'd known a forced route march was on the cards, I would have packed my folding bicycle.'

'Where would that have left me?' I said.

'Pushing me up that hill, of course. I'm all in favour of healthy exercise, but you can have too much of a good thing.'

'Someone will come,' I said.

'I blame you,' said Penny. 'All that effort you put into staying off everyone's radar. What if no one knows we've arrived? Don't be stubborn, darling. Get your phone out and tcll thc Lodge we're here. Before we die of exposure and end up with small animals gnawing at our bones.'

'A car will be with us in a few minutes,' I said calmly.

Her eyes narrowed. 'Is this down to your inhumanly fine senses? Or are you just being extra confident to annoy me?'

'Oh ye of little faith,' I said. 'Listen.'

Her head came up sharply as the sound of a car's straining motor finally made itself heard on the quiet evening air. Not long after, a car appeared quite suddenly over the crest of the hill and roared down the road to the station. Penny glared at me.

'Show-off!'

A suitably anonymous vehicle slammed to a halt before us. Not new enough to hold the eye or old enough to attract attention, it had probably started out a fierce crimson. But age and a complete lack of attention had reduced it to a two-tone mix of red and rust. I couldn't even guess at the make; which was probably just as well, as the maker would only have been embarrassed to acknowledge it. The engine cut off in a grateful sort of way, the door opened in a series of jerks, and the driver got out.

He turned out to be quite a large man for such a small car. He stayed where he was, looking us over unsmilingly. A stiff-backed man in his late fifties, grey-haired and impeccably shaved, handsome enough in a hard-used sort of way. He wore his tweed suit as though it was a uniform, along with sturdy, highly polished boots. Broad-shouldered and barrel-chested, he had large heavy-knuckled hands. Ex-military, and not that long ago. You can always tell. It's something in the bearing, and the way they look ready to shoot anyone who disagrees with them.

He looked me over first with his cold grey eyes, taking his time, and then Penny; before removing two photos from inside his jacket and comparing our faces with the ones in his hand. I had to wonder where he got them. There aren't many photos of me around, I've seen to that. He gave the matter some thought, before finally nodding briefly and putting the photos away. He strode forward and crashed to a halt right in front of us, as though in his mind he was still on a parade ground somewhere. I half expected him to fire off a snappy salute, or yell at me for having a button undone. When he finally addressed us, his voice had a surprisingly pleasant Scottish burr.

'Mr Jones, Miss Belcourt, welcome to Ringstone Halt. I am Donald MacKay, head of security at Ringstone Lodge. You've come a fair way to be here, I understand.'

'All the way from London,' said Penny. 'I was beginning to worry we'd have to spend the night here.'

'My apologies, miss. We were only alerted you were coming a short time ago.'

'Shouldn't we have code words, or recognition phrases?' Penny said brightly. 'Like "the snows are particularly bad in Moscow this year"?'

MacKay indulged himself with a thin smile, just for her. 'We do not burden ourselves with such things, miss.'

'Then why the photos?' I said.

'Electronic information can be hacked or subverted, Mr Jones,' MacKay said sternly. 'As well you know. I favour the old school, less to go wrong. And we are being especially cautious just at present, now that Mr Parker is a guest at the Lodge.'

'Would I be right in thinking you're late of a Highland Regiment, Mr MacKay?' I said.

He inclined his head, just a little. 'Indeed, sir. I had the honour to be Regimental Sergeant Major; until I was forced to retire because of my years. I was not ready to sit around the house and do nothing, so I made a new life for myself in security. There is always a place in the Security Services for an old soldier. They value experience. The Ministry of Defence put me in charge of Ringstone Lodge some three years back. And I am proud to say there has not been a single unfortunate incident on the premises since I took charge of things.'

'But you are . . . part of the Organization?' said Penny, dropping her voice conspiratorially even though we couldn't have been more alone on the surface of the moon.

'I have Organization clearance, miss,' MacKay said carefully. 'So I can remain in charge on those occasions when the

Organization finds it necessary to take over the Lodge from the Ministry.'

'Does that happen often?' said Penny.

'Often enough, miss.'

'And would I be right in thinking you've seen your share of strange and unusual things?' I said. 'Enough for the Organization to take notice of you?'

He shot me a quick glance. 'Aye, sir. I have seen my share, and some. There is not much that can throw me.'

'What have you seen, Mr MacKay?' Penny said winningly.

'Those are stories for another time, miss,' MacKay said firmly. 'For now, we must needs be on our way. The others are waiting.'

'Others?' I said.

'Not in public, Mr Jones.'

I thought that was pushing it a bit, under the circumstances, but I nodded and went along. MacKay picked up Penny's suitcase and carried it over to the car, with no visible signs of effort. He loaded it into the boot and then looked back at me and my backpack. I shook my head. He nodded, and gestured for us to get in the car. I beat Penny to the shotgun seat by just a few moments and settled smugly into place with my backpack on my lap, while Penny dropped scowling into the back seat. MacKay ignored all of this, as though such childishness was beneath him. He took his time arranging his long legs carefully behind the steering wheel, fired up the engine, and sent the car roaring back up the hill.

Heading for Ringstone Lodge, and everything that lay waiting there.

The road remained entirely untroubled by any other traffic, but MacKay still drove with the exaggerated care of a chauffeur, studying the way ahead with an unwavering gaze as though half expecting something untoward to be lying in wait around every bend in the road. We drove in silence for some time. MacKay didn't seem to feel the need to make conversation. The open countryside passed us by, grim and contemplative under the darkening sky, with no obvious landmarks or features of interest.

'Fill me in, Mr MacKay,' I said finally. 'What's the situation?'

'Much as you'd expect, Mr Jones.' MacKay's gaze didn't waver from the road ahead for a moment and his voice was entirely calm. 'Everything at the Lodge is secure, including Mr Parker. All is in order. We've merely been waiting on your arrival.'

'Is Parker behaving himself?' I said.

'He has been most cooperative,' said MacKay. 'Though he has not as yet had much to say for himself. Nothing of importance or substance. He is perhaps a little more at his ease than one might expect, given his present circumstances.'

'What sort of a man is Parker?' I said. 'How does he strike you?'

MacKay gave the matter some thought before answering. 'A man who knows things. The kind of things most men are better off not knowing. A man with secrets, his own as well as other people's. And most definitely a man who hoards such things to himself, like a miser, for when he might need to make use of them.'

'But what's he like?' said Penny. 'Funny, dour, argumentative? Charming?'

'He can be,' said MacKay. 'He is well trained, after all. But you can never trust a man like that, in anything he says or does. He will always have his own reason for everything.'

'Any sign of outside interest in the Lodge?' I said.

'No, sir. No one is supposed to know we have Mr Parker as our guest, though how long that will last . . .'

'Especially if he's right and there are traitors inside the Organization.'

'Do you think that is likely, Mr Jones?' said MacKay. He still didn't turn his head to look at me.

'Anyone can be turned,' I said. 'All it takes is enough pressure. Or temptation. But I don't know enough about the Organization, or its personnel, to know how likely that is.'

'Not many do, sir,' said MacKay.

'Who am I going to be meeting at the Lodge?' I asked, tacitly agreeing to change the subject.

'Only Organization-appointed personnel are in residence at

the moment, sir. The bare minimum necessary to debrief Mr Parker properly.'

'I'm surprised you haven't got an army surrounding the Lodge,' I said. 'A lot of really bad people have really good reasons to want our man silenced before he can spill whatever beans he has.'

'An army would only attract undue attention, sir,' said MacKay. Just a little condescendingly. 'We have the very best security measures in place, backed up by all manner of hidden unpleasantness. An army would have trouble getting in.'

Penny could tell I was getting impatient at having to dig answers out of MacKay and turned on the charm. She smiled winningly into the rear-view mirror, and leaned forward so she could breathe her words right into his ear.

'Who exactly have you got working for you at the Lodge, Mr MacKay?'

'Two guards, miss. Both supplied by the Organization. Alan Baxter and Karl Redd.'

'Have you worked with them before?' I said.

'No sir, I have not. But they have proved themselves to be most efficient.'

'What did they do before they came to the Lodge?' said Penny.

'One does not ask such questions, miss,' MacKay said firmly. 'We all know what we need to know, and only what we need to know.'

'But were they civilian security or military?' I said. 'You'd know, Sergeant Major.'

He nodded solemnly. 'Indeed I would, sir. And I would say not military. Though there is no doubt in my mind that they have both seen action in their time. Then there are the two interrogators, Doctor Alice Hayley and Doctor Robert Doyle. Again new to me and the Lodge, but both Organization people. Very highly qualified and experienced, I am given to understand. She is a fierce little body, the gentleman is more the academic soul.'

I couldn't help frowning. 'I can't believe the Organization would send you two entirely new people, not when there must be so many who've worked at the Lodge before.'

'If Mr Parker is right about rotten apples within,' MacKay said seriously, 'they would have to be very careful about who they chose.'

'I'm not sure I like the term interrogators,' said Penny, settling back in her seat again. 'Sounds too much like the Spanish Inquisition.'

'The Organization has access to techniques the Inquisition never even dreamed of,' I said. 'Given how steeped in secrecy they are, the Organization has always shown an unwavering dedication to getting the truth out of others.'

'You're really not selling me on this,' said Penny. 'No wonder you were so reluctant to come here.'

I shot her a warning glance. 'Trust me, nothing is going to happen at the Lodge that I don't approve of.'

'But how much ground does that cover?' said Penny. And she stared out her window, rather than look at me or MacKay.

'You should not feel sympathy for Mr Parker, Miss Belcourt,' MacKay said sternly. 'Given the kind of people he worked for, and the kind of things he did for them.'

Penny remained silent.

'Anyone else at the Lodge?' I said.

'Just our resident technician,' said MacKay. 'Philip Martin. He looks after our surveillance systems. He is MoD, but has been granted Organization clearance for this particular debriefing because bringing a newcomer up to speed on the Lodge's specialized equipment would take too long. Mr Martin has worked well for me these last three years, and I have no doubt as to his capabilities. I have been assured another quali-fied technician is on his way to spell Mr Martin, so he doesn't have to watch his screens twenty-four-seven. But it will be a while before the new man arrives.'

'Probably searching for someone they're sure they can depend on,' I said. 'That's the trouble with accusations, they make it hard to trust anyone. So that's it? No one else?'

'There are normally twenty-seven MoD personnel on site, but they have all been sent away for the duration,' said MacKay. 'Including the support staff. So we will have to mind for ourselves, the next few days.'

'They all just left?' said Penny, suddenly taking an interest again.

'No one argues with the Organization,' I said.

'Why?' said Penny.

MacKay allowed himself another of his thin smiles. 'A great many people would like to know the answer to that one, miss. If only for their own peace of mind. But when orders come down from on high, we do as we're told and trust there's a good reason for it. In the case of Mr Parker, it does make sense. If he is who he claims to be, we cannot allow anyone access to him who does not have the proper clearances. And if he is not, he could prove to be a very poisoned chalice. The less people are exposed to his deliberate disinformation, the better.'

'What is your own view of him?' I asked.

'He is . . . very polite, very eager to please,' said MacKay. 'No trouble at all.'

'You don't like him,' said Penny. 'I can hear it in your voice.'

'I believe we should all be very careful around Mr Parker,' said MacKay. And that was all he had to say.

We drove on, through increasingly bleak countryside. Just empty moors now, with no signs of life save for some stunted shrubs and patchy grassland. The skies were darkening into night, and a wind was rising. It felt like we were leaving the civilized world behind, to go to a place where only bad things happened.

'Why is it called Ringstone Lodge?' Penny said finally.

'After a circle of ancient standing stones,' said MacKay. 'Just over that hill to your right, miss. Ringstone Knoll.'

Penny craned her neck, but couldn't see anything. 'Are there stories about the stones?' she said hopefully. 'Druids and sacrifices and ghostly sightings?'

'Not as far as I know, miss.'

'But there is a history of hauntings at the Lodge?' said Penny. 'Things that go bump in the night?'

'The only spooks at the Lodge will be the agents who pass through on a regular basis,' I said. 'Right, Mr MacKay?'

I expected him to go along with my amused tone, but

MacKay surprised me by looking distinctly unhappy. He considered the question for a while. And when he finally answered, his voice, though steady, was troubled.

'Once, I would have agreed with you, Mr Jones. In my long career, in strange and often exotic places, I have encountered many odd things and seen more than my fair share of dead men . . . but never once did I see a ghostie. I would have said there was no such thing. Until quite recently, at Ringstone Lodge.'

'You've seen ghosts?' I said.

'There have been . . . occurrences.'

'How recently?'

'Very. But there are tales of unusual manifestations that go back generations. The Lodge has always had a bad reputation. As a place where the dead do not rest easy and the past is not always over, where spirits range the long marches of the night. I never took such tales seriously before . . . but I have experienced things at the Lodge in the last few days that I would not have believed if another man had told them to me.'

There was a long pause.

'Such as?' asked Penny.

'Sounds,' MacKay said reluctantly. 'Sightings. Things moving that should not. The Lodge has an unquiet feel these days.'

'But what kinds of sounds and sightings?' said Penny, squirming impatiently on her seat and leaning forward again. 'Are we talking headless figures, or dark shapes walking through walls?'

'Does your ghost carry its head under its arm, Mr MacKay?' I said. 'How does it see where it's going?'

'You are pleased to be facetious, Mr Jones,' said MacKay. He didn't sound pleased to have his judgement challenged. 'Whatever it is that walks in Ringstone Lodge, it is nothing so traditional. Nothing any of us can be sure of. Just . . . things heard in the early hours, or glimpsed out of the corner of the eye. Strange feelings and uncanny thoughts. You can believe it or not, as you please. But I believe we are not alone, at present, at Ringstone Lodge.'

'Are you the only one who's had direct experience of these phenomena?' I said.

'No, sir. Everyone present at the Lodge has seen or sensed something unnatural.'

'Including Parker?'

'He says not.'

'When exactly did these disturbances begin?' I asked.

'A night and a day before Mr Parker arrived, sir. Everyone else had left, and Mr Martin and I were preparing the Lodge for its new arrivals.'

'And you don't find that significant?'

'Of course, that was my first thought. But things have been happening for which I can find no rational explanation. For the first time in all my service at the Lodge, I do not feel safe.'

Given the kind of man MacKay was, I found that distinctly unsettling.

'And all of this started happening when Parker arrived?' I said.

'Mr Parker could not be responsible for any of this, sir,' MacKay said firmly. 'The first incidents preceded his arrival by many hours. And they did not cease after he was safely locked away.'

'It sounds like a distraction,' I said. 'Something to keep us occupied while an escape or an attack was being planned. I don't believe in coincidences.'

'No more do I, sir. But it has crossed my mind that the arrival of this bad man has awoken a more ancient evil. Stirred something from its long rest. I do not necessarily believe in ghosts, Mr Jones. But I am taking all of this very seriously. I do not like anything happening in my Lodge without my consent.' He smiled one of his thin smiles. 'Dead men walking are not conducive to good discipline.'

'I see your problem,' I said. 'More complications are the last thing we need. It's not like we can just call in a priest and have him exorcize the Lodge.'

'I personally have no truck with Roman ritual, being a firm Protestant,' said MacKay. 'But still, is there not some kind of professional help that the Organization could provide, Mr Jones? I have sent in several reports, but as yet all they've sent us is you. Do you perhaps have experience in this area?'

'Similar areas,' I said. 'I don't believe in ghosts.'

'That's all right,' said Penny. 'I'm sure they believe in you.'

'Really not helpful, Penny . . .'

'Anyway,' MacKay said heavily, 'it may well be that once Mr Parker has moved on to another establishment, it will all quieten down again.'

'If anyone could disturb the living and the dead, it's Frank Parker,' I said.

When we finally arrived at the gates of Ringstone Lodge, they were the kind that told you straight away what kind of visit you were in for. Tall and broad and heavy, with spiked steel bars so solid that you'd need a tank to get through them. And even then, it would have to be traveling at one hell of a speed. Brick walls stretched away either side, topped with long rolls of vicious barbed wire. I've seen prisons that looked more inviting. MacKay waited till the very last moment to slam on the brakes, and the car shuddered to a halt just short of the gates. Penny leaned forward again and stuck her head between mine and MacKay's, to study the Lodge.

'How utterly ghastly. What do the locals think of this place, Mr MacKay?'

'Local people won't come anywhere near the Lodge, miss. They know it of old, and its unwholesome reputation. It does help that the nearest village is some ten miles distant. We get occasional teenagers coming around, seeking to make a name for themselves by proving their courage, but our security measures are more than a match for them.'

He forced his door open, got out of the car, and moved forward to shout into the intercom at the gates. Penny looked at me. I looked at the Lodge. There was a pause, and then the gates swung slowly open and MacKay returned to the car. We drove through, and the gates slammed shut behind us. It took a while to get to the Lodge. The long gravel path passed through extensive grounds suitable for an old country estate. Wide lawns, neatly trimmed, with no flowerbeds, ornaments or garden furniture. In the distance dark woods cut off the view, holding shadows within. I turned round in my seat to look back at Penny.

'The open space is deliberate, to provide the Lodge's security people with an uninterrupted view. Nowhere for intruders to hide.'

'Apart from the trees,' said Penny.

'There are mantraps in the trees, miss,' MacKay said casually. 'And other things. Not a place for a wise man to go strolling.'

The gravel drive curved sharply around to conclude abruptly before a surprisingly pleasant-looking old-fashioned house. My first thought was that it might have been a family manor house, or even a country hotel, before the MoD took it over. Nothing about it to suggest the kind of things that went on inside these days. Which was, of course, the point. The house was large, and heavy with accumulated history. Generations had come and gone in Ringstone Lodge, and all of them had left their mark. The exterior seemed well-maintained, and I quickly spotted a whole bunch of concealed security cameras, as well as metal shutters stored in place above every window, ready to be brought down at a moment's notice. To seal the place up against outsiders and intruders. Or make it the perfect trap, ready to close on me the moment I walked inside and hold me there for as long as it took them to work out what to do with me.

MacKay brought the car to an abrupt halt directly in front of the main door, and was out of his seat and heading for the boot while Penny and I were still getting used to the idea that we'd arrived. I looked the Lodge over, bracing myself to walk into the jaws of the beast. I'd had nightmares about ending up in some place like this, strapped helplessly to a table while the doctors got out their surgical kits and trained interrogators asked me increasingly angry questions that I didn't have answers for.

Penny started to say something as I got out of the car. I'd spent most of my career confronting seriously scary things, and this was just another. I wouldn't allow anything to get in the way of doing my job. Not even myself. Perhaps especially not myself. I shrugged my backpack over one shoulder, in order to leave my arms free, and glared at Ringstone Lodge.

I could make out just two storeys, with windows that stared back at me like so many unsympathetic eyes in a cold blank face. An old house haunted by too many years of bad memories. I'd blown up and burned down places like this, in other countries. Sometimes just on general principles. Penny came and stood beside me, and held my hand.

'We don't have to do this,' she said quietly. 'If you're not happy about things, if this doesn't feel right, let's go back to the station. Tell them you're not feeling well. Tell them to get someone else.'

'If they really do have suspicions about me, that might be all the evidence they need,' I said, just as quietly. 'So, we go in. But Penny . . . If at any time I turn to you and say "Run!", don't stop to ask why. Just try to keep up with me.'

'Got it, Ishmael. But what on earth is that?'

I looked where she was looking. 'Well,' I said. 'It appears to be a cemetery.'

'They kill people here?' said Penny, her voice rising.

'Not recently,' I said. 'Not from the state of those headstones. They've been here for some time.'

I wandered over to take a better look, glad of the distraction. Penny stuck close beside me. It was getting seriously dark now, but the Lodge had its own exterior lighting. More than enough to hold back the night. The small graveyard had been tucked away unobtrusively around the side of the Lodge. Just a few dozen headstones, weather-beaten and speckled with mould. I walked along the rows, peering at the stones, trying to make out the faded names. Some of the dates went back to the seventeenth century. One stone, standing a little apart from the others, caught my eye. No name, no date. Just a single inscription: *God Grant She Rest Easily*.

'Some pour soul convicted of being a witch,' said Penny. 'That's an old prayer to keep a witch in her grave and prevent her rising up again to trouble the living.'

'The Ringstone Witch,' said MacKay. Penny jumped a little, I didn't. I'd heard him coming up behind us. MacKay came forward to study the headstones with us. 'Quite famous in her day, I understand. There were songs written about her. Long forgotten now, along with her crimes.'

'What is a cemetery doing here?' asked Penny.

'Once upon a time the Lodge was a family home, miss. And this was the family burying place. No one has been interred here for years. There was some talk of moving the bodies, it's not like there is any family left who might want to visit.'

'That's sad,' said Penny.

'Yes,' said MacKay, unexpectedly. 'It is. We should go in, Mr Jones. The others are waiting.'

'And Frank Parker,' I said.

'If that's who he really is,' said Penny.

'Indeed,' said MacKay.

He dropped Penny's suitcase at her feet, to make it clear he wasn't anyone's servant, and looked at me inquiringly. I nodded jerkily, and he led the way back to the front door. I followed him as casually as I could. It helped that Penny stuck close beside me. Hauling her suitcase along with her.

The main entrance hall turned out to be very comfortable, even cosy. A wide open space with thick carpeting, heavy antique furniture and nice cheery prints on the walls. All very bright and charming and agreeable, the smile on the face of the Medusa. A group of people stood waiting to meet us. They all had that look about them: fascinated to meet an actual field agent in the flesh, staring at me like I was some rare species in a zoo, and just a bit disappointed I wasn't Daniel Craig. None of them paid much attention to Penny. She frowned, she wasn't used to not being noticed. She shot me a look, and I managed a quick reassuring smile, just for her. I looked the group over, keeping my face carefully calm and unimpressed, and left it to them to make the first move. The first to step forward was a big brawny alpha-male type in his late twenties, squeezed into very tight clothes to show off his muscles. Dark hair, hard face, deep scowl. He thrust out a hand for me to shake.

'Alan Baxter. I'm here to make sure everyone behaves.'

'Good for you,' I said. 'I'm Ishmael Jones, and this is

Penny Belcourt. The Organization sent us to make sure you behave.'

Baxter went for the crushing handshake, putting all his strength into it. I shook his hand easily, not feeling any distress. His scowl deepened as he realized he wasn't getting anywhere, and he snatched his hand back. He looked to Penny, but she had already dumped her suitcase and placed both her hands firmly behind her back. She smiled at him brightly, but Baxter hardly gave her a glance before turning back to me. He looked me up and down, doing his best to make it clear he wasn't in any way impressed.

'Ishmael Jones . . . Never heard of you.'

'I should hope not,' I said. 'I am supposed to be a secret agent, after all.'

'I've got a job to do here,' Baxter said heavily. 'Don't get in my way.'

He sounded like he had a lot more to say on the subject, but the man behind him tapped him lightly on the shoulder. Surprisingly, Baxter immediately stepped back to let the other man take his place. A few years older than Baxter, he had colourless blond hair, pale-blue eyes and a cool, thoughtful air. He dressed well, if inexpensively. He smiled briefly at Penny and me, and his voice was quiet and easy-going.

'Karl Redd. Security. Good to have you here at last. We've been feeling a bit abandoned, all on our own. Good to see the Organization hasn't forgotten us. Hopefully we can get things under way now.'

His word were carefully considered and scrupulously polite, but I could sense a real strength in him held in reserve for when he needed it. Such men are dangerous, because they think before they act.

'We'll keep you safe while you're here,' he said. 'No one gets past us.'

'Well,' I said. 'That's good to know.'

Penny smiled radiantly at Baxter and Redd. 'Do either of you have a gun?'

'Of course,' said Baxter.

'It's part of the job,' said Redd.

And they both pulled back their jackets to reveal handguns

in shoulder holsters. Baxter started to reach for his gun, only to stop after a cold glare from MacKay.

'Don't you have a gun, Mr MacKay?' said Penny. 'You're an old soldier, after all.'

'I do not carry a weapon, Miss Belcourt,' said MacKay. 'I leave that to those who might need to use them. The Lodge does of course have its own armoury. For emergencies. I have the only key.'

'I'd like a gun!' the young man at the back said loudly. 'I'd feel a lot safer with a gun, especially now Parker's here, but they won't let me have one.'

'You stick to your computers, Mr Martin,' said MacKay. 'You are dangerous enough as it is.'

'You have no idea,' said Martin.

Dr Alice Hayley shouldered her way past Redd, to announce herself in a loud and carrying voice. A middle-aged black woman with close-cropped hair, sharp eyes and a severe mouth. She wore a smart suit, no jewellery, and didn't offer to shake hands. Or even try for a smile. She looked like she was waiting for me to say something wrong, so she could pounce on me. So, of course, I just smiled easily back at her.

'I don't know what you're doing here,' she said flatly. 'Neither Doctor Doyle nor I made any request for a field agent, and we certainly don't need another layer of authority. We know our job. We don't need anyone interfering. I don't see what you could possibly hope to contribute . . .'

'That's why I'm here,' I said. 'To ask the questions it would never occur to you to ask.'

Hayley looked disappointed that I wasn't going to dispute her authority, but I was too old a hand to show my cards that early.

'I trust you know better than to get in the way of the actual interrogations?' she said.

'I'm just here to oversee the operation and make sure everything goes smoothly,' I said. 'Though I will need to speak to Parker before you start.'

'I can't permit that,' Hayley said immediately. 'Establishing the proper relationship and rapport between interrogator and subject is a delicate matter. I won't allow you to jeopardize our work.'

'You don't get to permit or allow anything where I'm concerned, doctor,' I said patiently. 'I will decide what is and is not for the best. Feel free to make an official complaint about my attitude, if you like. Many have. See how far it gets you.'

Hayley glared at me fiercely, but had nothing else to say. She had the look of someone who preferred to nurse her grudges then attack from ambush. She turned to the man who had to be her colleague and he smiled back at her, entirely unperturbed. He then turned his smile on me; a short dumpy man in his fifties, with a gleaming bald head and a neatly trimmed salt-and-pepper beard. His suit was good quality, but a little faded. He had the look of a college professor who'd stayed on past his best days. His smile was an entirely professional thing, and didn't touch his eyes. He put out a hand, and I shook it solemnly. Like two boxers touching gloves before the fight begins.

'Doctor Robert Doyle,' he said breezily. 'Don't take any of this personally, Mr Jones. It's just that we're all very keen to get started. When we were brought in, we weren't told you would be overseeing things. Doctor Hayley and I are used to a certain level of autonomy . . . I'm sure we'll all work perfectly well together, once we've had a chance to get to know one another.'

He was going out of his way to be friendly and present himself as the reasonable voice, the man I could trust. I didn't buy any of it. His voice and his attitudes were practised things, the false face of the interrogator who wants you to have faith in him. The one who persuades you to say things that aren't in your best interests. I gave him my best false smile in return. Because I can fake it with the best of them.

Up close, I could smell gin on Doctor Hayley's breath. And the presence of tranquilizers in Doctor Doyle's perspiration.

I looked to the one man who hadn't introduced himself, slouching at the back and looking at everything except Penny and me.

'Philip Martin?' I said.

'Indeed,' said MacKay. 'Step forward and make yourself known, Mr Martin. Move yourself, you idle fellow!'

'I was never in the army!' Martin said loudly. 'Don't think you can order me around! I have qualifications.'

'Of course you weren't in the army,' said MacKay. 'Look at the state of you. None of the services would take the likes of you on a bet.'

Martin moved reluctantly forward and nodded grudgingly. His gaze lingered on Penny. He seemed the typical techie; early twenties, grubby jeans and trainers, a *World of Warcraft* T-shirt, and a baseball cap on backwards. He shrugged at me with a put-upon air.

'I'm the one who really runs things around here. The one everyone relies on to work miracles with outdated equipment and a limited budget. And do I get any thanks, any appreciation? The hell I do! Can we get this over with, MacKay? I want to get back to my screens, so I can keep an eye out for orcs and trolls.'

'How is the security situation?' said MacKay.

Martin glowered at him. 'Nothing's changed in the hour or so since you last asked. All my cameras and microphones are working, all the recorders are running, and my exterior sensors are functioning perfectly. No one can get in or out of the Lodge, or the grounds, without my equipment knowing all about it and raising all kinds of sweet merry hell. I've got it all running on cruise control for the moment, but never trust a computer to do a man's job. They're not sneaky enough. The sooner I get back to my screens, the better I'll feel and the safer you'll be. Can I go now?'

'How extensive is the surveillance coverage?' I asked. Because I felt I ought to say something.

Martin sniffed moistly and rattled through his answer at speed, half proud and half resentful at being made to sound off like a performing seal.

'There are cameras and motion sensors in place all through the grounds, and along the boundaries. There isn't an inch that isn't covered by something professionally suspicious. I can hear the grass growing and track the flight of butterflies. Nothing happens here that my machines don't know about.'

'Defences?' I said.

'Land mines,' said MacKay. 'Set off by contact or remote control, singly or in groups. So let me remind everyone once again to stick to the designated paths. Unless you want to find out just how high you can jump. There are also gas jets hidden throughout the grounds, ready to dispense everything from soporifics and hallucinogens to deadly measures, as required.'

'Deadly measures?' said Penny. 'What kind of intruders are you expecting?'

'The kind who come prepared for ordinary defences, miss,' said MacKay. 'But in a real emergency I would have Mr Martin place the Lodge in lockdown, and we would sit tight and wait for armed reinforcements.'

'Lockdown?' I said.

'All the doors are electronically locked,' said Martin. 'And steel shutters slide into place over the windows. Don't let the pleasant exterior fool you, Ringstone Lodge is a fortress.'

'Of course it is,' I said.

'How long would it take for help to arrive?' said Penny.

'An SAS contingent could be here in under an hour,' MacKay said calmly. 'And we are required to report every twelve hours, to give the All's Well. If we miss a report, the SAS are sent in automatically. So we make sure never to miss a report. Those gentlemen are not renowned for their sense of humour when it comes to being called out unnecessarily.'

'All of this, for just one man,' said Penny. 'Is Parker really that important?'

'He might be,' I said.

'This is all standard procedure, miss,' said MacKay. 'We have had some very important personages as our guests. Prominent enough to require such levels of protection.'

'When was the last time your defences came under attack?' I said.

'You will understand there are some questions I am not permitted to answer, Mr Jones,' MacKay said carefully. 'You would have to contact your superiors for such information.'

'And see how far that gets me,' I said.

'How long before my backup gets here?' Martin said loudly.

'I can't run everything on my own. Well I can, and I do, but even I have to sleep sometimes.'

'He's on his way,' said MacKay. 'Now contain yourself, you overpaid mechanic, and try not to let the side down in front of company.'

'I should have asked for another raise,' said Martin. 'You people don't deserve me, you really don't.'

'I often wonder what I did to deserve you,' said MacKay.

From the amicable way the two men snarled at each other, it was obvious they had years of shared experience behind them.

Martin looked at me squarely. 'I quizzed Headquarters about you once we were told you were on your way.'

'Even though you were instructed not to,' said MacKay.

'I like to know who I'm going to be working with,' said Martin. 'But interestingly, they wouldn't tell me anything about you. Almost as though they didn't know anything about you themselves.'

'Well,' I said. 'That's sort of the point of being a secret agent. We like to keep the element of surprise on our side.'

'Doctor Doyle and I have read your Organization file,' said Hayley.

'It made for very interesting reading,' said Doyle. 'What there was of it.'

'We have a great many questions to put to you,' said Hayley.

'Save them for Parker,' I said.

And there must have been something in my voice, because everyone looked away. MacKay cleared his throat.

'Mr Jones, Miss Belcourt, your mobile phones will not work inside the Lodge, for security reasons. If you need to make a call you will have to go outside, into the grounds. And even there, your conversations will be recorded. I should remind you that there are surveillance cameras in every room, including the living quarters. Everything is recorded, for later scrutiny. Our security cannot be compromised.'

'What about the bathrooms?' said Penny.

'Take a deep breath and try not to think about it,' said Martin.

'Oh, ick . . .' said Penny.

'Where's Parker?' I said.

'Down in the basement, sir,' said MacKay. 'Entirely secure behind thick stone walls, a great many steel bars, and an electronic lock that can only be opened from the main security centre. We are keeping Mr Parker comfortable enough, for the moment. He hasn't made any complaints. Not that it would do him any good if he did. He has frequently expressed his desire to get the process started. Perhaps he feels confession will be good for his soul.'

'I need to talk to him,' I said. 'Right now, Mr MacKay.'

Hayley started to say something, only to back down as Doyle put a hand on her arm. Interesting power dynamic there. I made a mental note to look into that later. MacKay produced an official file from a desk drawer and handed it to me. He'd clearly been expecting me to ask for it. The file was large and heavy. I leafed through it quickly, with Penny crowding in behind me and peering over my shoulder. Frank Parker's official file had little in it that I didn't already know, or at least suspect. There were half a dozen photographs, of six entirely different faces. I felt like wincing. After so many plastic surgeries, it would be a wonder if Parker had any working facial nerves left. If he wanted to raise an eyebrow, he probably had to give himself plenty of warning or use a wire. The file contained extensive reports on places he'd been and people he'd worked with, but only code names for his various cases. Never any details. I closed the file and handed it back to MacKay.

'There is a more complete file, of course,' he said. 'But that has been declared "Eyes Only" for the two doctors. So they can check details of past cases against what our guest tells them. If you wish to see that file . . .'

'I know,' I said. 'Talk to my superiors.'

MacKay put Parker's file back in the drawer and locked it. 'Now, if you will come with me, Mr Jones . . .'

'And me!' said Penny. 'We're a team.'

Hayley raised an eyebrow. 'Really?'

'Yes,' I said. 'I value her input.'

'It's true,' Penny said brightly. 'He does.'

'But not this time,' I said. 'Parker might say things to me, as a fellow agent, that he would never admit to in front of company. You can meet him later, Penny. After I've pulled a few of his teeth. You stay here and make friends. Or failing that, teach them a few useful tricks.'

'You will tell me everything later?' said Penny.

'Of course,' I said.

'I want to make it clear, here and now, that I officially object to this intrusion into our procedures!' Hayley said loudly.

'And now you've done it!' I said. 'Do you feel any better? Good. Now find something to keep yourself busy until I've finished with Parker. I recommend flower arranging. Very soothing to the troubled mind.'

No one so much as smiled.

'Tough crowd,' I said to Penny.

'Fuck them if they can't take a joke!' she said sweetly.

MacKay led the way down the backstairs. All bare plaster walls and rough stone steps, descending a lot further than I was comfortable with. The surveillance cameras observing our every move weren't even hidden down here. A narrow corridor with locked doors on every side finally brought us to the main detention cell. No door for Frank Parker, just steel bars. No privacy, and no chance for him to hide anything. All to put him in the right frame of mind, no doubt.

He was already standing on the other side of the bars, waiting to greet us. He seemed perfectly calm and relaxed. They'd let him keep his own clothes, but it was clear from the way his trousers drooped that they'd taken his belt. Just in case. He had no jacket, and looked a little chilly in his shirtsleeves. I glanced at his shoes; they were slip-ons. I turned to MacKay.

'Go back to the stairs and wait for me there.'

'Are you sure, sir?' He didn't actually raise an eyebrow, but he sounded like he wanted to.

'Three's a crowd.'

'As you wish, sir.'

He nodded to me, just a little stiffly, gave Parker a look that made it clear he'd better behave himself, and then disappeared back the way we'd come. I waited till I was sure MacKay was out of earshot, and then nodded to Parker.

'Hi. I'm Ishmael Jones.'

'Oh, I know who you are,' said Parker. He had a light, careless voice. 'Just as you know who I am.'

'Well,' I said. 'I know who you're claiming to be.'

The man before me looked to be in his late fifties. Several years younger than he was supposed to be. A little overweight, with receding hair, and a very ordinary-looking face that was completely unlike any of the photos in Parker's file. But then that was probably the point. Looking closely, I could see scars concealed in his face and neck, along with surgical implants designed to change the shape and structure of his skull. Whoever he was, he really didn't want to be recognized. He studied me carefully, dark eyes peering out of old scar tissue, like an animal from its cave.

'If I'm not Parker,' he said. 'Who am I?'

'A lot of people could have a vested interest in undermining the Organization through carefully tailored disinformation,' I said.

'But how many of them would be willing to place themselves in the hands of the Organization's interrogators?' he said.

'Why would Frank Parker be willing to do such a thing?' I said.

He shrugged, briefly. 'Penance, perhaps.'

'Penance for what?'

'I wondered who they'd send,' Parker said thoughtfully. 'I thought it might be the current Colonel, or perhaps another field agent, but I really didn't expect the infamous Ishmael Jones.'

'We've never met before,' I said. 'I'd know.'

'I know your reputation,' said Parker. 'You've made quite an impression in the darker corners of the hidden world. You look just like your photo. Even though it was taken a long time ago.'

'I'm amazed you were able to find one,' I said. 'I've destroyed most of the ones that have made it out into the world. Where did you find it?'

'In your Organization file, of course,' said Parker. 'Not the official one, I mean the one they don't let just anybody see.'

'Good thing there isn't much in it,' I said.

'More than you'd think,' said Parker.

'You don't want to believe everything you read,' I said.

There was a pause, as we looked each other over.

'You'd be surprised how many people are genuinely scared of you,' Parker said finally. 'Mostly because they can't figure out how you do what you do. Though I have heard things . . .'

'Oh yes?' I said politely. 'Such as what?'

'That would be telling.' He smiled, and winked roguishly. 'In my current situation, information is all I have to bargain with. I'd be a fool to give it away for free. Let's just say certain people have been studying you for some time. From a distance. You'd be amazed how much I know about you . . . Ishmael Jones.'

'You only think you know about me,' I said. 'Let's make a start. What can you tell me about the traitors inside the Organization?'

'Sorry,' said Parker. 'I'm not giving up anything until I have a deal in place.'

'You really think you're in a position to dictate terms?' I said.

'I have something the Organization wants,' said Parker. 'I'm sure the two doctors could get it out of me, in time. But you don't have time. The information I possess is very time-sensitive. So yes, I think they'll make a deal. Don't you?'

'How long has the Organization been compromised?' I said.

'Too long,' said Parker.

I looked at him for a moment.

'What exactly is the Organization? Do you know?'

'No,' said Parker. 'Even after all these years, I'm not sure anybody knows. Except for those at the very top.'

'It has been suggested to me,' I said carefully, 'that the whole thing might just be smoke and mirrors. That there is no actual Organization, just a handful of people running a gigantic bluff.'

Parker smiled. 'Wouldn't surprise me.'

'Then how can there be traitors?' I said.

'That's part of the information I'm selling,' said Parker.

'I'm not buying,' I said.

'You want to ask me something,' said Parker. 'Something specific. Be my guest, I'm not going anywhere.'

'Why did you leave the Organization?' I said.

He smiled, but there was no humour in it. He looked suddenly tired, and perhaps a little sad. Not that I trusted any of what I was seeing in his false face.

'One of these days you'll feel the need to walk away and leave it all behind. All the lies that are our life, all the compromises and small betrayals of everything we think we believe in, that break our spirit piece by piece. And then maybe you'll end up here, standing on my side of the bars, waiting to answer questions and hoping you can make a deal. We come home because it's the only place we can go where they're sure to take us in. Not because the Organization cares about us, but because we're valuable.

'I've worked for so many people, so many causes and ideologies . . . But in the end the Organization is family. They make us, they shape us, they hold the paperwork on our souls. Not surprising, really. It's the nature of our job that we lead isolated lives. Always on the move, never a chance to put down roots or get close to anyone.' He caught something in my expression. 'Oh, you think you've found someone. Make the most of it, Ishmael. It won't last.'

I didn't argue the point. 'Is there really no one in your life? What about family, friends, lovers? Even people like us can't move through the world without making some connections. Is there no one you'd like us to contact?'

He smiled. 'So you can check with them, to check up on me? No, there's no one. There was someone once . . . She left me after she became pregnant, and I wouldn't leave the spying game to be with her. How could I tell her it was all I knew? I could have tracked her down but she'd made her decision. And I didn't want to endanger her or the child by drawing attention to them. She chose to go and I let her. It was for the best.'

'There's nothing about that in your file,' I said.

'Not everything gets into the files,' he said. 'You should know that, Ishmael. Why are you here? I mean, why you of all people? And why are the interrogators taking so long to get to me? Come on, let's get this show on the road. I have so much to tell them, secrets like you wouldn't believe. In return for being allowed to retire and put all this madness behind me.'

'It's not that simple,' I said. 'You must know that. First you have to convince us you are who you claim to be.'

'Understandable,' said Parker. 'I often feel the same way when I look in the mirror. I've had so many faces, so many identities . . . How can I prove to you that I'm really Frank Parker?'

'You tell me.'

'I could tell you things about the Organization. Names, codes, protocols. Past and present.'

'How would you know the up-to-date stuff?'

'That's part of what I'm offering to trade,' said Parker. 'I could tell you the names of the past two Colonels. Oliver Cranleigh, and after him James Belcourt.'

I had to raise an eyebrow at that. 'I didn't know the name of my Colonel until he was dead.'

'Yes,' said Parker. 'I heard about that. And now there's a new Colonel. Would you like to know his name?'

'Maybe later,' I said.

'I could tell you why they're always called the Colonel.'

'I'm not that interested.'

'You would be,' said Parker. 'If you only knew.'

'You're tempting the wrong person,' I said. 'I have nothing to offer you.'

'You could get me out of this cell. Arrange for better treatment.'

'And why would I do that?'

'Because if you did, I'd tell you what I found out about the Organization that made me leave. It's too late for me, Ishmael, but you could still save yourself.'

'Tell me why you went rogue,' I said, 'and I'll think about it.'

Parker shrugged heavily. 'What I found out . . . didn't exactly come as a surprise. Not after some of the things the Organization had me do for them. Maybe I was just tired of what my life had become. But in the end, the new life I made for myself wasn't that different. Same puppet, different strings. Why do we do this, Ishmael? Why do we give our lives to shadows and lies?'

'Because it's a job worth doing,' I said. 'The Organization makes the work possible.'

'But what exactly is the job?'

'Keeping people safe,' I said. 'From all the things they don't need to know are out to get them.'

'I used to believe that,' said Parker. 'But . . . do we keep the general populace ignorant of all the dangers in the hidden world because they couldn't cope? Because they'd panic or go crazy? I don't think so. I think it's because that makes them easier for our lords and masters to control. We deny them knowledge because they might use it against those in power. We should tell people the truth. Tell them everything. And then, what would we need an Organization for?'

'Are we qualified to make a decision that big?' I said.

'If not us,' said Parker, 'then who? And if the Organization really are such saints and benefactors, with everyone's best interests at heart, why isn't anyone allowed to know who and what they are?'

'Do you know?' I said.

He smiled.

'Did you ever think you'd end up here?' I said. 'Deep in the bowels of the infamous Ringstone Lodge?'

'I asked to be brought here,' said Parker.

I had to raise an eyebrow. 'That has to be a first. Why?'

'I have my reasons.'

'Did you expect to find a friendly face here?'

'Something like that. How do you feel about being here, Ishmael Jones? Are you sure that when the time comes they'll just let you go?'

'Why would they want to keep me?' I said.

'Because you're the infamous Ishmael Jones.'

I have a lot of experience when it comes to hiding my true nature from the rest of the world. I was aware of the irony involved in my quizzing Parker over who he really was. But then who better than someone like me, who knows all the tricks? Did the Organization know that, and was that why they'd sent me? So many questions, and so few answers. Or at least none I could trust.

'Can you think of any way to prove conclusively who you are?' I said.

'No,' he said. 'I've destroyed my past quite thoroughly.

First, when I joined the Organization; and then later, when I had to hide from them. It wasn't difficult. It wasn't like there was anything I wanted to hang on to.'

'What about the child?' I said. 'We could always run a check on his DNA, to see if it matches yours.'

'No,' he said flatly. 'I won't put the child at risk by exposing him to our world. In the end, you people are going to have to decide just how badly you want the information I've got. You're just going to have to trust me.'

'Trust is a hard thing to come by in our profession,' I said.

'You should know, Ishmael.'

He turned away from the bars, sat down on his bed, and stared at the wall opposite.

'I have nothing more to say to you. Get out of here and send in the interrogators.'

'You're really prepared to tell us everything you've done?' I said.

'Everything.'

'Even the bad stuff?'

'Especially the bad stuff.'

Was he looking to do penance, or just bargaining for his own safety? I couldn't read his false face or his carefully controlled body language. He was an agent, after all.

'Are you sure that's all you want to say to me?' I said. 'Once I leave, the real questioning begins.'

'That's what I want.'

'You must be the first man in your position to say that,' I said. 'You know it will get rough.'

'Good,' said Parker. 'I deserve it.'

'Are your sins really so bad?'

'You have no idea.'

I left him sitting on his bed, staring at nothing, and went back to join MacKay at the foot of the stairs.

'Well?' said MacKay. 'What did he have to say?'

'Nothing I didn't expect,' I said. 'Nothing particularly useful.' I looked at MacKay. 'I take it there is a recording of our conversation?'

'Of course,' said MacKay. 'Cameras and hidden microphones.

I'm sure the two doctors are digging through your words for clues even as we speak. But if you knew that, why did you send me away?'

'To give Parker the illusion of privacy,' I said. 'To make it easier for him to open up to me.'

'And did he?' said MacKay.

'Hard to tell,' I said.

THREE
Haunted by More Than One Past

I thought about what Parker said, and what he didn't say, all the way back up the stairs. While MacKay maintained a respectful silence. Why had Parker decided to come back? What, precisely, had brought him back out of the shadows after all this time? And why had he asked to be brought to Ringstone Lodge, in particular? I had to smile, quietly, to myself. Parker had baited his hook very cleverly; even I was intrigued to find out what it was he had to tell us. But that wasn't my job. I wasn't here to learn the truth, just to keep the man alive while we figured out whether or not he really was Parker.

I had no idea. He sounded like the real thing, but an agent is an agent whoever he works for. And no one's more convincing than a con man with the very latest line in snake oil to sell you. The only way to beat the con is to not want whatever it is that they're selling.

Back in the entrance hall I found Penny had been left all on her own, sitting on a chair in the corner, one crossed leg idly swinging. She bounced up on to her feet, nodded to MacKay, and beamed happily at me.

'Welcome back! How was the underworld?'

'Not quite as illuminating as I hoped,' I said. 'Where is everybody?'

'Security "R" Us decided they just had to go check out the grounds and the perimeter,' said Penny. 'In case we were followed here from the station.'

'I think one of us would have noticed,' I said.

'Almost certainly,' said MacKay. 'But it is best to be sure, regarding such matters.'

'Baxter and Redd didn't try to bother you?' I said to Penny. 'Put on the pressure as to why we're here?'

'Oh sure,' said Penny. 'But I just went all girly on them and they didn't know how to cope.'

'What about Philip Martin?' I said.

'Gone back to his little hutch to keep his beady eye on everything.'

'I am going to have to take a look at this security centre at some point,' I said to MacKay.

'Of course, sir.'

'Doctor Hayley and Doctor Doyle are currently plotting together in the lounge,' said Penny. 'I was very pointedly not invited.'

'They'll be wanting to talk to you now,' said MacKay. 'About what you've learned from Mr Parker.'

Penny raised an eyebrow at him. 'They'd better not be planning to interrogate Ishmael. He really doesn't take kindly to that.'

'It's true,' I said. 'I don't.'

'I am sure it is all in the name of sharing useful information,' said MacKay. 'We belong to the same team, after all.'

'Really?' I said. 'I don't think Hayley and Doyle got that memo. But by all means, let's play nice and pretend we're all here for the same reasons. I have questions of my own, for those two. Lead on, MacKay.'

A few nicely appointed corridors later, MacKay ushered us into an extremely comfortable lounge. Big and airy, with the usual old-fashioned country-house furniture and a great bay window that looked out over the grounds. Fierce light from the overhead chandelier pushed back the growing darkness outside. Hayley and Doyle were sitting side by side on a large sofa, drinking tea out of delicate china cups. They looked up sharply as we entered, put their cups down on the coffee table before them and, ignoring both Penny and MacKay, fixed me with stern but anticipatory stares. For two such experienced interrogators, their faces and body language were surprisingly easy to read. Or maybe that was just me. Hayley was clearly brimming over with questions concerning things she thought she knew about me. Doyle was nervous about facing such an experienced field agent, and trying very hard not to show it.

Both of them made a point of not standing up as I entered, partly to remind me of their doctorly authority but mostly because it would have been difficult for either of them to get up out of the depths of the sofa and still retain any dignity.

An open laptop had been placed on the coffee table, next to a pile of old *Country Life* magazines. The sound had been turned down just before we entered. I caught a quick glimpse of the screen, showing me talking to Parker, before Hayley shut the laptop down completely. As though she didn't want me to see which part of the interview she'd been so interested in. I gave her my best enigmatic smile, to show her I could play the secrets game too. Doyle had a fat official file perched on one knee. The closed cover had the three red diagonal stripes that meant 'For your eyes only'. I dropped bonelessly into a chair facing the two doctors and arranged myself comfortably. Penny perched elegantly on the arm of my chair, crossing her long legs to show them off to their best advantage. But the doctors still only had eyes for me. I was their target. MacKay moved off a way to take up a position by the bay window, where he could watch us and look outside at the same time.

Hayley stretched out an imperious hand to Doyle, who handed over the official file without a murmur. Hayley opened the file and leafed through it, taking her time. Penny looked at me, to see how I wanted to play this. I just smiled and sank back in my chair. I was in no hurry. Hayley wanted to talk about what I'd learned from Parker, which meant she had to come to me for answers. But she was putting it off so as not to seem too eager, too needy. Doyle split his attention between Hayley and me, waiting to see which of us would speak first. I was very interested in the file. The three red stripes on the cover meant it contained information on Parker that the Organization felt I didn't need to know. And I wanted to know. I really don't like it when people keep things from me. I could have snatched the file away from Hayley and taken a look for myself; but that would only have led to raised voices and tears before bedtime, and I still had to work with these people. So I just settled comfortably in my chair and smiled easily at one and all. I could always steal the file later, if I needed to. But

I doubted there was anything in it to tell me why Parker had chosen to walk away from the Organization, or anything else I really wanted to know.

Doyle stirred restlessly, and leaned forward on the sofa to address me. 'Now you've spoken to our man of mystery, Ishmael, do you think he really is the legendary Frank Parker?'

'He sounds like the real deal,' I said carefully. 'But then if he's been properly coached by the opposition, he would do. Wouldn't he? He's saying all the right things, and holding back when you'd expect him to. But I am a little surprised that he's so insistent on talking to you . . .'

'We've already had a brief word with the man,' said Doyle. 'Exploratory talks, you understand, opening gambits and all that . . .'

'What did he have to say?' I said. 'Anything interesting?'

'Not really,' said Doyle. 'A very close-mouthed man, our Mr Parker.'

'I didn't have any problems,' I said. 'But then, we have more in common. Have you got any useful information out of him yet?'

'Nothing worth having,' said Hayley. She slammed the file shut and glared at me. 'We heard everything you said. The fascinating cut and thrust of clashing egos. He's hiding something.'

'Of course he is,' said MacKay. 'But not necessarily what we think.'

We all looked at him, but he had nothing more to say. He looked out the bay window at the grounds, as though expecting an attack at any moment. Hayley studied me suspiciously.

'Parker did seem to know an awful lot about you, Ishmael. Which is odd, considering the two of you have never met before. Officially. I wonder what he'll tell us about you, once we get to work on him?'

'I'm interested in that myself,' I said. I slouched down a little more in my chair, just to make it clear I wasn't intimidated by her tone. I looked thoughtfully at her, and then at Doyle. 'I don't know how high your security clearance goes, but I would advise you to be very careful over which particular cans of worms you choose to pry open. Apart from anything else, if there really are bad apples inside the Organization . . .'

'We only have his word for that,' Doyle said judiciously. 'It could just be a bargaining ploy to make us take him more seriously.'

'And encourage us to make him a better deal,' said Hayley.

'But what if it isn't?' said Penny. 'If you don't know how far up the rot goes? Who can you trust?'

'It does add a certain urgency to the situation,' said Doyle. 'But that could be the point. To hurry us into precipitous and unwise decisions.'

'You did get some interesting information out of the man,' Hayley said reluctantly. 'We've already had Martin contact Headquarters, suggesting that they set their hounds on the trail of the woman and child.'

'So you can access the child's DNA?' I said. 'Or so you can threaten them in order to put pressure on Parker? Nothing like holding a knife to a loved one's throat to bring a reluctant prisoner into line.'

'Exactly,' said Hayley.

Penny looked at her as though she was some kind of poisonous insect. Hayley didn't seem in the least concerned.

'Parker had to know our little chat was being recorded,' I said. 'And that you'd be bound to go after the woman and child once he mentioned them. I don't think anything he said, no matter how casual, was unintended. Perhaps he wants the Organization to find them for him, because he hasn't been able to do so.'

'Do you think that's why he came back?' said Penny. 'Because of them?'

'Possibly,' I said. 'But why now, after all these years? Doctor Hayley, Doctor Doyle, is there anything in Parker's unexpurgated file that I ought to know?'

Hayley's mouth tightened into a flat line and she met my gaze defiantly. In this at least she had the advantage and wasn't about to give it up. Then Doyle cleared his throat, and she shot him a glance of betrayal.

'Nothing particularly earth-shattering,' said Doyle. 'Just more details, on the various cases he handled.'

'Do you recognize any of these case names, Mr Jones?' said Hayley. 'The Inverted Pyramid in the Pacific, The Hidden Sixth Side of the Pentagon, The Occasional Cities of the Black Sun?' She watched my face carefully as she ran through the titles.

'You made those up!' said Penny. And then she stopped and looked at me. 'Those are real? Really?'

'Unfortunately, yes,' I said. 'I've heard of all of them, but I can't see a connection to anything I've worked on.'

'But you have heard of them,' Hayley said accusingly. 'Even though, technically speaking, you must know you're not supposed to have done so.'

'I hear all kinds of things, in my line of work,' I said. 'Gossip is what makes the secret agent's world go round. The trick is to tell people things that don't matter in the hope they'll tell you things that do. Of course, a lot of the time you don't know what really matters until you find out the hard way, much later. I don't see how any of those cases could possibly connect to what's happening here. And let's face it, you can cross-examine Parker all you like, hoping to catch him out in a detail here and a name there. But if he is a fake, you can be sure he'll have been very thoroughly briefed and you won't trip him up on anything that obvious.'

Hayley nodded reluctantly and put the file to one side.

'Frank Parker had an excellent record as a field agent,' said Doyle. 'A high success rate, with minimum exposure and an acceptable level of civilian casualties.'

'Which is not always the way,' said Hayley. 'I have read about what happened at Belcourt Manor, Mr Jones.'

'Change the subject,' I said.

Something in my tone must have got through to her, because she averted her gaze.

Penny fixed Hayley with her coldest stare. 'What does your file tell you about the kind of person Parker was? I mean, was he an honourable man? Could he have come back just because he discovered there were traitors inside the Organization?'

'He did imply he left because he found out the Organization wasn't what he wanted it to be,' I said. 'Perhaps he wants to save it from itself?'

'Honourable behaviour?' said Hayley, almost smirking. 'Rare, I would have thought. In your line of work.'

'Oh, you'd be surprised,' I said. 'What is a cynic after all, except a disappointed idealist? People get into our line of work for all kinds of reasons.'

'And you, Ishmael?' said Doyle, quite casually. 'What brought you into the hidden world?'

'I belong there,' I said. 'It feels like home.'

'We were assured we could expect your full cooperation,' Hayley said coldly. 'But I have to say you're not being very forthcoming.'

'I don't have to be,' I said cheerfully. 'I'm just here to oversee the process and make sure everything runs smoothly. Parker is the subject of your interrogation, not me.' And then I stopped and studied Doyle and Hayley carefully. 'Unless, of course, things have changed . . .'

'No, sir, they have not,' MacKay said immediately. 'You are currently in charge of Ringstone Lodge, with authority over everyone here. My instructions on that were most particular.'

'Good to know,' I said. I gestured at Parker's file. 'It could be that we're looking in the wrong place. It's always possible the answer lies in where Parker went after he left.'

Hayley opened the heavy file again, and turned to a section at the back. 'We have some information on that. Parker seems to have done secret work for all the usual subterranean groups, at one time or another. Quite often he would work for one side and then go do something for their opposite number. Almost as if he was trying to balance things out. Interesting.'

'But what kind of work did he do?' I said.

'Does it matter?' said Penny.

'It might,' I said.

'Information gathering and wet work,' said Hayley. 'He was very skilled at both.'

'Wait a minute,' said Penny. 'You mean . . .'

'Yes,' said Doyle. 'That much we can be sure of. Mostly, Frank Parker killed people.'

'Bad people?' Penny said tentatively.

'Good and bad, in as much as the terms have any meaning

in intelligence work,' said Hayley, almost offhandedly. She was working her way through the file, turning the pages more and more quickly. 'His targets included high-up personages and complete unknowns. He didn't seem to care who he was sent after, as long as someone was willing to pay to see them dead. Parker was a consummate professional, untroubled by any sense of conscience or morality.'

'But he stopped,' I said. 'Just gave it all up and walked away. Disappeared so completely even the most experienced people on both sides couldn't find him. So why did he stop?'

'Maybe he decided he had enough money,' said Doyle. 'But then later something went wrong, the money ran out . . . And that's why he's back.'

'Looking to sell his soul one more time,' said Hayley. 'In return for protection from the one Organization that could hide him from all the enemies he's made.'

'Could there be a clue in the new faces he chose?' Penny said suddenly. 'Character traits in common, for example? Perhaps they were the faces of people he wanted to be?'

Hayley and Doyle looked at each other, and then Hayley flipped back to the beginning of the file and the photos showing Parker's previous faces. She looked them over carefully, with Doyle leaning in close beside her.

'Interesting idea,' Hayley said finally.

Doyle nudged her arm and she reluctantly laid the file on the coffee table, in front of Penny and me. And then she turned away and rested her chin on her hand, staring off into space and thinking hard. Doyle watched her do it. I studied the various photos carefully, but couldn't see any connection between the faces.

'To change his appearance this completely,' I said finally, 'Parker must have undergone major plastic surgeries, including subcutaneous implants to change the shape of his face.'

Hayley looked at me sharply. 'Implants? Are you sure? No one said anything about implants.'

'It's what I would have done,' I said smoothly. 'Surgery just alters the outer appearance; you have to change the under-lying bone structure if you want to make yourself really unrecognizable. But why did he feel the need to change his facc that much? So he could tell himself he wasn't the person who'd done so many bad things? He said something to me about not liking to look at himself in the mirror. Check the recording and get the exact words.'

'All these faces have one thing in common,' said Penny. 'None of them look particularly happy.'

'You're right,' I said. 'Paging Doctor Freud . . .'

'But on the other hand,' said Doyle, 'our guest could be using these past faces to hide the fact that he isn't Parker.'

'The man in the cell has had surgery and implants,' I said. 'I saw the scars.'

Doyle frowned. 'Really? I couldn't see anything.'

'I have experience in these matters,' I said.

'Are you saying you've changed your face, Ishmael?' said Hayley.

I just smiled.

'Frank Parker is famously supposed to be unkillable,' said MacKay. 'If all else fails, we could try killing him. See if it takes.' We all looked at him. He took in our faces and shrugged. 'Just a thought.'

'I think we'll leave that as a last resort,' I said. 'Rather than risk losing the goose that could still lay golden eggs.'

'As you wish, sir.'

'I need to talk to Parker,' said Hayley. She closed the file with a snap. 'Really get to work on the man.'

She didn't actually rub her hands together in anticipation, but the sound of it was in her voice. Doyle nodded solemnly.

'He'll crack. They all do, in the end.'

Penny didn't even try to hide her distaste. 'Whatever happened to the Hippocratic oath?'

'Suspended,' said Hayley. 'For the duration.'

'The duration of what?' said Penny.

'Sorry,' Hayley said smugly. 'That's classified.'

I considered her thoughtfully. 'What exactly are your orders? To get to the truth? Or to break the subject? Because it does occur to me that if you were to decide this isn't Parker, then the Organization wouldn't have to take his accusations of traitors seriously.'

'Everyone here wants him to be the real Frank Parker,'

Doyle said firmly. 'Because bringing his valuable information to the Organization would be a success big enough to make all of us. Even apart from the traitors within, what Parker knows could bring down any number of important enemies and save the lives of many of our people currently out in the field.'

'Really?' said Penny.

'Of course!' said Doyle.

'The hidden world is in a constant state of undeclared war, Miss Belcourt,' said Hayley. 'You must have noticed. And in a war like ours, information is ammunition. If Parker really has what he says he has, then we want it. But if we get it wrong, if we let a fake get past us, the damage his disinformation could do to the Organization would be incalculable. He could spend years eating away at us from the inside. As a sleeper, a saboteur, an assassin . . .'

'So,' I said. 'No pressure, then.'

'Are you sure you don't want me to kill Mr Parker?' said MacKay. 'It wouldn't be any bother.'

'No,' I said firmly.

'We have to get back to Parker,' said Hayley. 'We were just starting to make some progress with him when word came that you were on your way and everything had to be put on hold till you got here.'

Hayley and Doyle stared at me challengingly. I just smiled, and met their gaze perfectly steadily.

Penny gave me a hard look. 'You're being far too casual about this, Ishmael. Would you let them torture Parker, if that was what it took?'

'Of course not,' I said.

No one in the room looked like they believed me. But I could hardly say to Penny 'It depends . . .'

'My associate and I have a long and successful record in getting the truth out of people, Penny,' said Hayley. 'This case may be a little more complicated than most, but we'll get there.'

'It's what we do,' said Doyle.

They exchanged tight professional smiles, the little black woman in the business suit and the dumpy college professor.

Sometimes the most frightening people can have the most ordinary faces.

'Whatever happened to showing good faith and winning a man's trust?' said Penny, stubbornly returning to her point. 'You never know, you might get better results out of Parker that way.'

'We don't have the time,' said Hayley.

'Or the inclination?' I said.

'We have to make a decision soon as to who he is,' said Doyle, 'so we can decide where to send him next.'

'What are the options?' I said.

'Just two,' said MacKay. 'Either we pass him on to a more secure location where he can safely unburden himself of all he knows. Or we bury him among the tombstones at the side of the Lodge.'

Penny was shaken by his bluntness. I wasn't.

'We need to get back to work,' said Hayley. 'Time is not on our side.'

'It never is,' I said. 'Go ahead. Don't let me keep you.'

Penny shot me a look, as though she'd still been half expecting me to stop them. To protect Parker from the nasty interrogators. But that wasn't what I was there for. I met Penny's gaze steadily. Her mouth tightened, and she turned away from me.

'Before you go, doctors,' said Penny, 'There's something else we need to discuss.'

'What?' said Hayley, with heavy patience.

'The hauntings,' said Penny.

'They need to get to work, Penny,' I said.

'I'm not stopping them! I'm just interested.'

I looked around. MacKay's face was unreadable, but interestingly Hayley and Doyle both looked unhappy. As though they really wished Penny hadn't asked them that question.

'No one in the Lodge has seen a ghost,' said Hayley. 'As such.'

'But there have been . . . unexplained incidents,' said Doyle.

'Things that go bump in the night?' said Penny.

'And in the daytime,' said MacKay.

'And you've actually seen these things?' I said.

'We have all seen or heard something,' said MacKay.

'I'm not convinced it's anything more than group hysteria, from all the pressure we're under,' said Hayley. 'Cabin fever.'

'What I find particularly interesting,' said Doyle, his professionalism coming to the fore almost in spite of himself, 'is that it's never anything you can put your finger on. Never anything definite or identifiable.'

'Do you believe in ghosts?' Penny asked bluntly. 'Ishmael keeps saying he doesn't . . .'

'I don't,' I said. 'I really don't. Why are you having such a hard time believing me?'

'How can you say that?' said Penny. 'After everything we've seen.'

'In all my time in the field,' I said, 'dealing with the darkest areas of the hidden world, I have never once encountered a ghost or a spirit. Or anything to convince me that the dead ever come back to bother the living.'

'But what about . . .?'

'Hush,' I said. 'Not in front of the children. I'm not convinced she was anything more than some kind of creature, perhaps an evolutionary offshoot.'

'Denial isn't just a river in Africa,' said Penny.

I looked at her. 'Sometimes I have no idea what you're talking about.'

'I am more than willing to entertain the notion that there is a scientific explanation for the . . . unusual things we have all experienced,' said MacKay. 'If only someone would provide one.'

'Dead is dead!' said Hayley.

'They are if I have anything to do with it,' I said.

'I still favour the idea that it's all some kind of psychic phenomenon,' said Doyle. 'The stone tape theory, with the solid structure of the Lodge playing back stored memories of past events.'

Hayley sniffed loudly. 'The world has enough strange things in it without dragging in pseudoscience.'

'And yet,' murmured MacKay, 'still, it moves . . .'

Hayley and Doyle looked at each other, and had nothing more to say. Penny looked at me triumphantly.

'Come with me, Mr Jones, Miss Belcourt,' MacKay said finally. 'It's time you visited Mr Martin in his security centre. He can present to you what evidence we have of the supernatural at play in the Lodge.'

'Good,' I said. 'Evidence is always good.'

And back through the pleasantly appointed corridors we went. With so few people in it, the Lodge seemed almost eerily quiet. Like walking through a hotel after all the guests have been evacuated. The absence of people can make just as strong an impression as a noisy crowd. Silence has a presence all its own. The security centre was tucked away just round the corner from the entrance hall, behind a closed, locked and heavily reinforced steel door. An ominous presence, in the country hotel setting. MacKay didn't even bother to knock, just leaned in close to the intercom grille.

'Mr Martin, you reprehensible creature! This is MacKay. Open up.'

There was a pause. During which I thought I detected a brief uncertainty in MacKay's face, as if there was a real chance Martin might not let us in, just to show MacKay up. And then there was the sound of several heavy locks disengaging, one after the other, and the door swung slowly back. I looked thoughtfully at the layers of steel upon steel that made up the door. I like to think there isn't any door that could keep me out if I just put my mind or my shoulder to it, but this one looked like it could give me some serious problems.

MacKay politely but firmly insisted on entering the security centre first, presumably to reassure Martin with a familiar face. Like a keeper at a zoo. Once we were all inside, and the door had closed itself firmly behind us, the room seemed uncomfortably small. It was packed with all kinds of surveillance equipment, a lot of which still had that bright shiny look that suggested it had come straight from its packaging. Some of the tech was so advanced I had trouble deciding what it was, and it's part of my job to be up to date on such things. Rows of monitor screens covered three of the walls, crammed together and showing detailed views of the interior and exterior of Ringstone Lodge, including the woods, the grounds and the perimeter walls. Which added up to a hell of a lot of hidden cameras.

Philip Martin sat in the middle of it all, on a battered old swivel chair that made soft protesting noises as he turned this way and that, his gaze jumping from one screen to another. He didn't get up to greet us as we entered, just nodded brusquely to MacKay and Penny, and scowled at me. There were no other chairs in the room, and it didn't look safe to lean on any of the equipment.

'All right,' I said. 'Show me everything. You know you want to.'

'Welcome to my world,' said Martin. 'I see all, hear all, and remain diplomatically quiet about most of it. Unless it's really funny. Watch, and wonder.'

His fingers moved quickly over the keyboard resting on his lap. The views on the screens zoomed in and out, closing in on individual trees in the woods or opening up to show whole sections of the grounds. Martin smiled proudly as he presented us with shuffled glimpses of room after room and all kinds of sounds picked up by hidden microphones. One screen hooked on to movement in the woods, and Martin zoomed in to show Baxter and Redd emerging from the dark shadows between the trees. Martin boosted the sound levels so we could hear what they were saying.

'Ishmael Jones!' said Baxter. 'I ask you! What kind of a name is that? If he's going to use a cover name, he could at least choose something that doesn't sound so obviously fake. Bloody field agents. Always looking down on the rank and file like us, who do all the real work. Ishmael Jones . . . He thinks he's so much. I could take him.'

'Pretty sure you couldn't,' said Redd. 'Field agents are supposed to be just a bit special when it comes to the old ultraviolence.'

Baxter growled and shook his head. 'They make that stuff up to scare the opposition. You watch how fast he backs down once I stand up to him.'

Martin shut down the sound. 'If he was any more alpha male, he'd sweat testosterone. You want to steer clear of him, Ishmael. He's trouble.'

'That's all right,' I said. 'So am I. Show me Frank Parker. What's he doing right now?'

'Not a lot,' said Martin.

He gestured to one particular screen. And there was Parker sitting on his bed in his cell, looking at nothing. He didn't seem to have moved since I left him.

'Now, that is spooky!' said Penny. 'A man in his position shouldn't be that calm. Not with all the things he's got to be worried about. If I was in there, I'd be climbing those walls by now.'

'Yes,' I said. 'But he's been trained. This is what I would expect to see from an experienced field agent. Show no fear, show no weakness. Give your interrogators nothing to work with. He has something they want, so that puts him in the driver's seat.'

'I could send Baxter and Redd down there, when they return,' said MacKay. 'Have them beat some of the cockiness out of him.'

'No you couldn't,' I said. 'Even allowing for his age, a trained field agent could still kick the crap out of a couple of standard thugs. And if by some chance one of them did get in a lucky shot and Parker fell and hit his head, a man with concussion isn't going to be answering any questions. I really don't think the Organization would be too happy about that.'

MacKay inclined his head. 'You are of course entirely correct, Mr Jones. I withdraw the suggestion.'

'First you want to kill him, and now you want him beaten up!' said Penny. 'Don't you like Parker?'

'He's a traitor,' said MacKay. And in his voice was all the merciless judgement of the old soldier.

I looked at Parker, sitting there in his cell. 'He's a professional. But whose professional? He came home to this country when he could have gone anywhere, sold his information to anyone. I think it has something to do with the woman and child he mentioned. The family he never knew.'

'I never knew my father,' said Martin. 'Grew up perfectly well without one. Families are overrated.'

I nodded, slowly. 'Hayley and Doyle said they'd already talked to him. Do you have that recording?'

Martin looked to MacKay. 'Doctor Hayley told me not to let anyone else see it . . .'

'Mr Jones is in charge,' said MacKay. 'Show him anything he wishes to see.'

Martin shrugged. 'So long as you keep the vultures off my back . . .'

His hands darted across the keyboard, and a screen suddenly cleared to show us Hayley and Doyle sitting together on the sofa in the lounge. They had Parker's unexpurgated file open on the coffee table before them. They seemed much more relaxed, on their own.

'This isn't what I asked to see,' I said.

'It's relevant,' Martin said quickly. 'Keep watching.'

'We've been through this, Alice,' Doyle was saying patiently. 'The Organization was very clear about which questions they want us to ask. We're supposed to compile a complete list of everyone Parker ever worked for, and details of all the missions he carried out for them.'

'We haven't got time for that, Robbie,' said Hayley. 'Let's just prove it's really him, and then someone else can dig out the rest.'

Penny looked at me and mouthed 'Alice' and 'Robbie'. As if she couldn't believe such cold-blooded interrogators could have such ordinary names.

'I'll be amazed if Parker tells us one thing he doesn't want us to know,' Hayley continued. 'That man is a professional hard case.' She stretched slowly, her face becoming almost sensuous as she savoured the sensation. 'I wonder how much we can persuade him to tell us about the traitors?'

'No, Alice,' said Doyle, smiling indulgently. 'Until we know for sure who we're dealing with, we can't even raise the subject. Or allow him to. We don't want him casting suspicions, in case it makes the Organization distrust perfectly good people. Which might be what this is all about, after all.'

'I love it when you boss me around, Robbie,' said Hayley. And she gave Doyle a surprisingly wicked smile before returning to the subject. 'It's the areas we're not supposed to get into that fascinate me. Aren't you tempted to ask him anyway? I know I am.'

'Of course I'm tempted,' said Doyle. 'But I'm not going to, and neither are you.'

'Don't be such a poop, Robbie. Why not?'

'Because I don't want to end up sitting in a cell next door to Parker, waiting for an interview with someone like us.'

'You always were the sensible one. But aren't you excited? This is the first time we've had access to an actual field agent. The knowledge we gain could be invaluable!'

'Yes . . .' said Doyle. 'Well . . . as long as we're careful, Alice. And I mean quite extraordinarily careful.'

'Of course, sweetie.'

They leaned towards each other, and Martin hurried to shut the screen down.

'Did they know they were being recorded?' said Penny.

'They should have,' said Martin. 'I told them every room in the Lodge is covered by hidden cameras and microphones. But it's hard to be on your guard all the time.'

'Love among the headshrinkers,' said Penny. 'The horror! I wonder if he psychoanalyses her in bed?'

'Before or after?' I said.

Penny grinned. 'Probably during . . .'

'Moving on,' I said. I looked to Martin, who was smirking broadly. 'Are you ready to show me the Parker interview now?'

'Hold on to your socks!' said Martin. 'This is the good stuff.'

The screen changed to show Hayley and Doyle standing together in front of Parker's cell. He stood on the other side of the bars, facing them calmly. Hayley gave him her best scowl, but if Parker was in any way intimidated he made a really good job of hiding it.

'I thought it would be you,' he said. 'Doctor Hayley, Doctor Doyle. You've made a name for yourselves these past few years. Not a particularly nice name, but I suppose that goes with the territory.'

'You must have known this was going to happen, Frank,' said Doyle. 'Interrogation and debriefing are standard procedure in cases like yours.'

'There are no cases like mine,' said Parker. 'And of course I knew, I've been looking forward to it.'

Hayley and Doyle exchanged a glance, and then Hayley fixed Parker with her best cold stare.

'Stand back from the bars now, Frank. And keep both your hands where we can see them.'

'I have been very thoroughly searched,' Parker said easily. 'Including all my important little places. I thought I was going to have to get engaged at one point. Yes, I know . . . standard procedure.'

He backed away from the bars, not taking his eyes off Hayley and Doyle, until he bumped against the rear wall of his cell. Hayley raised her voice.

'Martin, open the door.'

The lock on the cell door made a series of complicated sounds as Martin operated it by remote control, and then the bars slid smoothly sideways. Hayley and Doyle stepped inside the cell and the bars immediately slid back into position. Parker sat down on the bed, without asking for permission. He kept his hands ostentatiously in sight, clasped together in his lap, and smiled engagingly at Hayley and Doyle.

'Well, isn't this cozy? I would ask you to sit down, but I haven't been supplied with any chairs. There is the toilet, if one of you isn't too fussy. Or you could snuggle up beside me on the bed. No? Suit yourselves. Feel free to lean against the wall. Or not, as you wish. Now, what shall we talk about?'

Hayley stepped forward, taking the lead. Doyle stayed where he was, watching Parker carefully.

'Why have you chosen to come back now, Frank?' said Hayley. 'Did something happen?'

'I don't want to talk about that,' said Parker. 'I want to talk about what's wrong inside the Organization.'

'We're not allowed to discuss that,' said Doyle. 'You must understand, Frank, we're not cleared for that level of information.'

'Then send for someone who is,' said Parker. 'There are things the Organization needs to know. Urgently.'

'We've been given a list of things to ask you, Frank,' said Hayley. 'You have to give us something, so we can give you something.'

'No,' said Parker. 'Go back and talk to your superiors. Get all the clearances you need, or you're wasting my time. If you aren't up to this, pass me on to someone who is. I don't know how much time I've got before someone turns up at the Lodge looking for me.'

'You're perfectly safe here, Frank,' said Hayley.

'I know all about Ringstone Lodge,' said Parker. 'Everyone in our line of business does. Which means our mutual enemies will expect to find me here. I can't stay long. It isn't safe. For any of us.'

'You're in no position to make demands, Frank,' said Doyle.

'I think you'll find I am,' said Parker.

'We're here to get answers out of you,' said Hayley. 'And we're prepared to be very persuasive.'

'Get your clearance,' said Frank, 'And I'll tell you everything. All kinds of amazing things.'

'You assured the Organization you would cooperate, Frank,' said Doyle.

'I am,' said Parker. 'Ask me anything you like about my past. I can talk about that. Enough to convince you I'm me. But the real stuff, the reason I'm here, that's too important to put off for long.'

'Frank . . .' said Hayley.

'No,' said Parker. 'You're wasting time, and the Organization won't thank you for it. Not once they know what I know.'

Hayley and Doyle looked at each other, then moved back to the cell door. It slid open and they left. Parker waited till the bars had closed again, and then raised his voice after them.

'And when you come back, don't call me Frank.'

Hayley looked back at him. 'Why not? Isn't that your name?'

'Don't try to pretend we're friends. Call me Mr Parker.'

Martin shut down the screen. I turned to MacKay.

'You said he was being cooperative. No trouble at all, you said.'

'He was,' said MacKay. 'Right up to the point where they went in to talk to him. And even then he sounded like he was making sense.'

'Have Hayley and Doyle requested the necessary clearances?' I said.

'Of course,' said MacKay. 'They're still waiting for someone to make a decision.'

'Is that why you're here, Ishmael?' asked Martin. 'Do you have that level of clearance?'

'Sorry,' I said. 'That's classified.'

'What just happened there didn't go the way Hayley and Doyle thought it would . . .' Penny said thoughtfully. 'Could this be what Parker intended all along? Blow smoke in interrogators' eyes to keep them away from him?'

'Wouldn't surprise me,' I said. 'I really don't like how quickly that man was able to stop two trained interrogators in their tracks. Did you see how easily he took charge? Call me Mr Parker . . . That man has been very well trained.'

I stood and thought for a moment, considering possibilities, while the others watched me. Finally, I turned to Martin.

'Ghosts,' I said. 'You're supposed to have evidence of hauntings. Show me what you've got.'

Martin nodded quickly, and tapped away at his keyboard. 'No one wanted to believe anything supernatural was going on at the Lodge until I showed them what my systems had picked up. How much do you want to see? I've got hours of recordings. Nothing conclusive, I'll admit, but they are fascinating. With a heavy side order of downright disturbing.'

'Do you have evidence, or not?' I said.

'Well, yes and no. I've got evidence of something . . . As to what, you'll have to decide for yourself.' Martin nodded to a particular screen. 'OK, I've put together some edited highlights. Hang on to your undies, we are about to go full on spooky.'

The screen showed a long corridor with subdued lighting and two rows of closed doors facing each other. The time stamp in the bottom right hand corner said 23:45. MacKay leaned in close beside me.

'Upper floor of the Lodge. Living quarters for the support staff.'

'Hush!' said Martin. 'Listen . . .'

My head came up as I heard, quite distinctly, the sound of human footsteps progressing slowly down the corridor, with no one visible on the screen to make them. There was nowhere for anyone to hide, no shadows or blind spots, but still the footsteps carried on. Growing steadily louder and heavier.

Suddenly doors were flung open the whole length of the corridor, one after another, and people came stumbling out of their rooms in a variety of nightclothes. The sound of footsteps cut off the moment the first door opened. Men and women with confused expressions and serious bed hair looked up and down the corridor, shouting questions and accusations at each other. It was clear this wasn't the first time such a thing had happened. Some of the people looked angry, some looked frightened. All of them were taking it very seriously.

The scene changed. It was the same length of corridor, but now the time stamp said 3:17. Even though it was early in the morning, all of the lights were on. As if no one wanted them turned off. I studied the screen carefully. Nothing moved, and there were no footsteps. No sound at all. And then one of the closed doors suddenly swung open, all on its own. No one came out of the room. After a while, the door slowly shut itself again. Martin froze the image on the screen.

'No one saw that happen at the time,' he said proudly. 'I only came across it by accident, when I was checking some old recordings for technical quality. It made me wonder what else there might be, so I went looking. And I found this. Watch, and wonder. This is a bit special.'

Same corridor, time stamp 7:12. The electric lights had been replaced by daylight. Again, nothing happened for a while and then a dark human shadow appeared on one wall. It lurched slowly down the corridor, without anyone present to cast it. I leaned forward, intrigued. There was something wrong about the shape of the shadow, and the way it moved. And then it just disappeared. Martin punched the air, froze the screen, and spun round in his squeaky chair to grin triumphantly at us.

'Isn't that absolutely amazing?'

'Doesn't it scare you?' said Penny.

'Oh sure,' said Martin. 'If I'd been there when it happened, I'd still be running. But that is just so cool. I could make a fortune out of material like this! If I wasn't bound by the Official Secrets Act, of course. I mean, I am definitely not thinking of trying to sell it. I'm very scared of what the Organization would do to me if I tried.'

'I'm watching you, Mr Martin,' MacKay said darkly.

Penny looked at me. 'That was pretty creepy.'

I thought about it.

'And there's lots more,' Martin said happily. 'All kinds of sights and sounds. Add to that the way people have been feeling just recently . . .' He shot a glance at MacKay. 'People will talk to me when they wouldn't talk to you. Because I can't have them fired. All the staff have been talking about how some parts of the Lodge have started getting on their nerves. They've all been experiencing bad dreams, bad feelings . . . Sensing things, even when they can't see or hear anything. Cold spots. Feelings of not being alone. Things glimpsed out of the corner of the eye that are never there when you look at them directly. A sense of being followed . . . The staff were going out of their minds. When the order came through for them to vacate, you never saw people pack so quickly. Hell, I'll be amazed if any of them come back.'

'Doctor Hayley put it all down to cabin fever,' I said.

Martin snorted dismissively. 'One, she hasn't been here long. And two, that woman has the sensitivity of a brick. You saw the way that shadow moved! Did that look like cabin fever to you?'

'Could your recordings have been tampered with?' I said.

'I've checked everything,' Martin said firmly. 'No one could gain access to my systems without me knowing. All the data you've seen is completely accurate and entirely uncorrupted. You can check for yourself if you want, but I'm telling you . . . You won't find anything.'

'What else have you got?' I said.

'You mean, that wasn't enough?' Martin looked taken aback. 'Well . . . OK, there is this.'

The screen before us showed a series of different locations inside the Lodge, at different times of day. In each case, the lights were flickering. Sometimes they turned themselves on and off. When people were in the rooms while it was happening, they looked very upset. Not just scared. Terrorized.

'That should not be possible,' said MacKay. 'All the electric lighting in the Lodge is controlled by the security systems. Completely independent from all outside interference, for security reasons.'

'Could it be interruptions in the power supply?' I said.

'The Lodge has its own generator,' said MacKay. 'Any interruption or breakdown would set off all kinds of alarms.'

'Right,' said Martin. 'And there's been nothing. I've run scans on all my systems, and they're all perfectly clean. You can check for yourselves.'

'Have you seen anything strange or supernatural yourself?' said Penny. 'I mean, in person?'

'No . . .' Martin sounded a bit wistful. 'Not personally . . . But then I'm in here most of the time.'

'I'm still not convinced,' I said.

'No more am I,' said MacKay. 'But in my army days I did see my share of . . . unusual things. And I assume you have seen your share too, Mr Jones. So why not spooks and spirits?'

I didn't have an answer.

MacKay offered to spell Martin for a few hours so he could take a nap, but Martin didn't want to know. He said he wouldn't feel safe away from the screens. And, his look implied, neither should we. We went back into the entrance hall, and he immediately closed the door behind us. I looked around sharply as I heard footsteps approaching the front door from outside. Then the door was flung open, and Baxter and Redd came bustling in. They were laughing and joking together, but their easy manner disappeared the moment they saw us. Redd closed the door carefully, while Baxter nodded to MacKay, ostentatiously ignoring Penny and me.

'The grounds are empty, the perimeter is secure. Nothing moving. All quiet.'

MacKay nodded to me. 'The surveillance systems should be enough to detect anyone, but there is never any match for human senses and experience.'

'Have either of you seen any ghosts?' Penny said brightly. 'Inside the Lodge, or out in the grounds?'

'No,' said Redd. 'And neither has anyone else. It's all in their minds.'

'We were out there looking for real threats,' said Baxter. 'No one's supposed to know Parker is here, but that won't last.'

'Word always gets out,' said Redd.

'By then the interrogation should be over,' MacKay said firmly. 'And our guest's identity confirmed, one way or the other. Then he will be on his way somewhere else, and no longer our problem. We only have to keep him safe and secure for a few days.'

'If you aren't expecting enemy interest just yet,' I said, 'who did you think might be out there?'

'Ghost hunters,' said MacKay, his mouth turning down. 'They will keep filing questions about supernatural events at the Lodge under the Freedom of Information Act, and demanding access to the house to run their own investigations. Then they get terribly upset when they're turned down. Sometimes they try to sneak in with their own cameras and equipment to see just what it is we're hiding from them. Of course, they never get past the security measures.'

'Are you talking about the land mines?' said Penny. 'Or the gasses?'

'Neither, miss. That would attract attention. We just throw a good scare into them and they run like rabbits.'

'What do you do?' said Penny. 'Dress up in sheets and rattle some chains?'

MacKay smiled, briefly. 'I think that would only encourage them, miss.'

'So we're secure,' I said. 'Good to know.'

'Why are you so interested in ghosts?' said Redd.

'We've just been looking at Martin's evidence of hauntings inside the Lodge,' said Penny.

Baxter made a disgusted sound. 'Oh come on . . .'

'You're not a believer?' I said.

'I haven't seen anything in all the time I've been here,' Baxter said flatly. 'It's just nerves. Nothing out of the ordinary is happening. I'd know.'

'Mr Baxter is a very suspicious man,' MacKay said solemnly.

'You don't believe in ghosts?' said Penny.

'Of course not!' said Baxter.

'When we shoot people, they stay dead,' said Redd. 'That's sort of the point.'

'Is that all you've been doing while we were out working?' said Baxter. 'Sitting around watching television?'

'Just trying to get a handle on the situation,' I said.

Baxter moved forward so he could glare right into my face. I let him.

'We don't need you,' said Baxter. His voice and his face were deliberately unpleasant. 'You're just getting in the way. Why don't you go home and leave the real work to people who know what they're doing? Go back to wherever useless long streaks of piss like you belong.'

'Oh dear,' said Penny. 'Ishmael, please don't break him! We're guests here, and they might make us pay for breakages.'

'Break me?' said Baxter. 'Him?'

He stabbed a finger at me. I grabbed the finger and bent it back, using physical distress as well as leverage to force Baxter down on one knee. He gritted his teeth to keep from crying out at the pain and tried to break free. But he couldn't. Redd started forward, but MacKay stopped him with a look. I smiled down at Baxter.

'I am here because the Organization wants me here,' I said calmly. 'To challenge me is to challenge them. Do we understand each other?'

'Let me go!' said Baxter. His face was white with pain and wet with sweat. 'You bastard! I'll . . .'

I bent the finger back some more, just short of the breaking point.

'Yes! Yes, I understand!'

I let go of him and stepped away. Baxter snatched back his injured hand and cradled it against his chest, breathing hard. He glared up at me, and then surged to his feet. Redd was quickly there to take him by the arm and guide him away, murmuring soothing words. I watched them go. As they disappeared into the lounge, it was Redd who shot me one last look. He was the one who I thought would bear watching, the one who could be really dangerous.

Penny gave me a hard look. 'Was that really necessary?'

'Yes,' I said. 'You just can't talk to some people.'

'I am afraid you have made an enemy there, Mr Jones,' said MacKay.

'We were never going to be friends,' I said. 'But who knows, maybe I'll pull a thorn out of his paw later on.'

'I will speak with Mr Baxter and Mr Redd,' said MacKay. 'I will not have dissension in the ranks inside the Lodge.'

'Why was he so angry?' said Penny. 'Because he thinks Ishmael is usurping his place?'

'No, miss,' said MacKay. 'Because he does believe in ghosts and has seen and heard things, and he doesn't want to admit it.'

'What about Redd?' said Penny. 'Does he believe?'

'A very hard man to read is our Mr Redd,' said MacKay. 'He holds his thoughts close to his chest, along with his emotions. Now, the two of you must be tired after your long day's travelling. Perhaps you would like to take a rest in your room before dinner? Which will be in about an hour. Nothing special, since we are having to look after ourselves. But I can open a can and operate a microwave with the best of them.'

I looked at Penny and she nodded, so I allowed MacKay to lead us up the stairs at the back of the hall. I don't get tired, mostly, but Penny does.

Our room was on the upper floor, the same long corridor we'd seen on Martin's screen. The place where strange things happened. MacKay led the way, carrying Penny's suitcase as though it was full of nothing heavier than feathers. Penny looked around interestedly and I did too, but couldn't see or hear anything out of place. The lights were steady, and so were the shadows. The doors remained firmly shut. Everything was as it should be. I definitely didn't feel any uncanny atmosphere.

'Most of the rooms are locked up,' said MacKay. 'Until the staff return. A guest room has been prepared for you.'

'Just the one?' said Penny, mischievously.

MacKay stopped and looked back at us. 'That is what I was told. If one room is not acceptable . . .'

'It's fine,' I said.

'Just thought I should say something,' said Penny. 'I don't like to be taken for granted.'

'No one would dare,' I assured her.

MacKay took us to a room at the far end of the corridor, and opened the door and ushered us in. He dropped Penny's suitcase on the floor with a loud thud and gestured vaguely around the room as if introducing it to us.

'I will bang the gong in the hall when it's time for dinner.'

'Will Mr Parker be joining us?' said Penny.

'Only in spirit, miss.'

He inclined his head and left, closing the door firmly behind him. I dropped my backpack on the floor and wandered round the room checking it out, while Penny muscled her suitcase up and on to the bed. The room seemed comfortable enough, if essentially characterless. Just a neat impersonal setting, for people who wouldn't be there long. The adjoining bathroom was so small there was barely room to swing a toilet duck. Penny unpacked her suitcase, happily spreading its contents across the bed and around the room.

'Spotted anything out of the ordinary?' she asked, without looking up from what she was doing.

'Not so far.'

'Any surveillance cameras?'

'Of course,' I said. I pointed out the obvious one over the door, and the better-hidden one over the bed.

Penny pulled a face. 'OK, that's kind of creepy. I thought there'd be a way for us to turn them off. Since we're guests here, not prisoners.'

'There is,' I said. I opened my backpack, took out a pair of thick socks, and draped one carefully over each camera. 'See?'

Penny looked at each sock in turn, and frowned dubiously. 'Will they be enough?'

'They're heavy socks,' I said.

Penny peered into my backpack. 'You really did bring just a change of clothes. Tell me you brought some extra underwear, as well as socks.'

'Of course,' I said. 'But they don't block off surveillance so well.'

'You found those cameras pretty quickly,' said Penny.

'I have a lot of experience when it comes to finding hidden things. Particularly things other people don't want me to find. I could rip the cameras out, but they'd just install new ones the moment we leave the room.' I sat down beside her on the bed and leaned in close so I could murmur in her ear. 'There are bound to be hidden microphones, as well. So be careful what you say out loud.'

Penny grinned. 'You know I can get just a bit noisy, under the right circumstances . . .'

'Exhibitionist!' I said.

We kept our heads close together and our voices low.

'So,' said Penny. 'What do you make of the others?'

'Hayley and Doyle are clearly more than just work colleagues,' I said. 'And very keen to make a name for themselves. I have a feeling their ambitions may be more important to them than getting the truth out of Parker.'

'Well spotted,' said Penny. 'Did you also happen to notice that Baxter and Redd are an item?'

I looked at her. 'Really?'

'Yes, really. They way they looked at each other, they way they acted with each other. It was obvious.'

I shrugged. 'I was more concerned with whether or not they were going to beat the crap out of me.'

'Mr MacKay seemed nice enough. When he wasn't threatening to murder Frank Parker.'

'You mean polite. There's a difference. Still, a good man to have in charge. Especially if there's a crisis. I'm not so sure about Philip Martin.'

'Seemed like a typical techie geek to me.'

'One who believes in ghosts?'

'And tries to get recordings of them . . .'

Then we broke off, our heads snapping round, as outside in the corridor the sound of slow, steady footsteps grew louder and louder. Heading towards us. We were both up and off the bed in a moment, standing together facing the door.

'Could that be MacKay?' Penny said tentatively. 'Coming back to tell us something?'

'Doesn't sound like MacKay,' I said.

The footsteps were louder and heavier than any human being should be capable of making. Unless he was eight-foot tall and carrying an anvil in each hand. There was something oddly deliberate and measured about the sounds. As if whoever was making them wanted to be heard. They came closer and closer. I looked at Penny, but she seemed more intrigued than scared.

I moved over to the door as quietly as I could and took hold of the handle. I waited till the footsteps were right outside our room, then jerked the door open and charged out into the corridor. Penny was right behind me.

The corridor was completely empty, and silent. I looked from one end to the other, but there was no sign that anyone had ever been there. I felt the hackles stir on the back of my neck, like a cold caress.

'Could he have slipped into one of the other rooms?' said Penny.

'All the other doors are locked, remember?' I tilted my head back and sniffed the air. 'No human scents . . .'

'You're weird, sometimes,' said Penny. 'So, what do you think that was?'

'Obviously we're meant to think it was a ghost,' I said. 'Even if it is a bit early in the evening.'

'Is it?' said Penny. 'Remember that shadow on the wall in broad daylight?'

'My first reaction,' I said, 'is that someone is messing with us. Trying to keep our minds off Parker.'

Penny shrugged. 'Whatever it was, it's gone now. There's nothing we can do, so let's have a nice lie-down before dinner.'

'And get some rest?'

'Not necessarily . . .'

FOUR
Dead Man Walking

I dreamed of a time before I was me. Before there was any Ishmael Jones. I was staggering across a field in the middle of nowhere. Desperate to get away from something that would destroy me if I looked back. It was night and the sky was full of stars, looking down on me like friends I'd left behind. The full moon bathed the scene in a shimmering blue-white glare, watching over me like a single great eye. The whole world seemed fresh and new, but that was just me. Because I'd only just been born, and thrust into this world to survive as best I could.

The recently ploughed earth shook and shuddered under my feet. Behind me terrible sounds were abroad in the night, as something huge heaved and rolled, disturbing the earth as it forced its way underground. And despite everything my instincts were screaming at me, I stopped and looked back. To see the massive alien starship burrow deep into the dark earth, hiding its presence from the world.

I couldn't see the ship clearly. It was too big, too complex, for human eyes to cope with. Or perhaps it took more than eyes to comprehend all it was. The broken earth rose and fell like solid waves as the ship disappeared from sight, plunging down into the depths of the world. Into some dark and secret place no one would ever think to look for it. I turned away and staggered on across the open field. Some inner knowledge told me I needed to get away, get far away, before anyone came looking. I couldn't afford to be found until I had understood who and what I was now . . .

Things changed suddenly, as they do in dreams. I was somewhere else, in some hotel room, looking at my new face in a mirror. I'd travelled a long way before I got my head together, and I no longer remembered where that field had been. Or the marvellous alien ship that had fallen from the stars like an angel with broken wings, to crash in a field in south-west England. Leaving me as the only surviving member of its crew. Before it disappeared, the ship's transformation machine had changed me into a human being; altered everything about me, right down to the genetic level. So I could survive on this new world, as a human among humans. Except the mechanism had been damaged in the crash. The change was successful, but it had wiped all my old memories. So I no longer remembered who and what I was before I woke up as me.

I looked into the mirror, at the face the machine had given me. Just an ordinary man, with an ordinary face. Mid-twenties, unremarkable, nothing to make me stand out in a crowd. Then slowly the face faded away, leaving nothing behind. I stared into the dark depths of the empty mirror, and it seemed to me that something else was rising up out of that darkness. Another face, the face I had before I was born. And I knew I really didn't want to see it; I didn't want to know what was still hiding inside me.

I sat bolt upright in bed, making harsh incoherent sounds, shaking and shuddering. The guest room at Ringstone Lodge snapped into focus around me as Penny turned on the bedside light. I swallowed hard, my heart racing. While the thing I hadn't seen slipped steadily, blessedly, back into the depths of my mind. Penny took me in her arms and hugged me to her, fiercely, protectively. Murmuring comforting words, and reassuring me with her human presence. My breathing slowed and I stopped shaking. Penny let go and sat back, so she could look searchingly into my eyes.

'It's all right,' I said. 'I'm back. It's over.'

'No it isn't,' she said. 'You've been having that dream on and off for as long as I've known you. Is this why you never want me to sleep over?'

'Why should both of us have to suffer?' I said. 'It isn't fair on you to have to see me like this.'

'Like what?' she said gently. 'Being human?'

We shared a small smile. I lay back down again, and she

snuggled up against me. I put an arm around her shoulders and held her close. We were both naked. Me, because I hadn't brought any pyjamas; and Penny because she never wore any. She didn't like the way they crept up on her in the night while she slept and tried to wrap her up like a mummy. Penny rested her head on my chest and murmured reassuring things. I let her. Because I needed to hear them, and because she needed to feel she could help.

'Is it always the same dream?' Penny asked, after a while.

'Pretty much,' I said. 'Because it's not a dream, it's a memory. Trying to force its way back into my head.'

'How long has this . . . memory been troubling you?'

'Since I first arrived in your world. In 1963.'

'Would it really be so bad if you did remember?' said Penny.

'There's an old story,' I said. 'Of a wise man who woke from a dream of being a butterfly. But then he wondered, was he a man who'd thought he was a butterfly? Or was he a butterfly dreaming he was a man? Penny . . . Sometimes I wonder if I'm just something that dreamed it was a man and loved it. And I am so scared of waking up . . .'

'Hush, hush, darling.' Penny put her fingertips on my mouth to quiet me. 'You are Ishmael Jones, because that's who you chose to be. The man you made yourself into, day by day. Nothing else matters.'

But the nagging fear remained. What if I was not a man? What if I was just a cage for something worse?

We dozed for a while, and then we both sat bolt upright in bed as an alarm bell suddenly started ringing. Loud and strident and urgent. Penny looked at me.

'Does that sound like a fire alarm to you?'

I sniffed at the air. 'I'm not getting smoke, or anything burning. The alarm's coming from downstairs. I think it's Security throwing a tantrum.'

'Could Parker have escaped?' said Penny. 'Or been attacked?'

'Let's go ask somebody,' I said. 'It's not like either of us is going to get any more sleep.'

We were both quickly out of bed, and pulling on the clothes we'd left scattered across the floor on our way to bed. I finished

dressing first, because I don't care what I look like, and shot
a quick glance at the two socks to make sure they were still
covering the cameras. I unlocked the door, Penny breathing
impatiently on my neck, and we hurried out into the corridor.
My ears pricked up as I heard something new, underneath the
alarm bells.

'What are you hearing, space boy?' said Penny.

'People shouting and running about downstairs,' I said.
'Mr MacKay sounds very upset about something.'

Doctor Hayley and Doctor Doyle emerged from the room
next to ours. Bleary-eyed and confused, they looked like they'd
got dressed in a hurry as well. Hayley fixed me with a cold
glare, as if getting ready to accuse me of being responsible
for the commotion.

'What is it?' she said loudly. 'What's happening? Has something happened?'

'An alarm bell is ringing,' I said. 'Now you know everything
I do. Happy?'

'Damn it, Jones . . .'

'You don't look happy . . .'

'Ishmael,' said Penny. 'Look at the time. It's later than you
think.'

'Story of my life,' I said.

'No, really!'

She held up her wristwatch. I looked at it, and then at mine.
It was more than two hours since we'd retired to our room.

'MacKay said he'd call us down for dinner in an hour,' I
said. 'Why didn't he call us?'

'Ah,' said Doyle. 'That's our fault, I'm afraid. Sorry.'

Hayley shut him up with a look, and then nodded to me
grudgingly. 'I gave orders for dinner to be postponed. I decided
it was vital Doctor Doyle and I talk with Parker again. If only
to undo whatever harm you might have done. So I told MacKay
to hold off dinner until we returned. But by the time we were
done, we were both so tired . . .'

'All we could think of was getting our heads down,' said
Doyle.

'For a nap,' said Hayley.

'Of course,' said Penny.

'Did you get anything out of Parker, this time?' I said.

'Nothing useful,' said Doyle.

'We're wearing him down,' said Hayley.

'Are we?' said Doyle. 'Feels a lot more like he's wearing us down.'

'I think we need to make sure we still have a prisoner to interrogate,' I said. 'Alarm bells are often associated with prison breakouts.'

'Oh, shit!' said Hayley.

'Well, quite,' said Penny. 'Now if we've all finished quizzing each other, could we perhaps get a move on?'

'You are of course entirely right,' I said.

'Damn right!' said Penny.

I led the way, moving at some speed because no one ever sounds an alarm bell to tell you good things. Either someone had got in or someone had got out . . . Or something had happened to the most valuable man in Ringstone Lodge. Penny strode along beside me, matching me stride for stride, grinning broadly. She loved a mystery, and was always happiest when she was actually doing something. Hayley and Doyle hurried along behind us, determined not to be left out of anything. When we finally got to the bottom of the stairs, the first thing we encountered in the entrance hall was MacKay yelling at Baxter and Redd.

'I want the whole Lodge searched! Every room, every corridor, every nook and cranny! Kick in doors, look under beds, and tear down the shower curtains. And when you've done all of that, I want a full sweep of the grounds and the perimeter. Why are you still standing here? Go!'

MacKay was in full Regimental Sergeant Major mode, so the two big security men just nodded quickly and hurried off. I said MacKay's name loudly, to make myself heard over the alarm bells, and he swung round scowling fiercely. He started to say something and then broke off. He tilted his head back and raised his voice.

'Mr Martin! Turn that damned alarm off! I can't hear myself think.'

Martin must have been listening from his security centre,

because the alarm bell shut down immediately. The sudden silence was a relief.

'Why the electronic hysteria, Mr MacKay?' I said. 'What's the emergency?'

'Has Parker escaped from his cell?' said Penny. 'Or has someone broken into the Lodge?'

I looked at her reproachfully. 'I was about to ask that.'

'Keep up or get left behind,' Penny said ruthlessly. 'Well, Mr MacKay?'

'Frank Parker is dead,' MacKay said flatly. 'Murdered.'

Hayley and Doyle made soft shocked noises and looked at each other with wide eyes, like frightened children.

'Now we'll never know what he might have told us . . .' said Hayley.

'How was he killed?' I asked.

'Stabbed, in his cell,' said MacKay. 'Even though it was never unlocked.'

'Really?' said Penny.

'How is that possible?' I said.

'I don't know!' said MacKay. 'It should not have been possible for anyone to get anywhere near Mr Parker, let alone murder him inside a cell that couldn't be opened!' He shook his head, suddenly seeming tired and dazed. 'Nothing has made sense since that man got here . . .'

'Could it have been suicide?' Penny said tentatively.

'What? No . . . I don't think so, miss,' said MacKay.

'Could someone have been trying to help him escape?' I said.

MacKay shook his head again, more firmly. 'Whoever got in came here to kill him.'

'But the cell was never unlocked?' I said.

'No,' said MacKay. 'Mr Martin was most firm about that.'

'Could he have been stabbed through the bars?' said Penny.

'That doesn't seem likely, miss.' MacKay took a long, slow breath to calm himself. And just like that, his moment of near-panic was over and he was the professional old soldier again. 'When I went down to the cell I found Mr Parker lying on his bed, on his back, some distance from the bars. Looking quite peaceful. Apart from the knife sticking out of his chest.

There was no sign of any struggle. I believe he may have been stabbed while he was sleeping.'

'But that would have to mean someone got inside the cell,' I said.

'I have already conferred on this with Mr Martin,' MacKay said steadily. 'He was most emphatic. The cell can only be unlocked from his security centre; and every time the bars open, the event is logged and recorded by his computers. Mr Martin swears no one has been inside that cell since Doctor Hayley and Doctor Doyle finished their last conversation with Parker, over an hour ago. And besides, no one could reach the cell without being detected by the cameras and motion sensors that line the whole length of the basement corridor.'

'I'm trusting those computers less and less,' I said. 'It seems more and more likely they've been interfered with.'

'Mr Martin says not,' said MacKay. 'And he was very firm about it.'

'There's no way anyone could avoid the cameras?' said Penny. 'With inside information, perhaps?'

'I don't believe so, miss,' said MacKay. 'We need to talk to Mr Martin. If any of the computer systems have malfunctioned, he will know.'

'Lead the way,' I said. 'I'm just dying to talk to Mr Martin.'

'You go on without us,' said Hayley. She'd been quiet for some time, concentrating on Doyle, whose eyes were worryingly vague and confused. 'I'm taking Robbie back to the lounge. He needs to sit down and gather his thoughts.'

'Fine,' I said. 'But stay in the lounge. I mean it! Don't make me have to come looking for you.'

Hayley sniffed defiantly and led Doyle away. He went with her like a bewildered child.

The heavy steel door to the security centre was closed and locked. Penny and I stood back as MacKay announced us via the comm grille by the door. He waited, then hammered on the door with his fist and yelled into the grille again. The door finally opened, and we all filed in. Martin swivelled round on his squeaky chair to face us, grimacing apologetically.

'Sorry for the wait while I checked you out. I'm not feeling too trusting at the moment.'

'Same here,' I said. 'Why didn't you see Frank Parker being killed?'

'Because I wasn't here,' he said, avoiding my eyes. 'I was sleeping in the room next door. I didn't want to leave my post, but I had to. I was nodding off in my chair. Do you know how long I've been on duty? Tell him, MacKay. Ever since Frank Parker arrived!' He caught the look on MacKay's face and calmed down a little. 'I was promised backup so I could get some rest.'

'He's on his way,' said MacKay.

'I had to get some sleep,' Martin said sulkily. 'I have a cot set up in the next room, for emergencies. So I'm only ever a few minutes away from the centre. Everything should have been fine. All the systems were running on automatic, and I locked the door before I left. No one could get in or interfere with any of the systems without setting off a whole bunch of alarms.'

'What did trigger the alarm, in the end?' said Penny.

'I'll show you,' said Martin. 'But I don't want anyone saying it's my fault! None of this is my fault.'

'Get on with it,' said MacKay.

Martin fast-forwarded through a bunch of recordings on his screens, to prove no one had approached the Lodge through the grounds or entered the Lodge without being noticed. Then he switched to a screen showing Parker in his cell. He was lying on his bed, perfectly at ease, ankles casually crossed. Staring up at the ceiling, apparently entirely unconcerned by his situation. Perhaps because he thought he was safe in his cell.

And then all the screens went blank.

'Mr Martin!' said MacKay.

'The cameras just shut down!' said Martin. 'All of them! Which isn't supposed to be possible. All right, I suppose you could go round the Lodge smashing them with a hammer, but I'd notice that. No, every camera inside the Lodge shut down simultaneously, for a good ten minutes.' He gestured at Parker's screen. 'When I could see again . . .'

The screen showed Parker lying on his bed. His position hadn't changed, but now there was a knife buried hilt-deep in his chest. His eyes still stared up at the ceiling, but they weren't seeing anything.

'That's what set off the alarm,' said Martin. 'The cameras going down and coming back on again.'

'Someone must have hacked into your computers,' said Penny.

'Not past my firewalls,' Martin said firmly. 'And yes, before you ask, I'm already running full scans on all my systems. It'll take some time, but I can tell you right now no one got to them!'

'The cell was still locked?' I said.

'Yes!' said Martin. 'You could crash this whole room and that cell would still remain locked. Built-in security measure.'

'Could you force it open manually?' I said.

'If you had time and the right tools, probably,' said Martin. 'But that didn't happen.'

'What did you do after you returned to the centre?' said MacKay.

'The moment I realized Parker was dead, I checked every room in the Lodge on my screens,' said Martin. 'But there was no sign of any intruder, anywhere.'

'How could anyone have got to Parker?' I said. 'How could he be killed inside a locked room no one could enter?'

'I don't know!' said Martin. 'Maybe the ghosts did it.'

'Not funny, Mr Martin,' said MacKay.

'Wasn't meant to be,' Martin muttered. He sounded more confused than defiant. He swivelled back and forth in his chair, ignoring the noises it made, looking from one screen to another as if half expecting an answer to present itself. When that didn't happen, he reluctantly looked back at MacKay.

'We're in deep shit, aren't we? The Organization will have all our heads for this.'

'Not if we solve the mystery ourselves,' I said. 'Luckily for you, I'm pretty good at that. Mr MacKay, what have you been doing for the last few hours? Instead of making dinner, as you promised?'

'I was overruled on that by Doctor Hayley,' MacKay said

stcadily. 'While everyone was resting I patrolled the Lodge, as is my custom of an evening. Checking all the doors are locked and the windows are all secure. I saw nothing out of place, and heard nothing unusual.'

'Where were Baxter and Redd?' I said.

'Outside, most of the time,' said MacKay. 'I did question them, and they were both adamant they saw no sign of intruders in the grounds.'

'That's where they were, all right,' Martin said quickly. 'I had them on my screens. And MacKay. Everyone was where they were supposed to be.'

'Except you,' I said. 'How long were you gone?'

'It was just a quick break,' said Martin. 'Maybe . . . three quarters of an hour.'

'Long enough,' I said.

'The computers monitor everything,' Martin said stubbornly.

'Not this time, they didn't,' I said. I turned to MacKay. 'Where were you, exactly, when the alarm started?'

'In the kitchen, at the back of the Lodge,' said MacKay. 'Mr Baxter and Mr Redd had only just come back inside. It was getting cold, and they needed a break. I sent them to the lounge and said I would bring them some hot coffee. I was busying myself in the kitchen when the alarm sounded. I ran back here and found the door to the security centre was open. On entering, I discovered Mr Martin staring at a screen showing the prisoner dead in his cell. I immediately went down to the basement and checked on Mr Parker's condition. I came back up, yelled for Mr Baxter and Mr Redd, and sent them off to check for intruders. Then you arrived.'

'Did you go inside the cell to check on Parker?' I said.

'No, sir. I thought it important to preserve the crime scene. I did check the bars, to make sure they hadn't been tampered with.'

'So you can't confirm Parker is definitely dead?' I said.

'He has a knife sticking out of his chest!' said Martin.

'Appearances can be deceiving,' I said. 'In our line of work.'

'I was a professional soldier for many years,' MacKay said flatly. 'I believe I know a dead man when I see one.'

'Even so . . .' I said. 'I need to see the body for myself. Show me, MacKay.' I looked at Martin. 'You stay here.'

'Damn right!' said Martin. 'I'm not being caught out again.'

'I'm coming too!' said Penny.

'Are you sure?' I said.

'I've seen my share of dead bodies,' said Penny. 'Remember?'

'Of course you have,' I said. 'All right, come along. But watch where you step, I don't want any clues trampled on.'

'I will trample on your soft and delicate bits if you patronize me again,' said Penny.

I looked at MacKay. 'It's true. She would.'

I studied the backstairs carefully as we went down, but I couldn't see any footprints or physical evidence. But once we reached the basement corridor and approached Parker's cell, the smell of blood came clearly to me. And underneath that, other smells associated with sudden death. We finally stopped before the cell bars and looked at the body. Parker was dead. No question of it.

'Not much blood,' I said, 'for a chest wound.'

'The knife will be holding most of it in,' said MacKay.

I looked to Penny. 'You all right?'

'After everything I saw at Belcourt Manor, a knife in the chest is nothing,' Penny said steadily. She looked at MacKay. 'There's no way the killer could have reached him through the bars. He must have gone in. And since Parker was stabbed from the front, either he was attacked in his sleep . . . or he knew his killer and believed he had no reason to fear him.'

'Let's hope it's that straight forward,' I said. I gave the steel bars a good rattle, but they didn't budge. I nodded to MacKay. 'Open it up.'

MacKay started to say something, and then stopped as the bars slid smoothly to one side. Martin was listening. I stepped inside the cell, and then looked back as MacKay and Penny started to follow me in.

'Not just now,' I said.

Penny looked like she wanted to argue, but didn't. MacKay just nodded. I leaned over the body lying on the bed and studied it carefully. Parker had been stabbed once. No defence wounds on the hands or arms, suggesting no struggle. But I didn't think he'd been asleep when it happened. He was laid out too neatly on his bed. No matter how sudden the attack, you'd expect some thrashing around. And besides, all field agents learn to sleep lightly. Parker would have heard the cell opening. No, he knew his attacker and let him get close . . . And afterwards the killer took time to arrange the body. Which might turn out to be significant, or might not. Killers follow their own logic.

I got down on my knees and studied the floor carefully. Moving slowly around the cell a few feet at a time, checking everything. I couldn't see a single footprint anywhere, which suggested the killer had cleaned up after himself. This had been no impulsive killing, no moment of madness or passion. Someone had planned Parker's death down to the last detail. I leaned forward and sniffed the floor, but I couldn't detect any trace of soap or bleach.

When I was finished with the floor, I got to my feet and examined every surface close up. If I concentrate, I am able to see fingerprints. A talent I prefer to keep to myself. I did tell Penny once and she asked if I could see DNA traces . . . I almost said something very rude. I may be an alien visitor from another world, but I'm not Superman.

No fingerprints and no blood drops, which meant the knife had plunged into Parker's chest once and then stayed there. I studied the knife hilt. Nothing special about it; not military issue, or special forces. Would probably turn out to have come from the kitchen . . . Where MacKay said he was when the murder took place. A kitchen knife would seem to indicate the killer was one of us in the Lodge, because an outside killer would have brought a weapon with him. But why a knife? Rather than strangling or a blow from a blunt instrument? A knife suggested anger and a personal grievance. Someone who needed to see the knife going in. However, a knife also suggested control. Because beating Parker to death might have been even more satisfying to someone who hated him, though far more messy. The killer would have been bound to get blood on him and on his surroundings.

So this was a carefully planned murder, by someone in the Lodge . . . Unless that was what the killer wanted us to think.

Unless everything here had been carefully staged, by a professional, to make it look like an inside job.

I looked Parker's body over carefully. I didn't bother to check his pockets. Security would have emptied them before he was put in the cell. I was more interested in the clothes; but the killer hadn't left any trace on them. Nothing I could see or smell. Up close, all the changes Parker had made to his face leapt out at me, reminding me there was always the chance this wasn't Parker. Could he perhaps have been killed because Hayley and Doyle were getting too close to the truth, and discovering this wasn't Parker after all? I finally straightened up again, and sighed heavily.

There was nothing in the cell or on the body to help me understand who had killed Parker, or why. I'd have to wait for someone to send in a forensics team with the proper equipment. See if they could find something I'd missed.

The only thing I could be sure of was that whatever Parker knew, whatever information he hoped to trade, it must have been really important. Something worth going to all this trouble to silence him. Because whoever did this had to have been a professional.

I'd barely stepped back into the corridor before Martin locked the cell again from his security room. MacKay and Penny looked at me expectantly, but I just shook my head. I had nothing to say, for the moment. I was thinking. I headed back to the stairs, and Penny and MacKay followed after me. I didn't need to look back to know they were exchanging glances.

There was no sign of Baxter and Redd in the entrance hall, so I went to the lounge. Where Hayley was doing her best to comfort an almost hysterical Doyle. He was sitting right on the edge of the sofa, rocking back and forth, wringing his hands. Hayley sat beside him, patting his arm and talking brightly. He didn't seem to hear her. Neither of them so much as glanced up as we entered the lounge.

'Our careers are over!' Doyle said tearfully. 'We're ruined! Getting answers out of Parker would have made our reputations, but this . . . Why did the bastard have to go and die on us? What are we going to do?'

'Hush, Robbie,' said Hayley. 'Everything's going to be all right.'

'No it isn't!' said Doyle. 'They'll blame us for this, you know they will.'

Hayley shot a glare at me. 'I won't let that happen.'

'What's wrong with him?' said Penny. 'Mister Big Tough Interrogator.'

'He's in shock,' Hayley said shortly. 'We've never had a patient die on us before.'

Penny raised an eyebrow. 'He's a patient now, not a prisoner!'

'It was our job to keep him alive,' said Hayley. 'He's no use to any of us dead.'

Baxter and Redd finally showed up to join us. MacKay gave them both a hard look, and they shook their heads quickly.

'The grounds are clear and the Lodge is empty apart from us,' said Redd. 'Nothing to suggest anyone got in.'

Baxter took in the state of the two doctors, sniffed loudly and, ignoring Penny and me, addressed himself directly to MacKay. 'This place is a fortress. Which means the murder has to be an inside job. Someone in this room is the killer.'

'I notice you're glowering at me in particular,' I said.

'Everything was fine here until you turned up!' said Baxter.

'Yes . . .' I said. 'I noticed that too. Maybe someone decided Parker needed to be silenced before he could open up to me.'

'What makes you think he'd talk to you, rather than us?' said Hayley.

'Because I've walked in his shoes,' I said.

MacKay raised his voice. 'Mr Martin, put the Lodge on full lockdown. Do it now!'

The whole house shook to the sounds of straining machinery, as heavy steel shutters ratcheted down to cover all the windows and the outer doors locked themselves. Doyle chuckled suddenly. A lost, joyless sound.

'Like nails being hammered into a coffin lid. Burying us alive . . .'

'Somebody shut him up,' said Baxter.

The last shutter slammed into place, the machinery ground

to a halt, and suddenly it was extremely quiet. We all looked at each other.

'I certainly feel so much safer now,' I said. 'Locked in here with an unknown killer. Who may or may not have unfinished business.'

Baxter scowled at MacKay. 'You should have given us some warning!'

'Why?' said MacKay. 'So you could leave? I don't think so. You said it yourself, Mr Baxter. This had to have been an inside job. Therefore all of us are suspects.'

'Does this situation remind you of anything, Ishmael?' said Penny.

'Yes,' I said. 'Let's hope for a better outcome this time.'

'What's he talking about?' said Redd.

'Belcourt Manor,' said Hayley. 'One of his cases. A massacre.'

'Another group of suspects, trapped together in one place,' I said. 'I caught the murderer eventually, but not before they killed everyone except Penny and me. Not one of my finest hours.'

'Stop it!' Penny said firmly. 'You did all you could. More than anyone else could have managed against that monster.'

'We're locked in for the night,' said Doyle, in the same sad, lost voice. 'Rats in a trap. We're all going to die.'

Hayley was already pouring him a large brandy from the cut-glass decanter on the coffee table. It didn't look like Doyle's first. She forced the glass into his hand and made him drink some.

'Mr Martin!' MacKay said loudly. 'A message should have gone out automatically once we entered lockdown, but just to be on the safe side contact Headquarters yourself. Make sure they know what's happening here.'

'Isn't that a bit like bolting the stable door after the horse has been stabbed?' said Penny.

'No,' I said. 'We need backup here as soon as possible. Before our killer finds a way out.'

'Not possible,' said MacKay. 'Not while lockdown is in place.'

'He's already managed several impossible things,' I said.

'I thought that was your line of business,' said Hayley.

'How could anyone kill Parker, not be seen, and not leave any trace behind?' said Penny. 'It's just not possible!'

'Unless it was the ghosties,' said MacKay. He only half sounded like he was joking. And from the way the others were looking, I had to wonder if they preferred that idea to one of them being the killer.

'I think we could all use something to eat and drink,' I said. 'Help settle our nerves.'

'The kitchen is open,' said MacKay. 'I will prepare something.' He raised his voice. 'You too, Mr Martin. This is no time for anyone to be on their own.'

'I'm not leaving the security centre!' said Martin. His voice didn't seem to come from anywhere in particular. It was just suddenly there in the room, with us. I looked around, but couldn't see a hidden speaker anywhere. And I'm usually pretty good at spotting such things.

'You'll be much safer with us, you miserable specimen,' said MacKay.

'I'm not going anywhere while my computer scans are still running,' said Martin. 'And I'm perfectly safe where I am, behind this solid-steel door. No one's going to get to me without using heavy-duty explosives or a bazooka. And I think I'd spot that on my cameras.'

'Then stay where you are,' I said. 'When I want you, I'll come and get you.'

Penny leaned in close, to murmur in my ear. 'I knew he could hear everything, but I didn't know he could talk to us as well.'

'I get the feeling there's a lot he can do that he doesn't like to reveal.'

'Who do you think is the killer?' said Penny.

'Not me,' I said. 'And probably not you.'

'Well,' said Penny. 'That's a start.'

We hurried through the empty corridors of the Lodge with MacKay leading the way. We all stuck close together, like sheep who'd just been alerted to the presence of a wolf. Baxter and Redd kept a watchful eye on every door we approached, braced for any sudden appearance, but they hadn't drawn their guns yet. I wondered why.

'Why haven't you drawn your guns?' I said.

'Because we're professionals,' said Baxter, not even glancing in my direction. 'We don't go blasting off at every shadow.'

'And because we're short on ammunition,' said Redd. 'All we have is what's in our guns at the moment. No reloads. I wouldn't want to waste a bullet on something that wasn't worthy of it.'

'They are also under my orders not to use their weapons unless they absolutely have to,' said MacKay. 'Ringstone Lodge is a listed building, with a great many important and expensive antiques.'

'Really?' said Hayley. 'Protecting our lives isn't considered as important as protecting the fixtures and fittings? To hell with that! You go ahead and fire at anything you like, boys. They can bill me.'

'I haven't seen anything worth shooting at yet,' said Redd. 'How about you, Bax?'

'Not a damned thing,' said Baxter. 'How about you, Mister Big Secret Agent Man?'

'We're safe enough for the moment,' I said. 'There's no one else on the ground floor.'

MacKay glanced back at me. 'How can you be sure?'

'Because that's my job,' I said.

Baxter rolled his eyes, and Redd looked like he wanted to. Penny dropped me a wink. Hayley looked worriedly at Doyle, whose gaze seemed further away than ever.

'How much further to the kitchen?' she said.

'Almost there, Doctor Hayley,' said MacKay.

The kitchen turned out to be a small but spotlessly clean affair on the far side of the Lodge. MacKay bustled around, organizing hot coffee and sandwiches for all and making a cheerful clatter. He seemed relieved now he had something practical to do. Everyone grabbed chairs and settled down around the single long table. Fortunately there were enough chairs to go round. Because no one wanted to go off on their own to find an extra one, if only because they didn't want everyone else talking about them while they were gone. Baxter and Redd sat together; and Hayley sat with Doyle, who was still holding on to his empty brandy glass. Penny sat with me. And for a while we all just sat and looked at each other, thinking our own thoughts, trying to spot a murderer in a familiar face.

Baxter was scowling so hard he was probably hurting his forehead. Redd sat stiffly with his arms folded, hard to read as always. Doyle had an almost fey look to him, as though all the things he'd thought he could depend on to make his world make sense had been taken away. Hayley studied us all carefully, trying to crack open our facades with her professionally trained mind. Penny just looked terribly interested in everyone. She was probably the only one there who didn't feel threatened. Partly because she trusted me to protect her; but mainly because after the slaughter she'd witnessed at Belcourt Manor it would take a lot more than a dead man in a locked room to throw her.

MacKay finally set three plates of roughly cut sandwiches down on the table before us. He stepped back and looked at us expectantly, but nobody made a move.

'What more do you want me to do?' said MacKay. 'Cut off the crusts for you? Get stuck in, there's a fine selection. I even managed a few vegetarian ones for you, Mr Redd.'

'Not really hungry, right now,' said Redd. 'But thanks for remembering.'

There were a few murmurs from around the table, indicating that no one had much of an appetite. I shrugged, and grabbed the nearest sandwich. MacKay nodded to me approvingly.

'Every good soldier knows it's wisest to eat when you can, because it might be some time before you get another chance.'

'I thought that was sleep,' I said.

'That too,' said MacKay.

He took a sandwich and sat down at the end of the table, so he could watch all of us at once; giving the impression of a man who had done all that could reasonably be asked of him, and it would be a brave soul who asked for anything more.

Penny watched me eating. 'Any good?'

'Not bad. You want a bit?'

'Really not hungry, just at the moment.' Penny wrinkled her nose. 'How can you eat, at a time like this?'

'You heard the old soldier. Got to keep the energy levels up when you're chasing the bad guys.'

'You're just sitting there?'

'My thoughts are racing.'

'You're a field agent,' Hayley said to me, thoughtfully. 'I suppose you're used to sudden death.'

'It's part of the job,' I said. 'Coping with it, and causing it.'

'Do you want to go down to the cell and examine Parker's body, Doctor Hayley?' said Penny.

'No,' said Hayley. 'Robbie and I aren't used to bodies. I never saw a dead man before.'

'I thought you were both doctors?' said Penny.

'Of the mind, not the body,' said Hayley. 'We're both academics. Robbie was perfectly happy in his ivory tower until I met him and dragged him out into the real world. Perhaps I should have left him there. He's not made for situations like this.'

Doyle raised the brandy glass to his mouth and, finding it was empty, put it down again. He didn't seem to know what to do with the glass, so Hayley took it away from him and poured out some coffee from the pot MacKay had prepared. She put the cup in front of Doyle, but he didn't even look at it.

'What are we going to do?' he said plaintively.

'I'll think of something,' said Hayley. 'You know me, Robbie. I always think of something. Now drink your nice coffee.'

'I don't want it.'

'Drink it anyway.'

'Don't shout at me!'

'Sorry! I'm sorry, Robbie. It's just . . .'

'I want to go home,' said Doyle.

'So do I,' said Hayley. She looked round the table. 'It's just shock. We'll both be fine. In a while.'

Baxter and Redd looked like they might be ready to say something about that, but MacKay shut them up with a look. Then he turned his attention to me.

'I was given to understand,' he said steadily, 'that Mr Parker was unkillable. And yet he died so easily . . .'

'Just goes to show,' I said. 'You don't want to believe everything you hear about field agents.'

'Even though there are all kinds of strange stories,' Hayley said pointedly, 'about the kind of people it takes to go out into the darker places in the world and wrestle with monsters?'

'Right,' said Redd, fixing me with a cold contemplative gaze. 'I've heard stories about the mysterious and enigmatic Ishmael Jones. I can't believe half of the things you're supposed to have done.'

'Then don't,' I said. 'You'll sleep better that way.'

'You'd have to be more than human to do everything I've heard,' said Redd. 'So what are you, really?'

'Very good at my job,' I said.

'But will you be able to identify the murderer?' said MacKay.

'Eventually,' I said. 'It's what I do.'

'Don't think you're going to pin any of this on me!' Baxter said loudly. 'Nothing that's happened here has been my fault.'

'But it was your job to protect Parker,' I said, in my most infuriatingly reasonable tone. 'To keep him safe, from all his many enemies.'

'Our job was to protect the Lodge from outside attack,' said Baxter, leaning forward aggressively. 'This was an inside job.'

'Had to be,' said Redd. 'Inside information, all the way. Our killer knew where to find the victim, and how to avoid the surveillance. Which means it has to be one of us. Sitting right here at this table.'

'Why would any of us want to kill him?' said Hayley.

'Perhaps someone here knew him from before,' said MacKay. 'Someone with a grudge.'

'More likely one of us is in the pay of the opposition,' I said.

'Who are the opposition?' said Penny, trying to keep up.

'Right now, any of the people Parker used to work for,' I said. 'He must have known something that someone couldn't afford us to know. Unless . . . the killer is working for one of the traitors inside the Organization, who's desperate to keep his identity from being revealed.'

'Either way, it's still not my fault,' said Baxter. 'Or Redd's.'

'Thanks for remembering me,' said Redd. 'Now cool it, Bax. No one's pointing the finger at either of us.'

'He is,' said Baxter, settling reluctantly back in his chair. 'Mister High-and-Mighty Field Agent.'

'I'm not blaming anyone, just yet,' I said. 'We're all under suspicion simply because we're here.'

'And all of you are outsiders,' MacKay said slowly. 'Only Mr Martin and I are regular Ministry of Defence personnel assigned to the Lodge. Everyone else was brought in specially, just for this operation.'

'So only you and Martin could really be capable of an inside job,' said Redd. 'Because only you know the layout and work-ings of the Lodge well enough.'

'All the other Lodge personnel are in the wind at the moment,' I said. 'The opposition could have got to any of them and forced or bribed the necessary information out of them. The first rule of any professional agent is to muddy the waters and confuse the situation. To distract the inquiring gaze away from what's really going on. Just because this looks like an inside job, doesn't necessarily mean it is.'

'So there could still be an intruder at large somewhere in the Lodge?' said Penny. 'Just waiting for a chance to kill us all, one by one?'

'There is no one else in the Lodge,' Martin's voice said loudly. 'If there was, I'd be seeing them on my screens.'

'Good to know you're still with us,' I said. 'Can you speak to us from any room in the Lodge?'

'Pretty much,' said Martin. 'Why?'

'Just thinking,' I said.

'About what?' said Baxter.

'Motive,' I said. 'I believe this murder was personal. That Parker was killed for who he was, not what he was doing here.'

'If it really was Parker,' said Hayley.

'Of course,' I said.

'I've been thinking about that,' said Penny. 'If we can't be sure Parker was Parker, how can we be sure anyone here is who they say they are? I mean we're all strangers to each other, only brought together for this particular mission. We've just been taking it for granted that all of us are who we claim to be.'

I nodded slowly. 'Normally there'd be a briefing file, with names and photos. But this was all put together in such a hurry . . .'

I could see suspicions growing in everyone's faces. No one actually pushed their chair back from the table to put more room between them and everyone else, but they all looked like they wanted to.

'I've known Bax for years,' said Redd. 'I can vouch for him. And he can vouch for me.'

'But who vouches for the two of you?' Penny said sweetly. 'How long have you been working at the Lodge?'

'Not long,' said Redd. 'We were called in at the last moment, to provide special security for Parker.'

'Did you check their IDs when they arrived?' I asked MacKay.

'Of course,' he said. 'And confirmed their arrival with Headquarters.'

'But IDs can be faked,' said Penny.

'How do we know that's really MacKay?' Baxter said craftily.

'I have worked here for three years,' MacKay said coldly.

'MacKay has,' I said. 'But how do we know you're him?'

I turned away from him to look steadily at Hayley and Doyle. 'The Colonel told me to expect two new interrogators at Ringstone Lodge, but he never mentioned any names.'

'Robbie and I have all the proper accreditation papers,' Hayley said coldly.

'Papers mean nothing,' I said. 'I've lost count of the number of false identities I've used. And it's always possible that you could have ambushed the real Hayley and Doyle on the way here, killed them and taken their place.'

'But . . . we didn't!' said Hayley, her voice rising. 'This isn't fair! How are we supposed to prove we didn't do something?'

'You can't,' I said. 'See? Isn't this fun? Paranoia, a game the whole family can play.'

'I can vouch for MacKay,' said Martin, his voice coming out of nowhere again. 'We're both on record as part of the Ringstone Lodge staff.'

'Ah yes,' I said. 'The man whose cameras can't be trusted. Whose records can therefore no longer be relied on.'

'I'm the only one you can rely on,' said Martin. 'Because I'm the one who sees and hears everything. Mostly because there's nothing else to do except sit and watch and listen.'

'What about our right to privacy?' said Penny.

'What about your right to survival?' said Martin. 'It's not like I care what any of you get up to. You'd be surprised how fast voyeurism can become boring when it's all you do, day in and day out. I'm with you all the time because somebody has to be. Your very own guardian angel.'

'Except when you're sleeping,' I said.

'Sleep,' Martin said wistfully. 'I dream of sleep.'

'We must wait for the reinforcements to arrive,' said MacKay. 'They can sort out who we really are.'

'If we're alive when they get here,' I said.

'Why shouldn't we be?' said MacKay. 'Lockdown is in place, none of us are going anywhere.'

'I'm more concerned about what happens when the SAS turn up,' said Redd. 'What if they decide to shoot everyone just to be on the safe side?'

'Those gentlemen do have a reputation for being very thorough,' said MacKay. 'But standard procedure after a lockdown means they will bring a full investigatory team with them. And they will get to the bottom of things.'

'Being the suspicious soul that I am,' I said, 'can I just check something? You have had a response to your emergency alert? You are sure Headquarters knows what's going on here? The urgency of the situation?'

'Mr Martin?' said MacKay, addressing the ceiling.

'Yes, I have received an acknowledgement,' Martin said coldly. 'I'd have said so, otherwise. Reinforcements will be here inside an hour. We can hold out that long, can't we?'

'It occurs to me,' said Redd, 'that if one of us is the

killer, whoever it is can't afford to be here when the SAS arrive.'

'We're locked in,' said Baxter. 'Remember?'

'But if he kills the rest of us,' said Redd, 'then all he has to do is go to the security centre and raise lockdown from there. That's where the controls are. Right?'

I looked at MacKay. 'Well? Is he right?'

'Yes,' said MacKay, reluctantly. 'Lockdown can be raised from the security centre. If they know the correct codes.'

'They've known everything else they needed to know,' said Penny.

No one else had anything to say. Everyone was thinking hard. Including Baxter, who looked like he was finding it a bit hard going. Even Doyle emerged from under his cloud, for the moment.

'So we can get out?' he said slowly. Picking on the only thing that mattered to him. 'We can leave, if we have to?'

'Hush, dear,' said Hayley. 'None of us are going anywhere.'

'But we could get out,' Doyle insisted. 'We don't have to stay in this terrible place, locked up with a killer. I think we should all leave right now. It's not safe here, for any of us.'

'Where would we go, Doctor Doyle?' MacKay said patiently. 'We could drive to the railway station, but there are no trains running at this hour. Do you really think we would be any safer standing around on a deserted platform all night? We could try for the nearest town, but it is many miles away. And anyone could be lying in wait along those deserted roads.'

'The killer could have planted explosives in our one and only car,' I said, not wanting to be left out of the general gloom and doom. 'To take us all out if we tried to leave. It's what I would have done. And anyway, you're all missing the point.'

'What point?' said Baxter.

'None of you are going anywhere,' I said, 'Because I won't allow it. You are all suspects, and it's my job to see that potential suspects don't just disappear into the night from a crime scene.'

There was a long pause as they all looked at me.

'You really think you can keep us here?' Baxter said truculently.

'Yes,' I said. 'Don't you?'

'Brave words,' said Redd. 'From a man without a gun, to two men with guns.'

'You really think that makes a difference?' I said.

'Oh for God's sake!' said Penny. 'Just whip them out and measure them. Slap them down on the table so we can all have a good look. Men! The sooner scientists come up with a viable alternative the better.'

Hayley surprised me with a brief snort of laughter. MacKay looked quietly pained. Baxter and Redd glanced at each other, then sat back in their chairs with their arms folded stubbornly.

I looked at Penny. 'I really have no idea what you're talking about.'

'Maybe not,' said Penny, 'but they do.'

'We need to do this by the book,' I said. 'We can't prove or disprove who we are, so let's stick to the simple things. Starting with alibis. Where were we all when Parker experienced stabbing pains in the chest?'

'Bax and I were together all the time,' Redd said firmly.

'Well of course you'd vouch for each other,' said Hayley. 'How do we know you're not working together?'

'How do we know you and Doyle aren't?' said Redd. 'And Jones will swear he was with his girl. So much for alibis.'

'His girl?' said Penny, dangerously.

'I was alone,' said MacKay. 'But I was in full view of the Lodge cameras at all times, as I am sure Mr Martin can attest.'

'Damn right!' said Martin. 'If attest means what I think it means.'

'We were all inside the Lodge when Parker was murdered,' I said. 'With the cameras offline for a good ten minutes, that's more than enough time for any of us to get down to the cell, do the deed, and get back again.'

'I don't like this,' said Doyle. 'Not trusting each other. What if this is what the killer wants, to turn us against each other?'

'Welcome back, Doctor Doyle,' I said. 'That was surprisingly lucid. Are you feeling better now?'

He smiled weakly. 'As well as can be expected. You've been

through something like this before, at Belcourt Manor. I read the file. What do you think we should do?'

'We need to stick together,' I said. 'Keep an eye on each other. No one goes off on their own, because that's a good way to get picked off. If you need a toilet break, wait till we all need to go.'

'He's right,' said Penny. 'Listen to him. I've seen what happens when the group doesn't stick together.'

'What did happen at Belcourt Manor?' said MacKay.

'People died,' I said. 'Because they didn't do what I told them to do.'

'If my parents had listened to Ishmael, they'd still be alive,' said Penny. 'Listen to him. He knows what he's doing.'

'But then you would say that, wouldn't you?' said Redd.

'The only way to stay safe,' said Hayley, 'is to figure out who the killer is ourselves. Find him, lock him up, sit on him till help gets here. Come on, we can do this! We're all professionals . . .' She smiled briefly. 'If we are who we say we are.'

'Where do we start?' said Penny.

I looked thoughtfully at Hayley and Doyle. 'You were the last ones to see Parker alive.'

'But he was still alive when we left,' said Hayley. 'Martin's records will confirm that.'

'She's right,' said Martin, without waiting to be asked.

'What did you talk about?' I said.

'That's classified,' said Hayley.

'Even now?' said Penny.

'Especially now,' said Hayley.

'Just bullshit,' said Doyle, staring into his cup. 'Nothing that mattered. Nothing you could trust.'

'Hush, dear,' said Hayley. 'Drink your coffee.'

'We only agreed to work for the Organization because it seemed like a step up to better things,' said Doyle.

Hayley put a hand on his arm, and he stopped talking. And perhaps I was the only one to notice just how hard she squeezed his arm.

'You have to get back to the security centre!' Martin said suddenly, his voice almost hysterically loud and urgent. 'Right now!'

'Calm yourself, Mr Martin,' said MacKay, just a bit wearily. 'What is the matter now?'

'You have to see this! Something's happened.'

'What could be so important?' I said. 'Parker's not going anywhere.'

'That's what you think,' said Martin.

We hurried back through the Lodge, pounding through the empty corridors as fast as we could without leaving anyone behind. MacKay led the way again, but this time we were all keeping a watchful eye on each other as well as our surroundings. When we finally arrived at the security centre, the door swung open before us. Martin had been watching and waiting. We hustled into the centre and pretty much filled it wall to wall. Martin bounced impatiently on his swivel chair.

'It happened again! One of the screens went blank when I wasn't looking!'

He pointed a shaking finger at one particular screen, showing Parker's cell. The bars were still closed, but the bed was empty. There was no trace of Parker anywhere in the cell. The bedclothes looked undisturbed, as though he'd just got up and walked away.

'He was gone when the cameras came back on!' said Martin. 'And now I can't find him anywhere in the Lodge.'

'He must be somewhere!' said MacKay. 'He can't have just vanished.'

'I thought you were keeping an eye on Parker?' I said to Martin.

'I can't watch all the screens at once,' he said defensively. 'I just keep up a regular routine to make sure I cover all of them in turn. But when I looked back at this screen, it was blank. The camera covering the cell had shut itself down. And while I was struggling to get it up and running, the system started working again all on its own and the cell was empty!'

'Whoever took the body can't have got out of the Lodge,' I said. 'We're still locked in. We are still locked in, aren't we?'

'Yes!' said Martin. 'We're still sealed up tight. But so was Parker's cell . . . The computer records swear it hasn't been opened.'

We all took a good look at the rows of screens, but there was nothing to see. The whole house was still and quiet and empty. Just as I expected. Someone was running a game on us.

'Shouldn't the alarms have gone off?' said Redd.

'If anyone opened the cell, yes,' said Martin. 'But it was never opened.'

'You're not making sense, Mr Martin,' said MacKay.

'I know!'

'At least we can be sure none of us were involved,' I said. 'We were all together in the kitchen when it happened.'

Everyone looked startled, and then relaxed a little.

'Unless . . . the killer has an accomplice,' said Hayley. 'Someone able to remove Parker's body while we were all busy giving each other an alibi.'

She turned to look at Martin. And, one by one, so did everyone else. He glared back at us defiantly.

'My presence in this room is recorded by the computers. Every time that door opens and closes, the computer time-stamps it. You can check the permanent record for yourselves, if you want.'

MacKay reached out a hand, and Martin handed over his keyboard. MacKay slowly entered a series of commands, pausing to remember the correct passwords, until the required information flashed up on one of the screens. MacKay studied it, and then gave the keyboard back to Martin.

'The computers confirm Mr Martin never left the centre. They also confirm Parker's cell hasn't been opened since I let you in to examine the body, Mr Jones.'

'The computers should have sounded an alarm the moment someone started down the corridor to that cell,' I said. 'Are you sure no one can override the Lodge's systems from outside?'

'Yes!' said Martin. 'Positive!'

'Then there must be an intruder inside the Lodge,' Baxter said flatly. 'Hiding in some secret place no one else knows about.'

'But we checked everywhere, Bax,' Redd said patiently. 'So did MacKay, and he knows this place better than anyone.'

'It's the only answer that makes sense,' Baxter said stubbornly.

'Unless Parker got up and walked away,' said Penny.

We all stopped and looked at her.

'The stories say he's unkillable,' said Penny. 'What if the knife in the chest didn't kill him, after all? What if he just bided his time, then got up and walked away? And now he's let loose in the Lodge, looking for the man who tried to kill him. Looking for revenge . . .'

There was a long and very uncomfortable silence, as everyone considered that idea and decided they really didn't like it.

'I want to go home,' said Doyle.

'You have the most experience with the darker corners of the world, Mr Jones,' MacKay said slowly. 'Is such a thing possible?'

'I've seen stranger things,' I said.

'Ghosts?' said Baxter. 'Men who can't be killed? Stick to what makes sense! You know the Lodge inside out, MacKay. It's an old building. Could there be hidden rooms, secret passageways?'

'I never heard of any,' said MacKay, 'But it is a possibility, I suppose. We'll just have to search the Lodge again, top to bottom. Mr Baxter and Mr Redd, you will take the upper floor. Look for hidden doors and sliding panels. You have my permission to be as rough and destructive as you see fit. I will take the ground floor. Mr Jones, Miss Belcourt, take the basement. Doctors, I think it best you find a room and barricade yourself in till we have determined the truth of the situation.'

'What did I just say about sticking together?' I said loudly. 'Splitting up is always going to be a bad idea.'

'The security of the Lodge must come first,' said MacKay.

He strode out of the centre, with Baxter and Redd all but treading on his heels. Hayley and Doyle looked at each other.

'We'll go back to the lounge,' said Hayley. 'Stay out of everyone's way. Join us there when you're finished.'

She left, pushing Doyle ahead of her. I looked at Penny.

'Why does no one ever do what I tell them to?'

'I don't know,' said Penny. 'Maybe you should go on a course.'

'Excuse me?' said Martin. 'What am I supposed to do?'

'Keep an eye on everyone,' I said. 'And yell out if you see anything.'

'Like what?' said Martin.

'I think you'll know when you see it,' I said.

I led Penny out of the security centre. The door started closing before we were even properly outside.

'First it's ghosts,' said Penny. 'Now it's a dead man walking. What next? The old Ringstone Witch rising from her grave?'

'Hush,' I said. 'You never know who might be listening.'

FIVE

Who's That Knocking at the Door?

Out in the entrance hall I paused for a moment, feeling the weight of history pressing down on me. For many years Ringstone Lodge had stood alone, miles from anywhere, the better to preserve its secrets. And once it became an interrogation and debriefing centre, there was no telling how much pain and horror these old walls had soaked up. All the years, all the people who had passed through, and the things they said and did to each other . . . Could this old house be haunted by so much awful history?

Considering how many strange things I'd dealt with in my time, why was I finding it so hard to accept the possibility of ghosts? If aliens and monsters were real, why not the walking dead and spirits from the vasty deeps? Was it simply that I couldn't stand the thought of all the people I'd killed for the greater good coming back to accuse me? All the men and women with bloody holes in their chests and backs, or with heads lolling limply on their shoulders from snapped necks, all the burned bodies and waterlogged corpses . . . What would I say to them if they stood before me?

I like to tell myself I've never killed anyone who didn't need killing; anyone whose death didn't make the world a better and safer place. But how could I trust my morality when I couldn't even trust my own memory? Sometimes I wonder whether I might be the biggest monster of them all . . .

Penny waited patiently at my side, and finally put a hand on my arm. 'Don't frown so hard, sweetie, you'll give yourself wrinkles. What are you thinking about?'

'The past,' I said. 'And how it has a way of creeping up on you.'

'I wish you wouldn't freeze me out, Ishmael,' she said. 'How can I help, if I don't know what the problem is?'

'Not every problem has an answer,' I said. 'But I will tell you one thing, we are not going down to the basement.'

'We're not?' said Penny. 'MacKay seemed very certain that we were.'

I smiled at her. 'You know I don't react well to authority figures. Especially when they start barking orders at me.'

'I had noticed, yes. But you must admit he has a point. Things happened down in the basement that we don't understand yet. I know you don't want to admit it, Ishmael, but given that the killer left no physical evidence behind, isn't it possible that Parker could have been killed by a ghost?'

'If he'd been frightened to death, maybe,' I said patiently. 'But whoever heard of a ghost stabbing someone?'

'Why are you so resistant to the idea that this spooky old place might be haunted?' said Penny. 'After everything we've seen . . .'

'There's no need for a supernatural explanation, when there are so many real-world suspects,' I said. 'A lot of people have a lot of good reasons for wanting Parker dead. That's why we were sent here, after all.'

'The Organization must have suspected there was some otherworldly aspect to this case,' Penny said stubbornly. 'Or why would they have chosen you?'

'Yes,' I said. 'I'm still thinking about that.'

'If we're not going down to the basement,' said Penny, 'where are we going?'

'To check the doors,' I said. 'Make sure they really are properly locked and secure. It occurred to me that if someone has hacked into Martin's computers, they could have taken control of one particular door and its cameras so they could come and go unobserved.'

'If there's a door that hasn't been affected by the lockdown,' said Penny, 'then our killer could escape at any time, long before reinforcements turn up!'

'Sometimes,' I said, 'It's all about crossing the i's and dotting the t's.'

'Alien!' said Penny.

*　　*　　*

We started with the front door. I checked it carefully, but couldn't see any sign of it being tampered with. It was very thoroughly locked, and while I rattled the door for all it was worth, just on the off chance, I couldn't budge it an inch for all my strength.

'Very solid door, that,' Penny said solemnly.

'Very,' I said. 'And a lot heavier than its size would suggest. Wouldn't surprise me if it had a solid-steel core.'

'Could you break it down?' asked Penny. 'If you had to? If something messy hit the fan and we had to leave in a hurry?'

'Probably,' I said.

We made our rounds of the ground floor, but it turned out there was only one other exterior door. And the back door turned out to be just as heavy and just as locked. All the time we were going back and forth, I kept waiting for Martin to say something; to challenge us over where we were and what we were doing, and why I wasn't following MacKay's instructions. But he never said a word. I could hear Baxter and Redd searching through one room after another, but I couldn't hear anyone else. All the corridors were equally empty, and almost suffocatingly quiet. The Lodge had the feeling of a very large house with very few people in it. Like we were just mice in a maze; moving this way and that, with no idea of what was really going on.

'All right,' said Penny, when we finally returned to the entrance hall. 'What now? Check all the windows?'

'No,' I said. 'A window without a shutter in place would be far too easy to spot.'

'Maybe we should go down to the basement,' Penny suggested tactfully. 'What if there's a hidden way in? Some secret tunnel connecting the basement to the grounds? That would explain how the killer was able to get to Parker without being noticed or detected.'

'Good idea,' I said. 'In a house this old, a few architectural secrets should come as standard.'

And that was when Baxter and Redd came striding into the entrance hall, having completed their search of the ground floor. I'd gone out of my way to avoid them, in the name of peace and quiet and not brawling in public. But now here they were standing right in front of me. And not looking at all happy about it. Baxter was scowling, as usual, while Redd was as coldly unreadable as ever. It bothered me that, while I usually had a pretty good idea of what was passing through Baxter's mind, I had no idea at all of what was going on behind Redd's enigmatic features.

'Why aren't you down in the basement, where you belong?' Baxter said accusingly.

'We're just going there,' said Penny. 'Have you found anything?'

'No,' said Redd. 'If anyone else is inside the Lodge, they're really good at moving around without leaving any traces. Could be a ghost, or it could be a trained professional. Like an Organization field agent, for example.'

'Right!' said Baxter, fixing me with his fiercest glare. 'What are you doing here? Spying on us? The ground floor is our responsibility; we don't need anyone looking over our shoulder.'

'Damn right!' said Redd. 'Unless, of course, you're trying to hide some piece of evidence from us.'

'This is what the killer wants,' I said steadily. 'Wasting time arguing with each other, instead of working together to find him.'

'But what if he doesn't need finding?' said Redd. 'What if he's been right under our noses all along?'

'If you've got something to say,' I said, 'say it. I'm listening.'

'Everything was fine till you got here,' said Baxter. 'The field agent with the mysterious background, the trained killer with more dirty secrets than the rest of us put together.'

'What is your problem?' Penny said sharply. 'You've had a mad on for Ishmael ever since we got here.'

'Bax applied to be a field agent,' said Redd, 'and the Organization turned him down. Never said why, but then they don't have to. I told him he was too clean for the kind of dirty work they do.'

'We don't need you here!' said Baxter, glaring right into my face. 'We're all the security the Lodge needs.'

'Really?' I said. 'The man you were supposed to protect was killed while you were busy seeing ghosts around every corner.'

'I didn't see any ghosts!' said Baxter. 'There aren't any ghosts.'

And he jumped me, his heavy hands reaching for my throat. He looked ready to do me some serious harm, so I quickly stepped inside his reach, grabbed two handfuls of his shirtfront, and threw him across the hall. He flew through the air surprisingly gracefully, given his size and weight, and hit the floor really hard. He rolled painfully for several feet, before coming to a halt. I expected the impact to slow him down, maybe even knock a little sense into him, but he just shrugged it off and scrambled up on to his feet again. He looked even angrier, if that was possible, and now he was grinning savagely. This was what he'd wanted all along: an excuse to beat and break and humiliate me. To prove to himself that he was the better man, more than a match for any damned field agent.

He took up a practised martial arts stance and came at me again, more cautiously this time. He struck out at me with vicious speed and strength, his blows and kicks demonstrating reasonably good form; but to me, he might as well have been moving in slow motion. I avoided most of his attacks, and blocked the others with enough strength to make him grunt with pain as well as surprise. And then I grabbed his shirtfront again, and threw him across the hall the other way. He landed harder this time, and took longer to get up on to his feet. He was breathing hard. I wasn't. He came forward again, and I wondered if I was going to have to do him some serious damage to stop him. I didn't want to have to do that. In his own obnoxious way, Baxter was just doing his job. And taking down one of our own people would have been exactly what the killer wanted.

So I waited till Baxter was almost upon me and then hit him once, swift and hard, right under the breastbone. He never saw it coming, never had a chance to defend himself. My fist slammed in deep, driving all the breath out of him. He stopped dead in his tracks, his eyes squeezing shut as all the colour drained out of his face. His legs gave up and he suddenly sat down on the floor, like a small child who'd just run out of steam. I waited a moment, to be sure it was all over, and then looked to see what Redd was doing.

He started towards me, his face set and cold, and Penny stepped forward to block his way. He gestured sharply for her to stand aside, but she shook her head, smiling sweetly. Redd looked at her with an almost indifferent anger.

'Get out of my way, girl. This is none of your business.'

'Ishmael is my business,' said Penny. 'He belongs to me, just like Baxter belongs to you. I think we should all calm down and behave like grown-ups. Don't you?'

'Move!' said Redd. 'Or I'll hurt you.'

'Not on the best day you ever had,' said Penny.

He grabbed for her wrist, to throw her out of his way. She seized hold of his arm, swept around, and threw him neatly over her shoulder in a perfectly executed judo throw. He flew through the air and slammed into a wall, hitting it so hard even I winced. He slid down the wall and sat on the floor, dazed. Penny marched forward to stand over him, both hands planted on her hips. She sniffed coldly.

'You can learn all kinds of useful things at a really good finishing school,' she said. 'So don't try anything like that again, or I will show you the special ball-breaking kick the nuns taught me at St Theresa's School for Exemplary Youngsters.'

She turned her back on Redd and came back to me, smiling brightly. I nodded approvingly.

'I knew you'd come in useful for something.'

'Have you quite finished playing with your little friend?' said Penny.

'I think he's had enough,' I said. 'I'm not a violent man . . .'

'Oh I think you are, really,' said Penny.

'Only when I have to be,' I said. 'This hasn't solved anything.'

'Probably not,' Penny conceded. 'But at least they'll now keep their distance while they're being mean to us.'

I picked Baxter up effortlessly. He made a low noise, as though he'd like to protest but didn't have the strength. I carried him across the hall and set him down next to Redd, who looked like he was still trying to figure out what had just happened. I arranged them neatly side by side and then stepped back. Baxter and Redd glared up at me, like I'd cheated. Which, strictly speaking, I had. They were used to human opponents.

'If I really was the killer, you'd both be dead now,' I said. 'Think about it.'

I turned away, and Penny raised an eyebrow.

'What now? Down to the basement in search of hidden tunnels?'

'No,' I said. 'The lounge. I think we need to have words with Doctor Hayley and Doctor Doyle.'

'I've got a few good words for them,' said Penny. 'But what if they don't want to talk to us?'

'I can be very persuasive,' I said. 'When I put my mind to it.'

Penny shrugged. 'Let's just hope it doesn't involve throwing more people around. I'm pretty sure that's not conducive to a good working relationship.'

'Almost certainly not,' I said. 'But if they should act up, you take Hayley and I'll hide behind you.'

'Not a chance,' said Penny. 'I get the feeling she could be seriously scary if she put her mind to it.'

'Of course,' I said. 'She's an interrogator.'

When I slammed open the door to the lounge and marched in without knocking, Hayley and Doyle both looked round quickly. As though they'd been caught doing something they shouldn't. They clearly hadn't expected to be interrupted. They were sitting on the big sofa again, with a whole mess of papers spread out on the coffee table. They put down the ones they'd been studying, and stood up to face us. Hayley had her usual aggressive face on, while Doyle looked calmer and more collected now he'd got something useful to occupy his mind.

'What are you doing here?' said Hayley.

'Keeping busy,' I said. 'What are you doing?'

Hayley and Doyle couldn't help glancing at the papers laid out on the coffee table. I stepped forward for a better look, and Hayley moved as though to stop me. I gave her a look, and she stepped back again. You don't get to be an experienced interrogator without being able to read people's intentions. I looked at the papers; copious handwritten notes on everything they'd seen and heard, and what they thought it meant. Most of it was in the same hand. Hayley's, most likely.

'Why aren't you using your laptop?' said Penny.

Hayley glanced across at it, lying closed at the far end of the coffee table. She shrugged, stiffly.

'It occurred to me that if our killer has been able to hack into Martin's computers, he'd have no trouble getting into mine. It's easier to keep paper private.'

'Unless someone walks in on you unexpectedly,' I said. 'I think you'd better talk me through this, Doctor Hayley. It's good to share.'

She sighed and sat down on the sofa, and after a moment Doyle did too. Penny and I sat down beside them, after Hayley made Doyle budge up to give us some room. I leafed quickly through the papers, with Penny leaning in beside me. It was all very detailed, very businesslike. Treating murder like just another puzzle to be solved. I started to say something, and Hayley quickly put up a hand to stop me. She gestured for all of us to lean in close and put our heads together. Penny looked at me and I nodded.

'Why are we doing this?' I asked politely.

'So we can speak privately,' said Hayley, her voice little more than a murmur. 'I don't want Martin hearing what we have to say.'

'Why not?' said Penny. 'Don't you trust him?'

'I don't trust anyone here,' Hayley said coldly. 'But especially not Martin. It could explain a lot, if someone has paid him to be not quite as attentive as he should be. But even if he is on the level, he's still a sneak. I don't want him running to MacKay and telling tales out of school. Robbie and I have been comparing notes on events, interpretations and possible motivations . . . and we think we know who the killer is.'

'You've got a suspect already?' said Penny. 'Cool! Who is it?'

'MacKay,' said Doyle.

I looked at Penny and she looked at me, and then we both looked at Hayley and Doyle.

'Why?' I said.

Hayley counted off the points on her fingers. 'Only MacKay has access to all areas of Ringstone Lodge. Including the security centre. He's always very good about waiting for Martin to open the door for him, but he once let slip to me that he has a master key for every lock in the building, for emergencies. He knows the Lodge inside out, which means he could know special places where he could hide himself away any time he feels like it. And he's an ex-soldier. He'd know how to kill a man with a knife, silently and effectively. If he can open the security centre door, he might well be able to do the same for the cell in the basement and know how to wipe all traces of what he'd done from the security systems. He was here before Martin, after all. Who knows what backdoor commands he might have installed in the computers?'

'And, of course, Parker wouldn't have been surprised to see MacKay,' said Doyle. 'Until it was too late.'

'Not bad,' I said. 'Logical, hangs together well. Makes sense, mostly.'

'We never miss Agatha Christie on television,' said Doyle. 'We love all her mysteries . . . Not for the murders, you understand, but for the problem-solving element.'

'The only thing missing,' I said, 'is motive. What reason could MacKay have to kill Parker?'

Hayley and Doyle looked at each other.

'You said it yourself, Ishmael,' Hayley said finally. 'A lot of people wanted Parker dead, before he could talk about all the things he'd done for them. All of them ready to pay good money to have Parker silenced. MacKay isn't a young man any more. He put off retirement once, but age is creeping up on him. He can't have many years left at Ringstone Lodge, and he must know it. This kind of pay-off would mean his inevitable retirement could at least be comfortable. But now I have a question for you.'

'Go ahead,' I said generously. 'You're on a roll. Go for it, ask me anything. Don't let me stop you.'

'Why did you bring Penny to Ringstone Lodge?' Hayley said flatly. 'What purpose does she serve?'

'I am decorative and functional,' Penny said sweetly. 'I can do many things, including brightening a room just by being in it.'

'It's true,' I said. 'You'd be amazed what she can do.'

'Organization field agents always work alone,' said Doyle. 'Everyone knows that. So what is she really?'

'She's my partner,' I said.

'I'm his better half,' said Penny.

'She keeps me human,' I said.

'You were the only agent to work in the field with the previous Colonel,' Doyle said heavily. 'Why did he decide it was necessary for him to involve himself in the dangers of fieldwork? And why choose you, out of all the field agents at his command?'

I looked thoughtfully at Doyle. 'How do you know about the cases the Colonel and I worked on together?'

'It's in your file,' said Hayley. 'Along with some other interesting facts. You first joined the Organization in 1963. Which would make you a contemporary of Frank Parker.'

'Except there's a good forty years difference between the way you look,' said Doyle. 'What happened? Was your plastic surgery much more successful than his?'

'Perhaps,' I said carefully, 'I am not the first agent to use the Ishmael Jones name.'

Doyle and Hayley looked at each other.

'Of course,' said Hayley. 'I knew there was no way any one man could have done all the things Ishmael Jones is supposed to have done.'

'It does make sense,' said Doyle.

'Now answer the question,' said Hayley.

'Sorry,' I said. 'What question was that?'

'Why, out of all the field agents at his disposal, did the previous Colonel pick you to work with?' said Hayley. 'Especially when he shouldn't have been out in the field himself anyway?'

'That sounds less like a question,' I said, 'and more like an accusation. I worked with the Colonel on occasion because that was the way he wanted it. Beyond that, I never asked and he never said. Now I work with Penny, because that's the way I want it. And as long as I continue to get results, the Organization doesn't give a damn how I do the things I do.'

And then I stopped and looked up, as the lights in the lounge flickered for several moments, before becoming steady again. Penny and I stood up and looked around the lounge. The lights flickered again, more noticeably this time. As though someone was nudging the switches. Hayley took in the look on our faces and rose to her feet, followed immediately by Doyle.

'What is it?' said Hayley, not bothering to keep her voice down any more. 'What's wrong? The lights? Just faulty wiring? You have to expect things like that in a house this old.'

'That's not all you can find in some old houses,' said Penny. 'Martin warned us about this.'

'Warned you about what?' said Doyle.

'He's seen lights flickering before,' I said. 'And lights turning themselves off and on, for no good reason. He says he's checked, and there's nothing wrong with the wiring or the generator or main systems. He blames . . . not necessarily natural means.'

'Ghosts?' said Hayley. 'Martin thinks the spirits of the dead are running around turning the lights on and off? What does he think they'll do next? Tie our shoelaces together when we're not looking?'

'But it would be very bad if the lights went out,' said Doyle. 'That would be horrible.'

Something in his voice made all of us turn to look at him. Doyle was peering around the room with almost childlike fear and anticipation. All the colour had disappeared from his face, and his mouth was trembling. The progress he'd made from his previous fright had been undone in a moment. Hayley patted him comfortingly on the shoulder, but he didn't seem to notice.

I looked carefully around the lounge. The lights were steady again now, bright and cheerful. But the darkness beyond the great bay window was worryingly complete. I couldn't even make out a glimpse of the grounds beyond. I was seized by a sudden certainty that the world outside was gone, swallowed up by the dark, and only we were left in this small island of light. Something cold settled in the pit of my stomach, and my hands clenched into fists. Hayley gave us all her fiercest scowl.

'This ghost nonsense has got to stop!' she said loudly. 'Whatever people might be seeing or think they're seeing, there's nothing supernatural going on here.'

'That's not what you said earlier,' said Penny.

'That was then,' said Hayley. 'We have a real problem now, with a real murderer somewhere at large in the Lodge. We can't allow ourselves to be distracted by such . . . fancies.'

'I was always afraid of the dark, as a child,' said Doyle. 'Back then there were no street lights where I lived, so when my mother turned off the bedroom light it was very dark. And I would lie there too scared to sleep, worrying that the rest of the world had gone away and I was all that was left. Sometimes a car would go past in the road outside and for a moment my room would be full of light and sound and hope; and then the car would move on, taking its light and sound with it, and I would be left alone in the dark.'

We all looked round sharply, turning to face the door as we heard footsteps outside the lounge, heading down the corridor towards us. The same kind of footsteps Penny and I had heard outside our room, up on the top floor. Slow and deliberate, and far too heavy to be human. Doyle made a soft desperate sound, and Hayley grabbed hold of his arm with both hands. None of us took our eyes off the door as the footsteps drew steadily nearer, heavy and deliberate, and invested with terrible intent. Penny moved in close beside me, her face set and determined.

And yet, for all the sound and fury of the footsteps, I couldn't feel any vibrations through the floor. Steps that heavy should have made a hell of an impact, and the vibrations should have carried on through the wooden floorboards . . . But I wasn't picking up anything, as though whatever was making the footsteps had no physical presence at all.

'Martin?' I said, raising my voice. 'Can you see if there's anyone outside the lounge? Martin!'

There was no response. Just the sound of the footsteps drawing menacingly closer.

'Why can't he hear us?' said Doyle. His face was wet with sweat, and there was a lost, fey look to his eyes that I really didn't like. 'Martin said he had microphones in every room. He must be able to hear us!'

He jerked his arm free of Hayley and waved his hands above his head, trying to attract Martin's attention.

'Robbie, no!' said Hayley. 'We don't need Martin. We can handle this.'

Doyle's arms dropped to his sides. He was breathing heavily. And when he looked at Hayley, his eyes were full of terrible apprehension.

'It's out there,' he said. 'And it wants in.'

'What does?' said Hayley.

'The dark,' said Doyle.

The footsteps crashed to a halt, right outside the lounge door. And then there was a long pause. Not a sound to be heard. Hayley and Doyle had their eyes fixed on the door. Penny and I glanced at each other, and I was surprised to find a mischievous gleam in her eyes. My heart warmed as I realized that out of all of us in the room she was the only one who wanted to open the door and see what was there. Just for the satisfaction of knowing. I grinned at her, and she grinned back.

Something knocked on the door. Loud, heavy knocks. But the door didn't shiver once in its frame. As though it felt nothing, as though the knocks had no physical impact. I headed for the door, and Penny was right there beside me.

'No!' said Doyle. 'Please don't open that door. Don't let it in.'

I stopped and looked back at him. 'Why not?' I said, as kindly as I could. 'What could be out there that would be so bad? If it's dark, we'll turn on some more lights. And if there is someone there, I'll deal with them. That's what I'm here for.'

'But there might be someone out there we really don't want to see,' said Hayley. Her voice was surprisingly unsteady. 'It might be Parker. Standing there, with the knife still stuck in his chest. Smiling, refusing to die, come to kill us.'

'You're getting as bad as Doyle,' I said.

'Why would Parker want to come after you?' said Penny. 'What would he have against you? You didn't kill him, did you?'

'No,' said Doyle. 'But we left him locked in his cage, trapped and helpless. Left him on his own with death coming for him and nowhere to run.'

'Who's there?' Hayley said loudly to the door, trying hard to sound angry instead of scared. 'Who's out there? Answer me!'

There was no response. No answer to her demands, no more knocking, no more footsteps. Just this feeling of a presence waiting on the other side of the door. Just a silence, that seemed to have a weight and a substance of its own. Pressing up against the other side of the closed door.

'Well,' I said, as lightly as I could, 'there's only one way to find out who it is.'

I walked steadily forward, with Penny only a step behind me. I stopped in front of the door and listened carefully, but couldn't hear anything. I took hold of the door handle and then looked at Penny, making sure she was braced and ready. She nodded quickly.

'Who do you think it is?' she said.

'I think . . . someone is messing with us,' I said. 'And I also think that when I get my hands on them they are going to be very sorry they ever thought this would be funny. Whoever is out there, I'm going to punch them in the head.'

'What if your fist goes right through them?' said Penny.

'If this is just an insubstantial ghost,' I said patiently, 'it wouldn't be able to knock on the door, would it? And it wouldn't need us to open the door. It would walk right through it.'

'For someone who doesn't believe in ghosts, you know an awful lot about them,' said Penny.

'It's hard to avoid ghost stories,' I said. 'Your culture is obsessed with death.'

'Maybe it is Parker,' said Penny, looking steadily at the door. 'A dead man walking, with murder on his mind. Not necessarily his own.'

'Then I shall punch him even harder in the head,' I said, 'for making our job more difficult.'

I jerked the door open and stepped out into the corridor. It was completely empty. No sign of anyone, anywhere. No sign to show that anyone had ever been there. The corridor stretched away before us, open and silent and not in any way menacing. It looked back at me quite innocently, as if to say, 'What are you looking at me for? I'm just a corridor.'

'Perhaps they ran away?' said Penny.

'No,' I said. 'We would have heard that.'

'What about that marvellous bloodhound nose of yours?' Penny said quietly. 'Can you smell anyone?'

'I can smell you, Hayley and Doyle,' I said. 'But not even a trace of anyone else. And I am definitely not picking up any of the distinctive odours you would expect to accompany a dead body.'

'Then what made all those sounds?' said Penny.

'Good question,' I said. 'It's like someone's trying to throw a scare into us . . .'

Hayley came forward, and looked cautiously out of the door and up and down the corridor. She still had one hand on Doyle's arm, keeping him close by her. Neither of them looked particularly relieved to see a completely empty corridor.

'We're not alone in Ringstone Lodge,' said Doyle. 'Something's in here with us.'

'Something,' I agreed.

'But you still don't think the place is haunted?' said Penny.

'I think someone wants us to think it is,' I said. 'I wonder why . . .'

The lights started flickering again. Not just in the lounge, but all the lights up and down the length of the corridor. Many seemed on the point of going out completely.

'Oh no,' said Doyle. 'Please . . . Don't let the lights go out! I don't think I could stand it.'

'I'm here with you. Show some backbone!' Hayley said sharply. She searched quickly through her jacket pockets. 'I've got an emergency torch here with me, somewhere . . . Don't let this get to you, Robbie. It's just someone playing games.'

'Almost as though someone is trying to get our attention,' said Penny.

'Or make a point,' I said.

'Did you feel that?' Doyle said suddenly.

We all turned to look at him. Doyle pulled his arm free of Hayley's grip and stumbled back into the lounge, looking quickly about him. Hayley went after him, like a mother in pursuit of a small child, but he barely noticed she was there. He waved one hand back and forth before him.

'What is it, Robbie?' Hayley said quietly. 'Did you see something? Hear something? What?'

'It just got cold,' said Doyle. 'Can't you feel it, Alice? It's suddenly very cold in here . . .'

I looked at Penny, and she looked at me.

'I don't feel any difference in the temperature,' I said carefully.

'Me neither,' said Penny. 'Maybe it's just in one place.'

'Maybe it's just in his head,' I said.

'A cold spot . . .' said Hayley. 'I've read about those. Sudden drops in local temperature, an energy drain to fuel some kind of manifestation.'

'Can you feel this cold spot?' I said.

Hayley shook her head reluctantly. 'No.'

She moved in close beside Doyle, trying to feel what he was feeling, though she obviously wasn't.

'How can you not feel this?' said Doyle. 'I'm freezing . . .'

'Then why isn't your breath steaming on the air?' I said.

'Look!' Doyle said, pushing back his sleeves. 'I've got gooseflesh!'

'I think your imagination is running away with you,' I said.

Doyle rounded on me. 'Monsters are real in your world? Horrible things watching us from the deepest shadows of the hidden world?'

'Yes,' I said. 'Monsters are real, sometimes. But just because some bad things exist, it doesn't mean they all do. Sometimes a legend is just a legend. Just because we're hearing and seeing things we can't explain, it doesn't mean there isn't an explanation.'

'Yes!' Penny said brightly. 'Ghosts.'

I looked at her. 'Am I going to have to throw a bucket of cold water over you?'

'Listen up!' Martin's voice said suddenly and we all jumped, just a bit. 'Pay attention! I need to tell you something.'

'Where the hell have you been?' I said. 'Did you leave the security centre again?'

'What? No!' said Martin. 'Of course not. I've been here all the time. I did have to use the commode, but it's on a swivel like the chair so I don't have to miss anything. Why?'

'Because we've been yelling our heads off,' said Doyle. 'Calling to you for help, and you didn't answer!'

There was a pause. And then Martin said steadily, 'I didn't hear you.'

'I was waving my arms around like an idiot,' said Doyle. 'You must have seen that!'

'I can't watch all the screens, all the time,' said Martin. 'I must have missed you. What's been happening?'

'The lights in here have been flickering,' I said. 'Though I notice that it seems to have stopped now. And then someone came walking down the corridor to bang on our door. But when I went to look there was no one there. Have you seen anyone moving around in this corridor?'

'No,' said Martin. 'Nobody. Damn! I miss all the good stuff. Let me just check the records . . . No, no sounds of footsteps or knockings. And no one moving anywhere near the lounge.'

'What about Baxter and Redd?' said Hayley. 'Are they still somewhere on the ground floor?'

'Yes,' said Martin. 'But nowhere near you.'

'Would your microphones actually be able to record ghostly footsteps?' Penny asked suddenly.

'Interesting question,' said Martin. 'I suppose if we were hearing them on some psychic level, instead of through our ears, then possibly . . .'

'Martin!' I said sharply. 'Concentrate! What did you want? You said you needed to tell us something.'

'Oh, yes!' said Martin. 'I've caught someone running around, on my screens. Or at least I think I have. The figure comes and goes so quickly that at first I wondered . . . No! There he is! I'm looking at him right now.'

'Who is it?' I said.

'I think it might be Parker,' said Martin. 'It's just a dim figure . . . but definitely not one of us.'

'What makes you think it's Parker?' I said.

'Well, who else could it be?' said Martin. 'I can't get a good look at him, he's moving too quickly. I'm just getting glimpses as he moves from one screen to another.'

'Is he setting off the motion trackers?' said Hayley.

'No,' said Martin. 'No, he isn't. Which is odd, because he should be. All my systems are working normally, there's not a red light anywhere.'

'It could be Parker's killer,' said Penny, 'if we're really not alone in the Lodge.'

'Ghosts . . .' said Doyle. 'The restless dead. Nothing rests easily at Ringstone Lodge . . .'

'I'm sure I've got a sedative about me somewhere,' said Hayley.

'Where is this person right now?' I said. 'Can you see him, Martin?'

'He's on the ground floor,' Martin said steadily. 'Or at least he was . . . I seem to have lost track of him for the moment. But the last I saw of him, he was very definitely heading in your direction – and I don't think it's because he fancies a nice sit down and a chat. Look, I don't think you should stay there. I don't know whether what I'm seeing is Parker or his killer, but either way it would be a really bad idea if you are still there when he turns up. So get out of there! Now!'

'Don't you start getting hysterical,' I said. 'Will everybody please calm down! I am a trained field agent, and I will handle whoever or whatever this is.'

'By punching it in the head,' said Penny.

'Always a good start,' I said. 'Doctor Hayley, Doctor Doyle, stay here in the lounge. I'll go see what's out there. You can lock the door after I'm gone.'

'I'm going too,' Penny said quickly. 'Whatever it is, I want to see it.'

'Of course you do,' I said. 'If you're very good, I'll let you punch him in the head as well.'

'You spoil me,' said Penny.

'I can't lock the door,' said Hayley. 'I don't have a key.'

'Then use furniture to barricade it,' I said. 'Pile up as much as you need to feel safe.'

'What if the lights go out?' said Doyle.

'I've got my emergency torch,' said Hayley.

'It's not a very big torch,' said Doyle.

'You're really starting to get on my nerves, Robbie!' said Hayley.

I set off down the corridor with Penny at my side. The lounge door slammed shut behind us. Followed by the sound of heavy furniture being dragged across the floor to push up against the door. I took a good look round, but there was no sign of anybody, living or dead. The corridor stretched away before me, completely quiet and utterly deserted. The old house seemed very still, as though expecting something to happen. Penny stood close beside me, waiting patiently.

'There must have been something out here,' she said finally. 'We all heard something.'

'Hearing isn't necessarily believing,' I said. 'But either way, there's nothing here now.'

'Martin seemed very sure someone was heading our way,' said Penny. 'But I can't hear anything. Can you hear anything, space boy?'

I strained my ears against the quiet. 'No, nothing. Just a few ticking clocks, one of which could use oiling.'

'Show-off!' said Penny.

'Well, if our intruder won't come to us, I think we should go looking for him.'

'Sounds like a good plan to me,' said Penny.

I set off down the corridor and Penny marched along beside me, matching me step for step. I loved the way she was always ready to throw herself into anything. Never a moment's doubt or hesitation. I liked to think it was because she had faith in my ability to deal with whatever happened, to protect her from anything; but as she'd already demonstrated to poor Redd, she didn't need anyone's protection.

'Are we heading anywhere in particular?' said Penny.

'Back to the entrance hall,' I said. 'We have to cover most of the ground floor to get there, and we'll end up not far from the security centre. So I can ask Martin a few pointed questions about this elusive intruder.'

'Are you sure you remember the way back?' Penny said doubtfully. 'It's a big house, and we took quite a few turns.'

'I remember all of them,' I said.

Penny looked at me. 'How?'

'I paid attention.'

'You can be very irritating on occasion, Ishmael,' said Penny.

Sometimes I have no idea what she's talking about.

* * *

But just a few corridors later I caught a familiar scent on the
air, from not far ahead. I increased my pace, as the heavy
coppery smell of freshly spilled blood became increasingly
clear. I rounded another corner and came to an abrupt halt, as
I saw Baxter lying on the floor with blood all over his chest.

Penny slammed to a halt beside me, swore briefly under
her breath as she saw Baxter, and then started to move forward
again. I stopped her.

'Is he dead?' she said, her voice quite steady.

'Yes,' I said.

'Are you sure? There might be something we could do . . .'

'No,' I said. 'He's dead. I can tell. You stay here, while I
check the body and the surrounding area.'

'I know, crime scene!' she said. 'I get it . . . Wait a minute,
can you hear anyone anywhere near here?'

'No,' I said. 'It's just us. And him.'

I moved forward, slowly and carefully, checking the heavy
carpet for drops of blood or foot imprints, but there was
nothing. No sign to show anyone had ever been here. Our
killer was very good at covering his tracks. The corridor was
long and narrow and completely deserted. No nearby doors
leading off, nowhere for the killer to be hiding. He'd just done
his work and left. I knelt down beside the body and looked it
over.

Baxter was lying on his back. His eyes were open and
unblinking. He'd taken a single stab wound to the heart. There
was blood all over his chest, but no knife left in the killing
wound this time. No defensive wounds. Baxter knew who
killed him and had let the killer get close. I couldn't see him
doing that with a walking dead man, so that would seem to
rule out Parker. Unless Parker had just appeared before him
out of nowhere . . .

A thought occurred to me, and I checked his shoulder holster.
It was empty. I checked the floor around the body, but there
was no sign of the gun anywhere. So, the killer had a gun
now. I stood up and turned to Penny.

'Dead. One stab wound to the chest, just like Parker.'

'So whoever it is didn't just come here to eliminate Parker,'
said Penny. 'Unless . . . the killer got trapped in here when

the Lodge went into lockdown. But then why would he hang around after his work was done? Surely a professional would know better? Perhaps he wants to kill us all in case Parker told us something!'

'You're really getting the hang of this deduction thing,' I said. 'At least there's nothing impossible about this murder. No locked door. Someone just walked up to Baxter and killed him where he stood.'

Penny frowned. 'But who would Baxter trust to let him get that close?'

'Good question,' I said. 'And I have another. Why didn't Martin see this happening on his screens and sound the alarm?' I raised my voice. 'Martin! Baxter's been killed. I'm with the body . . . Martin! Damn, he's not hearing me again. Someone must have taken control of his systems and is turning them on and off as necessary.' I stopped, and looked thoughtfully at Baxter. 'Why kill him? I mean, why him specifically as opposed to the rest of us?'

'Because he was on his own?' said Penny. 'Because he was just in the wrong place at the wrong time and saw something he shouldn't have?'

'But where's his partner?' I said. 'Those two are never apart.'

We both looked round sharply as we heard approaching feet. But these were perfectly normal sounds, entirely human. I could feel the vibrations through the wood of the floor. And all I had to do was sniff the air to know who it was.

'It's Redd,' I said to Penny.

He came round the corner quite casually, then stopped as he saw us standing beside Baxter's body. He made a harsh animal sound of grief. I started to say something, and he stopped me with a gesture.

'Get away from him!' he said. 'Don't you touch him . . .'

I stepped back, and Penny did too. Redd came forward quite slowly, staring unblinkingly at the dead man, until finally he knelt down beside him. He stared at Baxter for a long moment, and I couldn't read a single thing in his expression. Redd reached out to touch Baxter's face, and then pulled back his hand.

'I told you not to go off on your own, Bax,' he said quietly, almost confidentially. He stared up at me accusingly. 'He was looking for you, because you humiliated him. It wasn't enough for you to beat him, you had to make it look easy. This is all your fault!'

'We were nowhere near here when this happened,' said Penny. 'We just found him. Ishmael and I were in the lounge, with Hayley and Doyle. You can ask them. Or Martin can confirm it.'

'Yes!' said Martin, his voice rising clearly out of nowhere. 'I was just talking to them all, in the lounge.'

'Oh! You're back again, are you?' I said.

'What do you mean?' he said. 'I haven't been anywhere.'

'I spoke to you just now and you didn't answer,' I said.

'Shut up!' said Redd. 'Just stop talking! Martin, did you see who killed Bax?'

'No,' said Martin. 'I'm sorry but I've been busy, trying to track an intruder on my screens. I never saw this.'

Redd took Baxter in his arms and cradled the dead man, rocking him gently back and forth like a mother with a sleeping child.

'He was a good soldier,' Redd said finally. 'Not very complicated, but then he didn't need to be. He had me for that. And he had the heart of a lion. He wasn't afraid of anyone. He would never have allowed anyone to get this close unless he knew them.'

'And trusted them,' said Penny. 'I mean he would never have let Ishmael or me get that close, would he?'

'Bax never trusted anyone,' said Redd. 'He had . . . issues. And he'd never have let Parker get anywhere near him, dead or alive.'

He kissed Baxter on the forehead, and laid him gently down on the floor. He got to his feet. He wasn't crying. His face was cold, set in harsh unforgiving lines.

'I'll get him for you, Bax, I promise you. Whoever did this, I'll find them. They won't get away with this, whoever they are.'

'The only one of us not accounted for,' Penny said slowly, 'is MacKay. Martin, where is MacKay right now?'

'Still upstairs,' said Martin. 'Checking the last few rooms. But I'm telling you, it wasn't MacKay I saw moving around. Someone else is locked inside the Lodge with us.'

'Just because you saw someone,' I said, 'it doesn't mean it was Parker. More likely it was Parker's killer. And now Baxter's. That could mean an intruder, or it could be one of us. You said it yourself, Martin, you haven't seen this figure long enough to identify him.'

'I know who it wasn't.'

'No you don't,' I said.

'The man I saw was moving too quickly to be human,' said Martin. 'I know you don't want it to be ghosts or anything supernatural, but . . . Wait a minute! MacKay just emerged from the last room. He's starting down the stairs to the entrance hall.'

I set off at a run, with Penny and Redd right behind me.

When we finally burst into the entrance hall, MacKay was standing at the foot of the stairs. He nodded coolly to us as we stumbled to a halt.

'Mr Martin has already informed me as to the situation,' he said flatly. 'I am sorry to hear that Mr Baxter is dead. He seemed a very conscientious young man. I understand he was killed in a similar fashion to Mr Parker?'

'Single stab in the heart, from the front,' I said. 'The killer took the knife with him this time.'

'And you saw nothing of this, Mr Martin?' said MacKay. 'What have you been doing?'

'I've been busy!' said Martin. 'A lot's been happening!'

'That is no excuse,' said MacKay. 'We will discuss this lapse in discipline at a later date.'

'You did it,' said Redd, stepping forward to fix MacKay with his cold eyes. 'There wasn't anyone else, so it had to be you. You killed my Bax!'

MacKay met his gaze steadily. 'Talk sense, man. I was upstairs until right this moment. Mr Martin can confirm that.'

'Well, no. Actually, I can't,' said Martin. 'I did see you there, but not all of the time. I've been having problems with my cameras.'

MacKay sighed, but didn't take his eyes off Redd. 'What reason could I possibly have to kill Mr Baxter? We were on the same side.'

'Were we?' said Redd.

'I did see MacKay upstairs,' said Martin.

'But not all the time,' I said. 'A lot of things have been going on that you haven't been allowed to see. Because someone has taken control of your systems.'

'No!' he said. 'I'd know.'

'You know now,' I said.

Redd threw himself at MacKay. The older man didn't fall back a single step. He met Redd squarely, grabbed his outstretched arm and swung him around, then held him helpless in a vicious armlock. Redd struggled, fighting MacKay with all his strength, but couldn't break the hold. MacKay, his face grim, piled on the pressure; until Redd's face went white from the pain.

'Stop fighting me, Mr Redd,' MacKay said sternly. 'I will break your arm if that is what it takes to restore discipline.'

Redd threw his whole weight against the hold, even though the pain must have been unbearable, but he still couldn't break free. MacKay piled on the pressure almost to breaking point before Redd suddenly ran out of strength and gave up. He stood still, his head hanging down. Sweat dripped off his face. MacKay let him go and stepped back, watching Redd carefully. Redd hugged his arm to him, and wouldn't look at any of us.

'Show me Mr Baxter's body,' said MacKay.

But when we got back to the corridor, the body was gone. As though he'd just got up and walked away . . . I had to get down on my hands and knees to find the impression in the carpet that showed a body had been there. Redd watched me do it. MacKay raised his voice.

'Mr Martin? What happened here?'

'I don't know,' said Martin's voice. He sounded almost on the edge of tears, from sheer frustration. 'I was watching you on the screens to make sure you were safe, not the body. Wait a minute, just . . . let me check the recordings. Oh hell, I don't believe it! All the cameras in your area shut themselves down for a while.'

'Your systems have been seriously compromised,' I said. 'Someone is turning them on and off at will.'

'Unless Parker took the body,' said Martin. He laughed for longer than was comfortable, and there was more than a touch of hysteria in it. 'A dead man . . . took a dead man for a walk!'

'OK,' said Penny. 'Someone needs a break . . .'

'But what if the ghosts killed Baxter, and then took the body?' said Martin, his voice rising.

'Mr Martin!' said MacKay. 'Get a grip on yourself, right now. You are talking nonsense.'

'You don't know what I've been seeing,' said Martin. 'All kinds of weird things! You've seen and heard strange things too, just recently. You know you have!'

'That is no reason to lose your reason,' said MacKay. 'We will deal with whatever is happening in a calm and disciplined manner.'

'Where's Bax?' Redd said suddenly. 'I want my Bax!'

And he went running off down the corridor, ignoring the rest of us as we called after him, and quickly disappeared from sight.

'A very disturbed young man,' said MacKay.

'I told you not to split up the group,' I said. 'This is what happens when you go off on your own. You get picked off. We need to get back to the lounge, join up with Hayley and Doyle, and then barricade ourselves in. Wait for the reinforcements to arrive.'

'I believe you are right, Mr Jones,' MacKay said wearily. 'I fear I no longer understand what is going on in my Lodge.'

SIX

Accusations, Denials and People Losing Their Heads

MacKay led the way, as usual, striding along. But his head was hanging down, staring at the floor rather than where he was going. He didn't look like an old soldier any more, just an old man who'd been hit too hard and too often. I knew how he felt. It wasn't enough that everyone in the house had some kind of alibi for Parker's murder; now I had ghosts and walking dead men to consider, along with bodies that disappeared the moment you took your eyes off them.

MacKay stopped suddenly and raised his head. 'Mr Martin! This is MacKay. Do you hear me?'

'I'm right here,' said Martin. His voice seemed to come out of nowhere, as always. 'I have all of you on my screen.'

'I am taking Mr Jones and Miss Belcourt to join the two doctors in the lounge,' said MacKay.

'I know,' said Martin. 'I was listening. Go ahead, don't let me stop you.'

'I think you should come and join us,' said MacKay. 'We have a great deal to discuss, and you need to be a part of those discussions.'

'You need me right where I am,' said Martin. 'Sitting in front of these screens, watching everything. Standing guard over you.'

'Mr Parker is dead,' said MacKay. 'So is Mr Baxter. Both of their bodies disappeared and you saw none of it.'

'That's not fair!' said Martin. 'It's not my fault. I can only do what my equipment allows me to do.'

'Exactly,' said MacKay. 'So come and join us in the lounge, Mr Martin. That is not a request.'

There was a pause; and I did wonder for a moment whether Martin would defy MacKay, so he could stay in the one place he felt safe. But when Martin finally spoke again he sounded resigned, as if he'd known this was coming.

'Give me a few minutes to put the system on automatic. So at least whatever I miss will be recorded and I can study it later. I'll catch up with you in the lounge. No, hold on – wait a minute! I knew there was something I wanted to ask you. There are guns in the Lodge. Right? Well, wouldn't this be a really good time to break them out? So we can defend ourselves?'

'He has a point,' said Penny.

'There are guns,' said MacKay. 'Securely locked up in the armoury. For emergencies only.'

'And this doesn't qualify?' said Penny. 'What are you waiting for, an attack on the Lodge by an army of flying monkeys?'

'I don't think adding guns to an already dangerous situation is a good idea,' I said carefully. 'People are nervous enough as it is, without having them shooting at shadows. Or possibly each other.'

'If someone wants us dead, don't we have the right to protect ourselves?' said Martin. 'Or are we all supposed to hide behind you if things get bad? You're the Big Bad Secret Agent, so you probably already have a gun. One of those special ones that can fire round corners, which you assemble out of six ordinary-looking objects.'

'I'm not that kind of secret agent,' I said. 'And I don't have guns of any kind. I prefer to work without them.'

'It's a wonder to me you're still among the living,' said Martin.

'He has a point,' said Penny. 'Don't you look at me like that, Ishmael. He does have a point!'

'Mr Martin, you may be right,' MacKay said heavily. 'But I am not yet ready to dispense deadly weapons to untrained people with unsteady hands. Come to the lounge and we will discuss the matter further.'

None of us had much to say as we made our way through the empty corridors of the house. The silence was oppressive, a nagging weight on nerves already stretched to their limits. It was like walking through a jungle where predators might be lurking around every corner or hiding in any shadow. I kept a careful watch on every door we approached, and my ears trained for anything to suggest we might be being followed. Penny kept trying to look in six different directions at once; not because she was frightened, but because she wanted to be ready if anything happened. The two murders hadn't upset her; just made her more determined. The horrors she'd endured at Belcourt Manor, where she'd been forced to watch helplessly as her friends and family died, had given her a driving need to see the guilty punished. MacKay didn't seem to give a damn about his surroundings. He just plodded along, lost in his own thoughts.

When we finally arrived at the lounge, I was surprised to find Martin already there waiting for us. Looking more out of place than ever in the old-fashioned corridors, with his grubby T-shirt and his baseball cap turned backwards. He gestured sullenly at the closed door.

'They won't let me in,' he said loudly. 'I knocked, announced myself properly and told them you were on your way, and they still wouldn't open the door!'

'I will attend to this, Mr Martin,' said MacKay. His back straightened with an audible snap as his military discipline reasserted itself, and he stepped forward to hammer on the door with his fist.

I looked thoughtfully at Martin. 'How did you get here ahead of us?'

'I've been working in this dump for years,' said Martin. He smirked, almost proudly. 'I like to go exploring during my off time and I've found all kinds of shortcuts. It's not like there's much else to do around here, after all, and we're not allowed to go into town – in case any of the staff have a few drinks and start chatting to the locals about what really goes on here. Not that any of the locals would talk to us . . . Half the time it feels like we're locked up along with the prisoners. And they get looked after better! You would not believe what gets brought in here to sweeten their natures and soften them up. Booze, drugs, women . . . Just for them! We never get a look in. If it wasn't for my unlimited access to webcam girls and cute-cat videos, I'd have gone crazy long ago.'

'Hush, Mr Martin!' said MacKay. He knocked again, the sound thunderously loud in the quiet. 'This is MacKay! Open the door, Doctor Hayley, Doctor Doyle!'

'Go away!' said Hayley's voice, from the other side of the door. 'We've put up a barricade and we're not taking it down. It's not safe out there.'

'Not safe!' said Doyle's voice.

'I know, dear, I'm telling them that.'

'Well, tell them to go away and stop bothering us.'

'I am, dear. You go and sit down and have a rest. You know your nerves aren't good.'

I was tempted to smash the door in and kick their barricade aside; but I didn't want anyone in the Lodge to know just how strong I was. I might need the element of surprise at some point. So I stepped in beside MacKay and nodded to him, and he stepped reluctantly aside.

'Doctor Hayley, this is Ishmael Jones,' I said loudly. 'Please let us in. Things have changed and we need to discuss them.'

'What things?' said Hayley.

'Baxter has been murdered. And his body has disappeared into thin air, just like Parker's.'

There was a long pause. I imagined Hayley and Doyle looking at each other, raising their eyebrows and shrugging a lot. Finally there was the sound of heavy furniture scraping across the floor, as the two of them laboriously dismantled their barricade. It took a while, but eventually the door opened. MacKay strode straight in, so quickly and authoritatively that Hayley and Doyle had to jump back out of his way. The shock of being so openly defied had brought MacKay's military aspect back to the fore, and he seemed to have completely shrugged off his former malaise. Martin slouched in after him, hands deep in pockets, looking like he'd much rather be anywhere else. Preferably somewhere with a bar. Penny and I brought up the rear, and I closed the door carefully behind us. Hayley immediately came forward, pushing a heavy table ahead of her, but I stopped her with a raised hand.

'No barricade for the moment, doctor. Just in case we feel the need to depart this room in a hurry.'

She looked at me suspiciously. 'Why would we want to do that? Aren't we safe in here?'

'I don't know, doctor. But I'd rather have the option and not need it, than need it and not have it.'

She sniffed briefly, abandoned her table, and turned her scowl on MacKay. Doyle came over to stand beside her so he could join in the scowling. They clearly still considered MacKay to be their chief suspect as murderer. They had made a pretty good case. MacKay couldn't have known that, but he did know a complete lack of trust when he saw it. He stared both the doctors down, unflinchingly, so they turned their glares on Martin. Who just dropped into the nearest chair and ignored them.

'Can we get on with this?' he said loudly. 'There are far more important things I should be doing, some of them even work-related.'

'If you're here,' said Doyle, 'who's minding the store? Anything could be going on out there and we wouldn't know about it.'

'The computers are in charge,' said Martin. 'The cameras are still watching and the microphones are still listening, so you'd better all be on your best behaviour. You never know what might end up on YouTube if you annoy me sufficiently.'

'The cameras haven't done a particularly good job of protecting us so far, have they?' Penny said sweetly.

Martin pouted, and sank sullenly down in his chair. When he wasn't lording it over the rest of us with the borrowed authority his computers gave him, it was easy to forget how young he was. Away from the security centre and very much out of his element, he looked more than a bit twitchy. Hayley and Doyle gave up on their glaring, as it wasn't getting them anywhere, and took up their usual positions sitting on the sofa. I couldn't help noticing they'd put away all their handwritten notes before opening the door. MacKay sat down stiffly in a chair next to Martin, in a way that suggested relaxing was against his religion. I pulled up a comfortable armchair so I could sit facing Hayley and Doyle; and Penny arranged herself elegantly on the armrest, draping her arm across my shoulders to balance herself as she did so. I looked at MacKay, and he nodded to me, so I brought Hayley and Doyle up to speed on what had been happening. Hayley looked more and more interested, while Doyle looked increasingly distressed.

'I have come round to your way of thinking,' he said, the moment I stopped talking. 'I believe we should all stay here in the lounge, with the door securely barricaded, and wait for reinforcements. Now Baxter is dead, that just proves the killer's work isn't done.'

'Do you really think it wise to remain cooped up in here, when one of us is almost certainly the murderer?' said MacKay.

Martin started to get up out of his chair, and then sat down again when MacKay looked at him. He scowled around him impartially, seeming even more twitchy.

'How long before the reinforcements get here?' I said.

'Maybe half an hour,' said Martin, not even glancing at his watch. 'We can hold out that long, can't we?'

'We're not all here,' Hayley said suddenly. 'Where's Redd?'

'Gone off on his own,' I said.

'And you let him?' said Hayley.

'Baxter's death upset him,' I said. 'I would have had to wrestle him to the ground and sit on him to stop him, and I don't think that would have improved his mood any. Did you happen to see where he went, Martin?'

'Upstairs,' Martin said immediately. 'He didn't look like he was in the mood for company. He seemed to be looking for something, but I couldn't tell you what.'

After that we all just sat around for a while, looking at each other and trying not to appear too openly suspicious of anyone in particular. The mood in the room was distinctly cold and uncomfortable, with suspicious looks and heavy thoughts on all sides. I sat with Penny, Hayley with Doyle, and MacKay beside Martin. Three separate groups, ready to throw out accusations or defences at a moment's notice.

'I want to go back to my screens,' Martin said finally. 'At least I'd feel like I was doing something useful.' He glowered at MacKay. 'You said you wanted me here so you could discuss things. Well, go on then, discuss.'

'We should pool whatever information we have,' MacKay said slowly. 'In the hope someone will bring something new to the table. Perhaps you would care to start, Mr Jones. You must have more experience of dealing with murders and mysteries than the rest of us.'

'This whole situation is one big mystery to me,' I said. 'It's been a difficult case, right from the start. Bodies that disappear, with no hard evidence, no clues and no clear motives. Without any of those traditional tools of the trade, any accusation is just guesswork. And all this ghost nonsense isn't helping. It's just getting in the way of working out what's really going on.'

'Are we not supposed to talk about all the weird shit that's been happening, then?' said Martin.

'Not if it gets in the way!' said Hayley. 'What matters is identifying the killer before someone else dies.'

'Before he makes more ghosts,' said Martin. 'Come on, people, feel the atmosphere. We're practically hip-deep in ectoplasm!'

'Then why haven't I met one?' I said. 'I've seen two dead bodies and heard everything short of a spectral soft-shoe shuffle, but I haven't seen anything even vaguely transparent.'

'What about the things I showed you on my screens?' said Martin.

'I haven't seen anything in person,' I said.

'Are ghosts persons?' Penny said vaguely.

'They used to be,' said Doyle.

'Stop that!' I said.

'They're probably scared of you,' said Martin. 'Mister Big Bad Secret Agent.'

'If the ghosts are a part of what's happening, we can't just turn our back on them,' said Doyle.

'Of course not,' I said. 'They might creep up on us.'

'Really not helping, Ishmael!' said Penny. She smiled encouragingly at Doyle. 'Are you feeling better now?'

'Better than I was,' he said, smiling weakly in return. 'I'm supposed to be the one who puts pressure on others. It never occurred to me how badly I might cope under pressure!'

'You're doing fine, dear,' said Hayley.

'No I'm not,' said Doyle. He didn't even glance at Hayley. Instead, his attention fixed on Penny. 'It's all about inner resources, you see. You can be as brave as you like when an interrogation begins, but no one ever really knows their true mettle until it's tested. That's what Alice and I look for and play on. The hidden weaknesses that the subject doesn't even know he has – till we find them and exploit them. Now someone is playing us, and it seems I am not the man I thought I was.'

'Stop it, Robbie!' said Hayley.

He finally turned to look at her. 'I'm sorry, Alice, but once this is over I'm going back to my old university and taking up my previous position again if they'll have me. Either way, I want nothing more to do with this appalling profession you brought me into. I'm leaving, with or without you.'

'Robbie, please. This is no time to be making life-changing decisions,' said Hayley.

'This is exactly the time,' said Doyle. 'When you're so scared you can't lie to yourself any more.'

'We will talk about this later, Robbie,' said Hayley.

'No, we'll talk about it now,' said Doyle. 'I was perfectly happy in my ivory tower until I met you. Because I wanted to be with you, I let you lead me out into the big wide world. But your world has been eating me alive from the inside . . . and I just can't do this any more.'

'I did all of this for you,' said Hayley, 'so we could have a good life together. Your work made our careers possible. You can't just walk out on me, after everything I've done for you!'

'Yes,' said Doyle. 'Look what you've made of me, Alice.'

He smiled at her sadly, while she looked at him with growing horror in her eyes.

I noticed Martin was looking at MacKay. It was obvious he didn't like to see the old man appearing so tired and beaten down.

'Cheer up, MacKay!' he said loudly. 'Look on the bright side, we're not dead!'

'But my career is at an end,' MacKay said heavily. 'Mr Parker died while under my care. Mr Baxter died while following my orders. No matter how this works out, our lords and masters will require my resignation. And without a job, I'm nothing. It's all I've got.'

'I thought that, too,' Hayley said quietly. 'The moment I heard Parker was dead, I thought whoever's killed him has killed my career . . . Such a selfish thing to think, when someone has just died.'

'I thought I had some good years still left in me,' said MacKay. 'But it seems I was wrong. I got old, and didn't notice.'

And then he broke off, as the mobile phone in his jacket rang loudly. We all looked at him as he sat up straight in his chair, brought out his phone, and checked the caller's ID.

'It is Mr Redd,' he said. 'Of course. Who else could it be?'

'I thought phones wouldn't work inside the Lodge?' said Penny.

'Security phones are exempt,' said MacKay.

'Why is Redd calling you?' said Hayley.

'Because he is not with us, I suppose,' MacKay said dryly. He put the phone to his ear. 'What is it, Mr Redd?'

He listened for a while, nodding occasionally, then turned off his phone. He looked at it for a long moment before putting it away. He seemed oddly unsettled. As though the strange situation he was in had thrown him another unexpected curve.

'Mr Redd says he knows who the murderer is. The only person it could be. He even knows how our killer is performing his nasty little tricks. But he isn't prepared to name this person over the phone. He will only tell me face to face.'

'How many times do I have to tell you people?' I said loudly. 'Breaking up the group and going off on your own is never going to end well! Look, if anyone is to go off and talk to Redd, it should be me. Because I have a much better chance of surviving whatever's lying in wait out there.'

'Unfortunately, Mr Redd was most emphatic,' said MacKay. 'He will only talk to me. He says if he sees anyone else, he will disappear again. If there is even a chance Mr Redd can name our killer, with hard proof to back him up, I have to listen. I have to do my job.'

'Of course you do,' said Martin. 'I'll go back to the centre, so I can follow you on my screens.'

MacKay paused, as he realized Hayley and Doyle were staring at him. 'Is there a problem, doctors?'

'We don't like the idea of you leaving,' Hayley said sharply. 'Because as far as we're concerned, you're still our main suspect. Maybe you just want to talk to Redd alone so you can be sure of shutting him up.'

'Mr Parker was in my care,' said MacKay, and his voice was a very cold thing. 'Finding his murderer is my responsibility.'

'You did threaten to kill him yourself, once,' Penny said diffidently. 'And offer to have Baxter and Redd beat him up.'

'That was part of the job then,' said MacKay. 'My job now is to see him avenged. I have to prove myself worthy of my position. One last time.'

'You talk as though leaving your job would be the end of everything,' I said.

'It would be,' said MacKay.

'What about your family?' said Penny.

'The army was my family for many years,' said MacKay. 'The only one I ever wanted. When they were forced to let me go, my old home turned out to be a place I no longer recognized, my blood relatives nothing but strangers. So I came here and made the Lodge my new home, and those who worked under me became the closest thing I have to a family. I should have gone with them when they left . . .'

And just like that, his relationship with Martin made a lot more sense. Their constant squabbling and then standing up for each other was typical father-and-son stuff, even if neither of them had ever openly admitted it to each other. Martin was already glaring at Hayley and Doyle.

'My screens showed MacKay was nowhere near Parker when he died.'

'But your systems are a mess,' said Hayley. 'Your cameras come and go, your surveillance is full of holes . . .'

'I would have to say you make a much better suspect than me, Doctor Hayley,' MacKay said sharply. 'You were failing to get anywhere in your interrogation. We all knew that. Mr Parker diverted your attempts to get inside his head, with ridiculous ease. You have already admitted that a failure to break him could mean the end of your career. But if he was to die before he could be made to talk, then it couldn't be your fault, could it?'

'Alice was with me, in our room, when Parker was killed,' said Doyle.

'But then you would say that, wouldn't you?' said MacKay. 'You would say anything for her, because she runs your life.'

'You are the only one with the means, opportunity and motive,' said Hayley.

'Hardly,' I said. 'Given that we still don't know how the murder was committed, or why.'

'Who do you think it is, Mr MacKay?' said Penny.

'Much as I hate to point the finger at a man who is clearly suffering,' said MacKay, 'I would have to say I have never been able to fathom Mr Redd. A man who has always held his emotions very close to his chest, apart of course from his obvious devotion to Mr Baxter . . . A man like that might be capable of anything. Especially if there was enough money involved.'

'And you still want to go up there and talk to him?' said Penny. 'On your own?'

'That is why I have to talk to him,' said MacKay. 'To hear what he has to say. It is always possible that he feels the need to make a confession.'

'But . . . unless you want us to believe there are two killers running around out there,' Penny said slowly, 'that would have to mean Redd killed Baxter as well as Parker. And I don't believe he would do that, no matter how much money was involved.'

'There's always you,' Doyle said bluntly.

Penny looked at him. 'What?'

'Yes,' I said, 'I would have to go along with that. What . . .?'

'We still don't know why you're here, really,' said Doyle, ignoring me to stare coolly at Penny. 'Why would an Organization field agent like Jones, one of those who famously work alone, turn up here with a partner? Except, of course, he did work with the previous Colonel, on cases so special we're not allowed to know the details. Are you here to do the things he can't, Penny? Are you a specialist? A professional assassin, perhaps?'

'Who do you really work for, Penny?' said Hayley. 'Not the Organization. We checked.'

'Why would I want to kill Parker?' said Penny. 'Ishmael and I were sent here to keep him alive.'

'I don't know,' said Doyle. 'Why don't you tell us?'

'Yes,' said Hayley. 'Tell us everything about you and Ishmael Jones.'

They leaned forward, fixing her with their gaze, their voices suddenly compelling. But Penny just laughed in their faces.

'I don't intimidate that easily,' she said dryly. 'I used to work in publishing.'

'She was with me, in our room, when Parker died,' I said.

'But then you would say that, wouldn't you?' said Hayley. 'And you're not above suspicion yourself, Ishmael. As more than one of us has already noted, Parker was perfectly fine until you arrived. You insisted on talking to him privately, against my wishes, and within a few hours he was dead. Coincidence? I don't think so.'

There was a long pause, as we all looked at each other.

'You have been very quiet, Mr Martin,' MacKay said finally. 'You've seen more of what's happened than all of us put together. What do you believe is going on here?'

'I'm not going to say anything,' said Martin. 'You'd only laugh at me.'

'I think I can quite definitely assure you that none of us are in a laughing mood, Mr Martin,' said MacKay. 'If you have a theory of your own, I am sure we would all like to hear it.'

'I think Parker's presence here did something to this house,' Martin said steadily. 'Something to wake the sleeping spirits of Ringstone Lodge. Until he came here, the old ghosts were quiet. But within hours of his arrival, all kinds of strange things began happening. I saw things, heard things, even managed to record some of them . . . I believe there was a power in Parker, something he acquired while operating in the darker corners of the world. I think he found something old and terrible, and made it a part of himself. He couldn't be killed, they said. What's a knife in the chest, to a man like that? And now he's out there, walking the corridors, looking to take his revenge on the people who locked him up and tried to kill him. Dead or alive, he walks . . . surrounded by spirits of the past, called up again by his power. The dead do not rest easily in Ringstone Lodge. They never have.'

There was another long pause, and then Penny turned to Hayley.

'Didn't you say earlier that you had some sedatives on you? I think someone here could use several.'

'Let me see what I've got,' said Hayley.

Martin scowled at MacKay. 'See? I told you. No one likes to hear things they don't want to be true.'

But as I looked round the room, it seemed to me they were all ready to believe at least some of what Martin was saying. Apparently I was the only one left who wasn't prepared to believe ghosts had anything to do with what was happening at Ringstone Lodge.

'Oh, Ishmael . . .' said Penny. 'I hate to be the bearer of bad tidings, but I think we've all missed something. Look at the bay window.'

We all turned to take in the massive window at the far end of the lounge. Outside, there was nothing but the night. Just darkness, pressing up against the glass. I looked at Penny.

'What am I missing?' I said. 'It's just night out there.'

'But that's the point!' said Penny. 'We shouldn't be able to see the darkness. The windows are supposed to be covered by steel shutters!'

We were all up out of our chairs in a hurry, standing together, staring at the bay window. The night stared back, giving nothing away. How could I have missed something so blatantly obvious? Because so much had been happening? Or because I'd wasted so much of my time and attention on stupid ghost stories? MacKay rounded on Martin.

'Why isn't that window sealed?'

'I don't know!' said Martin. 'It's supposed to be. According to my computers, all the shutters came down simultaneously the moment I hit lockdown. What was I supposed to do, go round the house checking every single window? Look, I need to get back to the security centre. Figure out what's gone wrong.'

'And now someone else wants to go off on their own,' I said. 'It's like being surrounded by lemmings.'

'We have to check,' said MacKay. 'Because if the computers were wrong about this, what else might they be wrong about?'

'Then we should all go, as a group,' I said.

'Can't be soon enough for me,' said Penny. 'I'll never feel safe in this room again, with that window open to the world. Anyone could get in.'

'Or out,' I said. 'Anyone could enter or leave through that window, as often as they pleased . . .'

'Do we have a clue, at long last?' said Penny.

'Do you know, I think we do,' I said.

'I love clues!' said Penny.

Hurrying back through the house to the security centre, I allowed MacKay to take the lead again, so I could hang back and keep a watchful eye on our surroundings. I didn't trust any part of Ringstone Lodge, and I reckoned I'd had enough surprises for one day. But when we got back to the security centre, the heavy steel door was standing wide open, leaving all the equipment unguarded. I thought MacKay was going to have an apoplectic fit, right there on the spot.

'I cannot believe you left the door unlocked, Mr Martin!'

'But I didn't!' said Martin, staring at the gaping door with horrified fascination. 'I always lock the place up when I leave, you know that.'

We all peered into the dimly lit interior, but none of us took a step forward. In the end, MacKay lifted his chin and strode into the security centre in a way that suggested he was more than ready to kick the crap out of any intruder he encountered. But he was only gone for a moment before he was back out again, shaking his head.

'No one's there. It's safe for you to go in.'

Martin ran past him, and we all followed after. Penny leaned in close beside me to murmur in my ear.

'Shame on you, Ishmael. Letting an old man like that take all the risks.'

'An old soldier like MacKay?' I said. 'I'd back him against anyone dumb enough to still be there.'

'If it had been me, I would have left a booby trap or two behind,' Penny said demurely.

'Same here,' I said. 'But if there had been any, MacKay would have seen them.'

'You can be very cold-blooded on occasion, Ishmael.'

'Just practical,' I said.

Once inside we all crowded together, partly for mutual support but mostly because the space was so limited and we were all afraid to touch anything in case we broke it. The room seemed entirely undamaged, with nothing obviously missing. Martin had already planted himself on his swivel chair, his fingers flying across the keyboard on his lap as he checked whether the intruder had planted anything nasty in his systems. MacKay carefully studied a screen at the far end of the room.

'Lockdown has not been raised or tampered with,' he said finally. 'The Lodge is still secure.'

'Apart from the lounge window,' I said.

'Mr Martin?' said Mackay.

'I'm working on it!' said Martin, scowling fiercely at the screens around him. 'Otherwise, everything's working normally.'

'Working normally?' said Penny. 'That doesn't actually impress me much. There are undoubtedly moles out there in the grounds wearing heavy sunglasses who see more of what's going on than you do.'

'Bit harsh,' I murmured.

'Well . . .' said Penny.

Martin looked like he wanted to say something harsh in reply, but then he caught my eye and didn't.

'If you locked the door when you left,' Hayley said slowly to Martin, 'who opened it? Who else knows the combination?'

'Only MacKay,' said Martin. 'And we were both with you in the lounge.'

'So how did they get in?' said Penny.

'Ghosts?' said Doyle. But even he didn't sound too convinced.

'This is all just distraction,' I said firmly. 'There's been too much of that already. Check your cameras, Martin. Where is Redd, right now?'

Martin stabbed a finger at one particular screen, showing Redd standing alone on the top floor right next to the room

Penny and I had been given. The door was open, as though he might have been inside and just come out again.

'What's he doing in our room?' Penny said loudly.

'He must have some reason to be there,' said Hayley.

'Is there anything you want to tell us, Mr Jones, Miss Belcourt?' said MacKay. 'Is there perhaps something in your room Mr Redd might have discovered that we ought to know about?'

'No,' I said.

'Then why is Redd there?' Hayley said accusingly.

'Don't you snap at me,' I said.

'Redd claimed he had evidence as to who the killer was,' said Doyle. 'He must have got it from somewhere.'

'Well he didn't get it from our room!' said Penny. She stopped, and looked at me. 'Did we lock our room after we left?'

'Yes,' I said. 'But then locks don't seem to mean much in this house. So did Redd unlock it? Or did someone else do it for him? And if I hear an answer that in any way contains the word ghosts, I will take a firm hold of that person and show them how to pass through a wall the hard way.'

'I cannot keep Mr Redd waiting much longer,' said MacKay. 'He might become impatient and disappear back into the house.'

'I still say talking to him alone is risky,' I said. 'Why would he want to talk to you, in particular?'

'Call ahead first,' said Penny. 'Tell him you're on your way, Mr MacKay, so he won't get twitchy when he hears footsteps coming. And then while you've got him, try a few pertinent questions. This whole thing feels like a trap to me.'

'You are of course entirely right, miss,' said MacKay. 'But the best way to walk out of a trap is to know you're walking into one.'

He got out his phone and called Redd, but the man on the screen didn't react. MacKay put the phone away.

'Mr Redd must have turned his phone off to avoid having to answer any awkward questions.'

'Hold it,' I said. 'Everything in the Lodge is overheard and recorded. And Redd knows that. So why is he insisting on talking to you alone, when he must know we'll hear every word?'

'I must be sure to ask him that,' said MacKay. 'And now, I think it is time for me to be on my way.'

'I'll be following you every step of the way on my screens,' said Martin. 'You won't be alone for a moment.'

'That is reassuring indeed, Mr Martin,' MacKay said gravely.

'If it does all go wrong, don't be afraid to shout,' I said. 'Even a trained soldier can be caught off guard. I can be with you in a few moments.'

'I do not believe I have anything to fear from Mr Redd,' said MacKay.

'Don't you?' I said. 'After you nearly broke his arm to make him behave?'

MacKay allowed himself one of his small smiles. 'Mr Redd is just a hired security man. I was a professional soldier in a Scottish Highland Regiment. I believe I can handle Mr Redd, if I have to.'

He nodded to all of us, and then marched out of the security centre like an old soldier who'd just caught a whiff of cordite in the air. He might have doubts about his job, but not his abilities. We watched MacKay reach the foot of the stairs and then proceed up them slowly and steadily. On another screen, Redd was still standing by the open bedroom door. Penny pressed in close beside me.

'Do you suppose he's been searching our room?' she said quietly. 'Opening our bags, and going through our things?'

'Let him,' I said. 'It's not as if he'd find anything.'

'But he might have been touching my personal things!'

'I doubt whether he's that interested in female underwear,' I said. I looked at Redd for a long moment. 'He's standing very still, isn't he? You'd expect him to be more nervous, up there on his own.'

MacKay appeared on a new screen as he reached the top of the stairs. He stopped there for a moment, staring thoughtfully down the corridor, before starting forward. Then every single screen in the centre went blank. Martin swore harshly, and worked frantically at his keyboard.

'Do something!' said Hayley. 'Get him back. We need to

know what's going on. Anything could be happening up there!'

'I know!' said Martin. 'I'm trying!' But nothing he did seemed to work. In the end he grabbed hold of his keyboard with both hands and shook it in sheer frustration. 'It's not responding! There's nothing I can do!' He looked at the blank screens. 'I promised I'd watch over him.'

'Go, Ishmael!' said Penny.

I raced out of the security centre, followed by Penny and then Hayley and Doyle. I soon left them behind as I sprinted across the entrance hall, reached the stairs and pounded up them two steps at a time. I was at the top before the others had even reached the bottom. I stood there looking down the long corridor, not even breathing hard. There was no sign of Redd anywhere, or MacKay. I strained my ears for the slightest sound, but there was nothing. I called out to MacKay. My voice fell flat in the quiet, and there was no response. I called out to Redd. Still nothing. Where were they? What were they doing? They had to know I was there.

'Martin?' I said. 'Can you hear me?'

'Yes,' he said immediately, his voice coming out of nowhere. 'I've got sound back, but no vision. I'm still working on that. What can you see?'

'Just an empty corridor,' I said. 'Tell the others to stay where they are. I don't want anyone coming up here until I'm sure it's safe.'

'Got it,' said Martin. I heard his voice again, at the foot of the stairs, telling the others what I'd just told him. No one argued. I moved over to the nearest door and tried the handle. It was locked. I kicked the door in. The locked shattered and the door flew open, almost tearing itself off its hinges. I stepped inside the room and looked around, but there was nothing to suggest it had seen any recent use. I came back out, walked over to the door opposite and kicked that in. Another empty room. I went back out into the corridor, and considered my options.

'It's Parker!' Martin's voice said suddenly. 'Some of my screens just started working and I can see Parker. He's there, with you!'

'Where?' I said, looking up the corridor and then back at the stairs. 'I don't see him anywhere.'

'He just went into your room,' said Martin. 'Hurry!'

I sprinted along the corridor, not caring that Martin could see how fast I was moving. It only took me a few moments to reach the far end. The door to our room was still standing open. I rushed in. The lights were on, but no one was there.

'I've got him!' Martin said excitedly. 'I can see him again. He's right at the top of the stairs.'

'What? How is that even possible?' I said. 'There's no way he could have got past me.'

'I don't know!' said Martin. 'But he's there, I can see him. And he's starting down the stairs, towards the others.'

Towards Penny . . .

I ran out of the room and raced down the corridor. I couldn't see anyone ahead of me. I charged down the stairs, but when I finally reached the bottom and lurched to a halt only Penny and Hayley and Doyle were there waiting for me. Looking surprised, and more than a little startled at the speed of my return.

'What happened?' said Penny. 'We heard you crashing about upstairs, but Martin said you wanted us to stay here.'

'Didn't you see him?' I said.

'See who?' said Penny.

'Parker!' I said. 'Martin caught him on his screens, coming down the stairs ahead of me.'

They all looked at each other, and then at me.

'No one's come down these stairs since you went up them,' Doyle said carefully. 'We haven't seen anyone.'

'I saw him!' said Martin's voice. 'I did! Or at least, I thought I did. I mean, I saw someone and I think it was Parker. Are you sure you didn't see anything, Ishmael? You must have been right behind him.'

'Nothing,' I said.

'He couldn't have just disappeared between the top of the stairs and the bottom,' said Penny. 'Could he?'

'Unless he's a ghost, now,' said Doyle.

'First he's a walking dead man,' I said. 'And now he's a ghost!'

'But he couldn't have disappeared between the top and bottom of the stairs!' said Penny. 'That's impossible!

'You're right,' I said. And I frowned, thinking.

'Ishmael!' said Hayley. 'What happened up there?'

'I didn't see any sign of Redd or MacKay,' I said. 'And they couldn't have come down these stairs without you or me seeing them. So where did they go? All the rooms on that floor are locked, and the stairs are the only way down.'

'If anyone's got a key to those rooms, it would be MacKay,' said Penny. 'Did you check all the doors?'

'No,' I said. 'I got distracted, chasing after people who weren't there.'

'He was there,' Martin said sulkily. 'Hold it! Some more of my screens just came back. I can see inside all the rooms on the top floor, and there's no one in any of them.'

'We were talking earlier about hidden passageways,' said Penny. 'Concealed doors and sliding panels in the walls. MacKay sent Redd and Baxter up to the top floor to look for them, earlier on. Maybe Redd found one and used it to hustle MacKay away.'

'Why would he want to do that?' said Doyle.

'If we're lucky, he just wanted to show MacKay how the murderer could be moving around and avoiding us,' I said. 'Hidden passageways would go a long way to explaining how our killer can appear and disappear so easily. And since the secret corridors would be the only place in the Lodge not covered by the surveillance systems, they would be the one place where Redd and MacKay could safely hold a private conversation.'

'And if we're not lucky?' said Hayley.

'Do you really need me to say it?' I said. 'Apparently you do. All right then, my apologies in advance to those of a delicate sensibility. A hidden passageway would be the perfect place to kill someone without being seen and then hide the bodies. Parker and Baxter's bodies may already be in there.'

'But I saw Parker!' said Martin.

'You saw somebody,' I said.

Interesting changes took place in the faces before me. Some of the tension dropped away, as they realized hidden doors and secret tunnels went a long way towards excluding ghosts as a viable explanation. Penny smiled brightly, Hayley nodded thoughtfully, and Doyle began to breathe more easily. Of course, that still didn't explain how anyone could disappear between the top and bottom of a staircase. I was still working on that one.

'The whole Lodge could be riddled with secret passages,' said Doyle. 'Didn't some old houses actually have hollow walls, for smugglers and the like?'

'There was no mention of that in the official family history of Ringstone Lodge,' said Hayley.

We all looked at her.

'I didn't know there was one,' I said.

'There's a copy in the library here,' said Hayley. 'Privately published. MacKay mentioned it. I made a point of reading it as soon as I arrived. I like to know as much as possible about any new place I have to work in.'

Doyle looked at her. 'You never told me . . . Did this official history mention the family ghosts as well?'

'Yes,' said Hayley. 'Which is why I didn't tell you. You've always had a thing about ghosts.'

'You should have told me!' said Doyle.

'What do we do now?' Penny said briskly. 'Go looking for Redd and MacKay? Tap on the walls and kick the panelling?'

'Martin!' I said loudly. 'Are you seeing Redd and MacKay anywhere?'

'Not so far,' said Martin. 'But a lot of my screens are still down. I need more time.'

'How much time do we have before the reinforcements get here?' said Doyle.

'Not long now,' said Martin. 'Doctor Hayley . . . Could you please come back here and join me in the centre? Something has just come up on one of my screens, and I'd value your opinion.'

'What is it?' said Hayley.

'Complicated . . .' said Martin. 'You need to see this for yourself.'

'Oh, very well,' said Hayley.

She started off, and then stopped and looked back as she realized Doyle wasn't going with her. She looked at him inquiringly, and he shook his head.

'I think I've spent long enough following you around, Alice.'

She reacted sharply, as though he'd slapped her. And then her head came up and she turned away, the set of her shoulders making it clear she wasn't prepared to beg. She strode off, not looking back once. I had intended to go with her, to see what Martin had discovered; but that would have meant leaving Penny alone with Doyle, and I didn't want her out of my sight. She liked to think she could look after herself, and most of the time she could. But I didn't trust this house. Or any of the people in it. So the three of us stood together, at the foot of the stairs. Nobody seemed to want to say anything. Finally, Doyle turned to Penny.

'You're not a professional assassin, are you?'

'No,' said Penny. 'Not even a little bit.'

'I didn't really think so,' said Doyle. 'It's just . . . when you're desperate for answers, you can find yourself clasping at some pretty unlikely straws.'

'How long have you and Alice been together?' said Penny.

'Almost fifteen years. She found me in my academic hiding place and brought me out into the world. Showed me places and people I'd never even dreamed of. I'd thought I would be alone forever, but she freed me from the prison I'd made of my life. And for that kindness I would have followed her anywhere.'

'What did you do, before?' I said.

'Linguistics,' he said. 'All very theoretical, nothing to do with the real world. Or so I thought. But Alice saw a value in my work . . . a chance to do something with it that mattered. The things we persuaded people to say saved lives and put an end to all kinds of evils. Or so we were told. It's taken me till now to understand the kind of person the job made me into.'

'Sorry to interrupt,' said Martin's voice, 'but is Doctor Hayley still there with you? I've only got sound in the entrance hall.'

'No,' I said. 'She left a while back. She should have reached you by now.'

'That's what I thought,' said Martin. 'But she isn't here. And she could hardly have got lost along the way . . . I'm looking at what screens I've got, and I'm not seeing her anywhere.'

A horrible suspicion was growing in Doyle's face. I started to say something reassuring, but he stopped me with a sharp gesture.

'Something's wrong,' he said. 'Something's happened to her.'

'Let's go to the security centre,' I said. 'She might have stopped along the way to look at something.'

I didn't believe that for one moment, but I didn't want him panicking. He nodded quickly, and Penny and I walked him back through the entrance hall. There was no sign of Hayley anywhere; but on the other hand, there were no signs of violence or an abduction. When we finally reached the security centre, Martin already had the door opening for us – a sign of how worried he was. He looked at me inquiringly as we walked in, and I shook my head. Martin sat back in his chair and looked quickly around the various screens. Almost a third of them were still blank.

'I've got the microphones open,' he said. 'But I'm not hearing her voice, or any signs of movement. I've called out to her, but if she can hear me she isn't answering.'

'Then where is she?' said Doyle.

He didn't wait for an answer, just turned suddenly and strode out of the security centre. He called out Hayley's name, increasingly loudly, to no response. Penny and I looked at each other, and went after him. We found him standing at the foot of the stairs, murmuring her name over and over. He turned to look at us, his eyes full of tears.

'I should have gone with her,' he said. 'But I wanted to hurt her, to make a point. I sent her away and now they've taken her.'

'Who's taken her?' I said.

'The ghosts . . .' said Doyle. He turned away and screamed up the empty stairs, 'Give her back to me!'

I had hoped the idea of secret passageways might distract him from his fixation with ghosts, but clearly it hadn't taken.

All his poise and self-confidence were gone again. His face was unhealthily pale, his chest heaved as he tried to get his breath, and his hands were trembling.

'She could have found one of the hidden doors,' said Penny, 'and gone through to see where it led. That is the kind of thing she'd do, isn't it?'

Doyle just shook his head miserably, refusing to be comforted.

I raised my voice. 'Martin! Hayley said she found the official history of Ringstone Lodge in the library. Do you know where the library is?'

'Of course,' said Martin. 'I've spent some time there. Did I mention how starved we are for entertainment in this dump?'

He gave me directions. I turned to Doyle.

'Come with us to the library,' I said. 'There's bound to be something in the official history about hidden doors.'

'The Lodge is full of secrets,' said Doyle. 'Bad things have happened in this house, and I think some of them are still happening. We should never have come here.'

The library turned out to be little more than a simple reading room with packed bookshelves and a few comfortable chairs. Very civilized and very quiet, an oasis of peace in a busy house. With just the one small window, covered by a steel shutter. The light was bright and cheerful. I parked Doyle in one of the chairs and looked around the shelves.

'Martin! Where can we find this family history? What's it called?'

'Beats me,' said Martin. 'I can't even remember the author's name. It was all a bit dry and dull, as I recall. But it is there, somewhere.'

'Terrific,' said Penny, revolving slowly in the middle of the room so she could take in all the shelves. 'Where do we start?'

'You take one side of the door and work your way round the room,' I said. 'I'll start from the other and we'll meet up in the middle.'

Penny looked to Doyle to ask if he wanted to help her. But he was sitting slumped in his chair, lost in his own miserable thoughts.

Most of the books turned out to be the usual suspects; neat leather-bound volumes of Dickens and Trollope, and assorted paperback editions of Agatha Christie and Dick Francis. The kind of books you order by the yard to fill up shelves. Along with a sprinkling of local histories, and a small collection of quite specialized erotica. In the end, Penny found the family history first. Under 'R', for Ringstone Lodge. She brought the book triumphantly over to the single reading table, and the two of us studied it carefully. A large square edition, with good paper and binding and a really ugly typeface. Old enough to predate desktop publishing, it was probably a vanity-press production. *The History Of Ringstone Lodge* covered several hundred years in barely two hundred pages. Penny found the index, which took her straight to the story of the Ringstone Witch – the woman who lay buried out back under the ominous tombstone.

'Her name was Hettie Longthorne,' said Penny, glancing quickly through the account. 'Accused of placing a murrain on the surrounding lands, so that all young things died and the crops withered in the fields. When she refused to remove it, or more likely said she couldn't, they hanged her.'

'But what's her connection with the Lodge?' I said. 'Why is she buried here, with such a high-born family?'

'If I'm reading between the lines correctly,' said Penny, 'I'd say Hettie must have been born on the wrong side of the blanket and never acknowledged. Not welcome at the big house during her life, but buried here afterwards because the family felt guilty over not speaking up for her.'

'Would explain why they felt a need to put that inscription on her tombstone,' I said. '*God Grant She Rest Easily.*'

'Supporting an accused witch at her trial would not have been a wise or safe thing to do in those days,' said Penny.

'Did the murrain disappear, after she was hanged?' I said.

'Doesn't say,' said Penny. She shot me a look. 'You don't believe in ghosts, but you do believe in witches?'

'Not necessarily,' I said. 'Is there a picture of this Hettie Longthorne?'

'Just an old woodcut from a local broadsheet published at the time,' said Penny.

I leaned in beside her for a look. The illustration showed a tall slender figure in a long black robe. Something in the way the figure stood made me think she would have been quite young. Not a crone in a witch's hat with a bubbling cauldron and a black cat. Just a young woman who stood accused. Perhaps because she was different.

'What does the book have to say about ghosts?' said Doyle.

Penny and I jumped, just a bit. Doyle had been quiet for so long we'd forgotten about him. He'd sunk right down in the big chair, as though all the strength had gone out of him. He looked lost without Alice to tell him what to do. There was nothing I could say to him. I liked to think Hayley was still out there somewhere, perhaps stumbling along some dark and cobwebbed secret corridor searching for an exit. Though that didn't seem likely. More likely she was just another dead body waiting to be found. But of course I couldn't say that to Doyle, so I nodded to Penny and she turned to the index again. And sure enough, there was a whole chapter on the ghosts of Ringstone Lodge.

Penny and I glanced quickly through it, summarizing aloud for Doyle's benefit. There were any number of reported sightings down the years, but nothing out of the ordinary. A lady in white and a phantom monk, a skull that was supposed to scream on significant occasions, and a bloodstain on an old stone floor that couldn't be cleaned away. All a bit generic, really, the kind of stories that accumulate around any ancient house. To raise a chill on a winter evening round the fire, or just so there was something to tell the tourists on open days.

'Martin thought Parker brought some kind of evil power with him,' I said finally. 'To disturb and raise up the Ringstone ghosts. But there's nothing here worth raising up. And I have to say, I never heard of Parker acquiring any kind of power out in the field. We might have worked in some similar areas, but he was basically just a spy. Stealing and selling information, and disposing of people with a price on their head.'

'Maybe he stole the wrong kind of information,' said Penny. 'Or made some kind of deal to become unkillable.'

'No such thing,' I said. 'No . . . I would have heard something, if Parker had that kind of power. You know how people in our line of work love to gossip. Is there anything in the book about the Lodge's ghosts terrorizing people recently?'

Penny leafed quickly through the pages. I shot another glance at Doyle. He really wasn't looking good, but then he'd been up and down a lot in the last few hours. He didn't have the constitution for this kind of work, or this kind of world. He'd bounced back before, but that had been with Hayley's help. I'd hoped bringing Doyle to the library with us might help him focus. But instead he looked . . . haunted.

'Maybe the ghosts have come under Parker's power,' Doyle said slowly, not looking up.

'What power?' I said, trying hard not to sound impatient with him. 'If he'd had anything, the Organization would know and they would have told me. And MacKay, so he could oversee whatever precautions were necessary to hold Parker securely.'

'There's nothing in the family history about ghosts acting up in modern times,' said Penny. 'It's all vague sightings, spooky old stories, and dire warnings about the perils of modernization.'

'Try the index again,' I said. 'See if there's anything on hidden doors or secret passageways.'

Penny sighed loudly, just to make it clear she wasn't my servant, and turned to the back of the book again.

'Someone is trying to distract us from the real problem,' I said. 'Parker's murder. Everything that's happened before and since is only important if it ties in to that.'

Penny closed the book with a snap. 'Nothing on sliding panels, priest holes or smugglers' storerooms. Of course, it could be that the family kept such things to themselves, because they felt it was no one else's business.'

'Where's Alice?' said Doyle. 'I want Alice.'

'Don't worry, Robbie,' said Penny. 'We'll find her for you.'

'Don't call me that,' he said. 'Only she calls me that.'

Penny and I exchanged looks. The man was falling apart right in front of us, but short of finding Hayley I didn't see what else we could do for him. Penny put the family history back on the shelf and looked at me thoughtfully.

'You keep saying we're being distracted. From what exactly?'

'From the facts of the case,' I said. 'Parker was murdered inside a locked room while under electronic surveillance. Everything that's happened since has been designed to keep us from thinking about that. If we could solve the mystery of Parker's murder, I'm convinced everything else would just fall into place.'

Doyle stirred in his chair, and looked directly at me for the first time. 'Are you saying Baxter's death and the disappearance of Redd and MacKay and my Alice are just . . . collateral damage? That they don't matter in your great scheme of things?'

'Of course they matter,' I said. 'It's just . . .'

Doyle surged up out of his chair. 'You worry about your theories. I'm going to look for Alice. Because somebody has to.'

He strode out of the library, and Penny and I had no choice except to hurry out after him.

But once we were on the other side of the door, Doyle didn't seem to know what to do or where to go. So I led the way back to the security centre, hoping Martin might have his screens working properly again. Doyle said nothing as we moved quickly through the empty corridors, his eyes lost and unbearably sad. We passed by the foot of the stairs leading up to the next floor, and came to a sudden halt. Because there on the bottom step, set carefully side by side, were two severed heads. Hayley and Redd. His face looked resigned; Hayley's looked quietly betrayed. Their unblinking eyes stared out across the entrance hall. Even as the anger hit me, I couldn't help noticing how cleanly the severing cuts had been made, to allow the heads to rest neatly on the step. Someone had taken their time, because they wanted to make an impression. And a statement.

Doyle sank to his knees facing Hayley's head, and sobbed like a small child. Penny put a comforting hand on his shoulder, but he didn't even know she was there. Penny studied the two severed heads with cold, furious outrage, her lips pressed tightly together. Angry not just because these people had been murdered, but at what had been done to them. Turning horror and loss into a sideshow attraction. Penny was never more angry than when she was angry on someone else's behalf.

I was angry because this proved I'd been right all along. This wasn't the work of a ghost, or any malevolent spirit of the night. Someone was playing games with us.

'It seems our killer has found another use for his knife,' I said, thinking out loud. 'He's escalating, piling horror upon horror, to keep us from thinking straight. It's just more distraction. But why? What is it that he's so desperate to keep us from seeing?'

'I can't believe how quickly this has all happened,' said Penny. 'So many deaths in just a few hours . . . We were only talking to Hayley and Redd a short time ago.'

'This is no simple stabbing,' I said. 'This took time and effort. Our killer has tried everything he could think of to scare us. Ghosts and disappearances and mysteries . . . and now he's gone for the gore.'

'Concentrate, Ishmael,' Penny said sharply. 'What do we do? Where do we go from here?'

'Our choice of suspects is shrinking,' I said slowly. 'We know it isn't us, and Doyle was in the library with us when all this was happening. So who does that leave? Mackay . . . and Martin.'

'Unless there is someone else in the house with us,' said Penny. 'Martin saw someone on his screens. Remember?'

'Yes,' I said. 'I remember.'

'MacKay's been missing for some time,' said Penny. 'More than enough to do something like this. And he was going to meet Redd.'

'Although Martin is supposed to have been in the security centre all this time,' I said, 'he could have left while we were in the library . . .'

'But both MacKay and Martin have alibis for Parker's murder,' said Penny.

'Yes,' I said. 'Annoying, that. But then I've never had much time for alibis. Far too easy to fake, for any number of reasons.'

'What if Parker really has come back from the dead and is walking around the Lodge looking for revenge?' Penny said stubbornly. 'Maybe that's why he insisted on being brought here. For a chance to kill all of us. We have to consider the possibility, Ishmael, after everything we've experienced . . .'

'It is a possibility,' I said. 'But not a good one. No, Penny, keep it simple. Someone in this house killed Parker for their own personal reasons. And they're still here, even though they could have got out at any time through the unguarded window in the lounge. So our killer must have stayed on for a reason. Because he has unfinished business . . .'

'Such as?' said Penny.

'He wants us all dead,' I said. 'So that when the reinforcements finally arrive there will be no surviving witnesses left to point the finger. He wants to vanish, leaving a mystery behind.'

Penny shuddered briefly, remembering. 'How much longer is it till the reinforcements get here?'

I checked my watch, and frowned. 'It's been well over an hour since Martin placed his emergency call. They should have been hammering on the door by now.' I raised my voice. 'Martin! Can you hear me?'

We waited, but there was no reply.

'His systems must be down again,' I said. 'We'd better go brace him in his hidey-hole and have him contact Headquarters again. See what's happening.'

'No one's attacked us yet,' said Penny. 'If it should turn out to be the unkillable Parker, could you take him? I mean, I know you're good, but . . .'

'It's not him,' I said. 'But if it was . . . I'm better than good. I'd rip his head off his shoulders and bounce it up and down the hall like a basket ball. See how he'd manage then. But it seems to me there's something distinctly sneaky about our killer. An undead, unkillable Parker wouldn't need to hide, would he? The real killer has been taking down people who didn't even try to defend themselves. Because they saw no reason to, until it was too late. And let us remember, these were all naturally suspicious people.'

'So what do you think is going on?' said Penny. 'I mean, really going on?'

'I don't know,' I said. 'I hate being in situations I don't

understand. And I'm no nearer understanding why people are dying in Ringstone Lodge than when all this started.'

I stepped forward to look at the severed heads more closely. Penny came round the other side of the quietly crying Doyle, so she could look too. We weren't being heartless, just focused.

'Where are the bodies?' I said finally. 'Redd and Hayley weren't killed here, or there'd be blood all over the place. And I would have heard or smelled something while that was happening.'

'Not in front of Doyle,' murmured Penny.

'I don't think he's hearing anything much at the moment,' I said.

And then Penny and I both looked up sharply, as we heard footsteps coming down the stairs. Heading straight for us. We stumbled back and looked up the stairs, and there was MacKay. Descending the steps with a cold, grim face and a gun in his hand. The gun was aimed unwaveringly at me. I stood very still, watching him carefully. MacKay finally came to a halt just a few steps above the two severed heads, and fixed me with a gaze as assured and implacable as a hanging judge's.

'It's you,' he said. 'You're the killer, Mr Jones. And I will see you dead for what you have done here.'

SEVEN
Nothing Stays Hidden

For a moment that stretched, we all stood our ground and looked at each other. A tableau of the living and the dead. The accused and his accuser, two wide-eyed witnesses, and two severed heads that weren't interested in anything any longer. MacKay looked at me with death on his mind, waiting for me to answer him, but I just looked right back at him. I could feel Penny trembling at my side, not with fear but with anger. Wanting to say something, do something, but not daring to as long as MacKay had his gun trained on me. Because she knew that whatever my origins might be, I was still human enough to die from a bullet to the head. MacKay's gaze never wavered, but in the end his expression turned sour and he snarled at the still sobbing Doyle.

'Hush your crying, Doctor Doyle! She cannot hear you.'

Doyle stopped. His tears didn't slow or die away, they just stopped as though he'd been slapped across the face. I glanced at him. His face was pale but his eyes were suddenly hot, full of an anger that needed to go somewhere. He looked at MacKay and then at me, and then at the gun in MacKay's hand. Doyle fell back a step, and then another, and MacKay let him. He kept his cold gaze fixed on me, and the gun in his hand never wavered once.

'I don't think you should be pointing that gun at Ishmael, Mr Mackay,' Penny said steadily. 'It's not safe. For you.'

'Don't interfere, Miss Belcourt,' said MacKay. 'This man is a murderer.'

'Of course he isn't a murderer!' said Penny. 'We were sent here to protect Parker. Remember?'

'What better cover?' said MacKay.

'Where have you been all this time?' I said. Keeping my

voice carefully calm and reasonable, with just a touch of 'Let's not do anything either of us might regret.'

'What happened when you went upstairs to talk to Redd?'

'You do not get to ask the questions, murderer!' MacKay's voice shook with barely controlled emotions. 'I should have known it was you. Everything was going just fine until you arrived. You'd not been in the Lodge a few hours before people started dying. I should have known . . . Only another field agent could have brought down someone as experienced as the infamous Frank Parker.'

'Who put these ideas into your head?' I said.

'Stop talking!' MacKay said loudly. 'It doesn't matter who. I have you now, and I will see justice done for the horrors you have perpetrated under my roof.'

There was a scuffle of movement behind me, and Penny cried out. I'd been concentrating so hard on MacKay I'd lost track of everything else. I'd just started to turn when Doyle plunged a hypodermic needle into my neck. The needle stung fiercely as it sank in, and Doyle slammed the plunger all the way home. He jerked the needle out of my neck and stepped back, smiling triumphantly. He was breathing hard, and his eyes were dangerously bright.

'Alice isn't the only one who likes to keep sedatives handy for emergencies,' said Doyle. 'For suspects who turn dangerous, to themselves or to others. The dose I've just given you would knock out an elephant. More than enough to keep you quiet until the reinforcements arrive.' He laughed softly. A dark, unpleasant sound. 'And when you wake up, I'll be waiting for you. To begin your interrogation.'

Penny made a soft, horrified sound.

'Well done, Doctor Doyle,' said MacKay.

He lowered his gun a little, and then he and Doyle looked at me expectantly. Waiting for the drug to kick in and for me to fall to my knees. Penny started towards me, and then stopped as I smiled at her reassuringly. I turned my smile on MacKay, and felt it become something different. Something dangerous. MacKay raised his gun to cover me again, but I didn't even look at it, holding his gaze with my own.

'I'm a field agent for the Organization,' I said. 'And we're protected against all kinds of attack. Including poisons, drugs and overexcited doctors.'

In fact, Doyle's sedative was useless against me because of my alien heritage. I might have been made over into a man, but there were other things hiding inside me. Protections against anything my new world might throw at me. I'm like a Russian doll with another face hidden inside another face: the wolf in the fold and the snake in the grass, and everything else you never see coming until it's far too late. I am human, but I'm other things too.

Penny laughed shakily, relieved. MacKay and Doyle looked at each other, and the certainty went out of them. I'd just changed the rules of the game, and they could tell. Doyle looked at the hypodermic in his hand as though it was an empty gun. He started to scrabble in his jacket pocket for something, perhaps a stronger dose, and Penny decided she'd had enough. She stepped quickly forward and slapped the hypo right out of Doyle's hand. It made delicate fragile noises as it skidded across the floor and hid itself in the shadows. Doyle looked after it and then looked back at Penny. His face turned ugly. He raised a hand to hit her, and I winced. On his behalf, not hers.

Penny kicked him square between the legs, with such vicious force I half expected something to break loose and go rolling across the floor. All the breath shot out of Doyle's mouth. His eyes squeezed shut from the horrid pain, tears streaming down his cheeks. He turned slowly and hobbled away, one painful step at a time, making small pitiful sounds. I almost felt sorry for him. Penny glared after him, and then turned her glare on MacKay, standing shocked and somewhat bemused on the stairs. He still had his gun aimed at me. Penny started towards him with a worryingly speculative look on her face, and I quickly raised a hand to stop her.

'That's enough, Penny,' I said. 'Thanks for the support, but I think I can take it from here.'

'Are you sure?' said Penny, still glaring coldly at MacKay. 'That gun doesn't frighten me.'

'That's because it isn't pointed at you,' I said. 'Let me talk to the man. I'm sure reason and common sense can prevail.'

'First time for anything, I suppose,' she said, unwillingly.

'But you listen to me, MacKay. If you shoot Ishmael, you'd better be really fast with your second shot. Because if you're not, I will beat you to death with my bare hands.'

MacKay just nodded. He was an old soldier and, while he recognized the cold intent in her words, he wouldn't let it move him one inch from what he intended to do. I took a step forward to draw his attention back to me. The gun rose just a little, to aim squarely at my heart. I fixed MacKay with my best commanding stare.

'What happened up there, on the top floor?' I said. 'What happened between you and Redd so that he ended up down here, like this?' I gestured at the severed head on the bottom step, but MacKay didn't look away from me for a moment. I pressed him, raising my voice. 'Was there an argument? A fight? What did he want to say that he could only say to you? And what did you do with his body?'

I hit him with one question after another, like a boxer throwing combination punches, but MacKay didn't so much as rock on his feet. And yet I could tell that some of it was getting through to him, though he answered me in a cool and distant voice.

'I did nothing to Mr Redd. I never even met him. When I arrived at the top of the stairs, he was nowhere to be seen. I walked all the way down the corridor to your room, and I didn't see anyone. The door was closed; and when I tried it, it was locked. Even though it had been open on Mr Martin's screen. Didn't you watch all of this?'

'No,' said Penny. 'All the screens went down the moment you got to the upper floor. No vision, no sound. I don't know where you people got this surveillance equipment, but I think you should ask for your money back. It's a disgrace.'

I smiled inwardly. I knew she was trying to distract him. I kept my voice calm and steady, and unyielding.

'What happened up there, MacKay?'

'I called out to Mr Redd,' said MacKay. 'He didn't answer. I used my master key to unlock the door to your room and went inside, but he was not there.'

'Our door was open before you went up,' said Penny. 'As though Redd had been inside.'

'Indeed,' said MacKay. 'But there was no sign to indicate he had ever been in there. I considered the situation. If he was not in the room and not in the corridor, where could he be? The answer came to me in a moment. I have always believed that a house this old must have secret passages in it somewhere. It is in the nature of a building like this. And it was the only way in which Mr Redd could have disappeared so quickly. The only way the murderer could be moving around and be sure of remaining unnoticed by any of the security cameras.

'So I went back out into the corridor, locked your door again, and started tapping the walls. Once I was sure what I was looking for, I found the hidden panel quite easily. Cunningly concealed in the woodwork of the wall at the far end of the corridor. Right next to your room. I soon found the trick of opening it, and uncovered the hidden passageway beyond.

'I went inside, closing the panel behind me, because I did not wish to be found or disturbed until I had fathomed its secrets and had some idea of who might have been using it. The tunnel led to other tunnels and secret rooms, and hidden passageways deep beneath the Lodge. I have been walking up and down in them for some time, seeing what there was to see and thinking about many things.'

'I told you there had to be secret passages here, Ishmael!' said Penny. 'All old houses have them. It wouldn't be fair if they didn't.'

'And then I found the awful evidence of what you had done, Mr Jones,' said MacKay. 'And I came down here to find you and put a stop to your madness.'

'Hold it!' I said. 'It's good to know what you've been up to all this time, but you make a far better suspect than me. You had all the time you needed to kill Redd and Hayley. You have a master key to unlock anything, including Parker's cell and that window in the lounge. You know about the secret tunnels. And none of your victims would have seen any need to defend themselves against you, would they? The man who's job it was to protect them? Finally, you have the best motive. You knew you were getting too old for your job. That the MoD would have to let you go soon, despite all your experience. So you reached out to the opposition for one last big payment, so you could at least live comfortably afterwards. How much did they offer you to silence Parker before he could speak? And are you on a bonus for the rest of us, or did you just get carried away?'

MacKay met my gaze squarely through all of this, still covering me with his gun. And despite all the accusations I'd hit him with, his confidence didn't waver once.

'You are the killer, Mr Jones. And you are not going to talk your way out of this.'

I saw his finger tighten on the trigger. Saw the decision to kill me, and to hell with the consequences, rise up in his eyes. I charged forward, crossing the distance between us in a moment, snatched the gun out of his hand before he could finish pulling the trigger, placed my other hand on his chest, and pushed hard. MacKay fell backwards on to the stairs, sitting down so heavily it knocked all the breath out of him. His eyes were still widening at how fast I'd moved as I stood over him, his gun aimed at his face, not even breathing hard. And then I stepped back, hefted the gun lightly in my hand, and grinned at Penny. She laughed out loud, and clapped her hands delightedly. I waggled the gun meaningfully at MacKay when he looked like moving, and he stayed where he was. He wanted to look furious, but he was too shocked and baffled at how quickly I'd turned the tables on him.

'How did you do that?' he asked shakily. 'I never even saw you move . . .'

'I'm a trained field agent. Remember?' I said.

He glared at me defiantly. 'Go on then, Mr Jones. Do it. Kill me. I'll not beg for my life.'

'How many times do I have to say this?' I said. 'I'm not the killer. And to prove it . . .'

I turned the gun round and offered it to MacKay. He looked at me, unable to believe it, and then he snatched the gun out of my hand and shot me at point-blank range. My more than human reactions kicked in, and I was already moving to one side as he squeezed the trigger. The bullet shot through the space where my head had been just a moment before. I grabbed the gun away from him again, and hit him sharply on the point of the jaw. His head snapped back, and he was unconscious before he hit the stairs. I stepped back again, and looked at Penny.

'Now that worked fine the last time I did it, at Belcourt Manor,' I said. 'Giving up the gun is supposed to win them over, as a sign of trust. Why did he try to shoot me?'

'Because he's an old soldier,' said Penny. 'And you don't get to be an old soldier by missing out on a chance to kill your enemy.'

'I suppose so,' I said. 'Spoiled a perfectly good gesture, though. Hold it! What happened to Doyle?'

We both looked around, but there was no sign of the doctor anywhere. The wide open hall was empty and almost unnervingly quiet.

'Oh hell!' I said. 'Not another unexpected disappearance while we were distracted! I'm starting to feel like I should search the floor for trapdoors. And I really don't think I could cope with another murder.' I looked at the gun in my hand, and then handed it to Penny.

'Here. You probably need this more than I do. Would you have any problem using it?'

She looked at the two severed heads, still in place on the bottom step despite everything that had happened around them.

'No,' she said firmly.

'Do you know how to use a gun?'

'Yes,' said Penny, hefting the gun in a familiar way. 'I took some lessons at a private shooting club in London once I'd decided I was going to work alongside you as a spy girl. I thought one of us ought to know what to do with a gun.'

'I do know,' I said. 'I just prefer not to use them, whenever possible. Guns make it far too easy to make the kind of mistakes you can't put right afterwards. And they tempt you into dramatic gestures, when a little thought and some careful diplomacy would probably get you further.'

'We don't all have your built-in advantages,' Penny said dryly. 'How are you feeling? Did that sedative have any effect on you?'

I considered for a moment, then shook my head. 'Whatever

was in that needle, my system seems to have given it a good kicking. I feel fine.'

'What are we going to do with MacKay?' said Penny.

'Well to start with, you can point that gun somewhere else,' I said. 'We are not shooting him.'

'I never said we should,' said Penny. 'I was just . . . covering him. In case he woke up suddenly and decided he was in a bad mood.'

'We can't leave him here,' I said. 'It wouldn't be safe.'

'I don't think he's the murderer,' said Penny. 'He seemed very convinced it was you.'

'Yes,' I said. 'I wonder who convinced him?'

'We could always take him to the security centre, put him in with Martin. They could look out for each other.'

'Put our two best suspects together?' I said. 'I don't think so. I don't trust Martin any more than I trust MacKay.'

'I heard that!' said Martin's voice.

'Welcome back!' I said. 'How long have you been listening?'

'Long enough,' said Martin.

'Did you see what just happened here?' said Penny.

'Oh yes,' said Martin. 'Every bit of it. I never saw anyone move that fast in my life, Ishmael. You were just a blur on my screen. Does the Organization supply you with special drugs to supercharge you? And if so, can I have some? And what do you mean, you don't trust me? I'm the one who's been supplying you with useful information on everything that's been happening.'

'Don't take it personally,' I said. 'I don't trust anyone. Save for Penny, obviously.'

'Nice save, sweetie!' said Penny. 'I hardly had to glance at you at all.'

'To hell with both of you!' Martin said loudly. 'I'm going to lock myself inside the security centre and not come out again until the cavalry gets here. I know when I'm not appreciated. And don't come banging on my door begging to be let in when someone's after you, because I won't listen. Even if you're being pursued by the headless bodies of Redd and Hayley carrying chainsaws. So there!'

'About those reinforcements,' I said. 'Why aren't they here

yet? You said they could get here in under an hour once an emergency call had gone out, but it's been a lot longer than that and no one's turned up yet. What's happened to them? Hello? Martin? Oh hell, he's gone again . . .'

'Either his systems have crashed or he's not talking to us,' said Penny.

'A good way to avoid answering questions,' I said. 'We've got to put MacKay somewhere safe. Even if Martin stays locked up in his centre, Doyle's still out there somewhere.'

'You don't trust him either?' said Penny. 'All right, he stabbed you in the neck with a needle, but he was understandably upset at the time. And he was quite definitely with us in the library when these new murders took place.'

'It's a bit late to start defending the man now,' I said. 'After you gave him the full force of your famous St Theresa's kick. I felt the impact all the way over here.'

Penny shrugged, unmoved. 'He hurt you. I won't stand for that. But a moment's panic isn't enough to mark a man as a murderer. And you saw how upset he was over Hayley's death.'

'He could have been faking it,' I said.

'If he's that good an actor, he should be on the stage,' said Penny. 'And anyway, if he was a professional agent like you, I wouldn't have been able to take him down that easily.'

'Probably not,' I said. 'Still, he ran away.'

'Maybe his survival instincts finally kicked in,' said Penny. 'Because let's face it, if he isn't the killer he might as well have "Future Victim" tattooed on his forehead. And anyway, I still think there's someone else inside the Lodge with us.'

'Are we talking about Parker, the walking undead, again?' I said.

'It could be him,' Penny said stubbornly. 'Or there could be some other person, some assassin sent by the opposition, coming and going through that window in the lounge and using the hidden tunnels MacKay found to get around. Martin keeps saying he's seen someone on his screens who isn't one of us. If it's not Parker . . .'

'Let's take MacKay upstairs,' I said. 'We can put him in our room. It has no windows and we can use his master key to lock him in.'

'Does it have to be our room?' said Penny. 'He might wake up and start going through our things . . .'

I looked at her. 'What is this obsession you've got with people going through your luggage? What have you got hidden in there that you don't want anyone else to know about?'

'Don't you question me, Ishmael Jones! A woman's suitcase should be inviolable.'

Some arguments you just know aren't going to go anywhere useful. I gestured at MacKay.

'I'll take his shoulders, you take his legs. After we've dropped him off, I think it's our turn to go exploring the secret tunnels.'

Penny tucked her gun into the back of her belt, just so she could clap her hands again, grinning from ear to ear.

'About time! It's not a proper country-house mystery if there aren't sliding panels and secret passageways. Everyone knows that.'

'Did Belcourt Manor have any?' I said. 'I never thought to ask at the time.'

'A few,' said Penny. 'They didn't really go anywhere. Daddy had all the entrances bricked up and sealed before I was born. Apparently they made the old place terribly draughty.'

'Help me shift the old soldier,' I said.

Penny hesitated, looking at the two severed heads on the bottom step. 'What do we do with them?'

'Leave them,' I said. 'They're not going anywhere.'

We carried the unconscious MacKay up the stairs to the next floor. At least, the two of us started carrying him; until it became clear MacKay's dead weight was too much for Penny to manage. She didn't actually say so, but the unladylike grunts and increasing bad language made it clear she was having problems. So I threw MacKay over my shoulder and trudged up the stairs. Penny followed on behind, saying nothing very loudly. I paused at the top of the stairs, just in case, but the corridor was empty. It stretched away before us entirely untroubled by people or ghosts, and there wasn't a moving shadow anywhere. The two doors I'd kicked in were still standing open; the rooms beyond were quiet and empty. I strained my hearing against the hush, but all I could hear was Penny's harsh breathing behind me.

I hurried down the corridor, MacKay bouncing uncomfortably on my shoulder, until we got to our room. The door was standing half-open. I stood and looked at it for a long moment. I was sure MacKay said he'd locked it after he left. I put one foot against the door and kicked it open. The door slammed back against the inside wall, the flat heavy sound echoing loudly. Inside, all the lights were burning brightly. More than enough illumination to show no one was home, or rummaging through our things. Penny leaned in close and peered past me.

'What are you looking for, Ishmael?'

'Just one thing in this whole mess that makes sense,' I said.

'It's only a mess until you understand it,' Penny said wisely. 'Have you really no one in mind for the murderer? You sounded very convincing when you were accusing MacKay.'

'That was just to hold his attention,' I said. 'He's a good suspect, but I'm still working on a few ideas. I think the key to all of this was the way Parker disappeared between the top and bottom of the stairs, even though I was right behind him.'

'That was just impossible!' said Penny.

'Yes,' I said. 'It was.'

Penny sighed, and looked round the room. 'We didn't get to spend much time here, did we? And in the meantime, who's been sleeping in our bed?'

'If three bears should turn up,' I said, 'you have my permission to shoot them.'

'I don't suppose there's any porridge, is there?' said Penny. 'I'm feeling a bit peckish.'

'Would it be OK if I was to take MacKay in and dump him on the bed?' I said. 'Only he isn't getting any lighter, you know.'

'Go ahead,' said Penny. 'Don't let me stop you. You're the one hanging around in the doorway talking about bears.'

I dropped MacKay on to the bed and arranged him reasonably comfortably, while Penny quickly checked her various pieces of luggage for signs of tampering. MacKay made a few growly noises in his sleep, but showed no intention of waking up. When I hit people, they stay hit.

'Someone's taken your socks off the security cameras,' Penny said quietly. 'I'm not sure if that means anything, or not.'

'It might,' I said.

Penny waited. 'Well?'

'Let's go check the secret tunnels,' I said.

'Let's,' said Penny.

I searched through all of MacKay's pockets to find his master key, and of course it had to be in the last pocket I looked in. Just the usual electronic key card. We went back out into the corridor and I closed the door and locked it, slipping the master key into my back pocket, just in case it might come in handy later. Penny and I stood before the end wall and looked it over carefully. It didn't take me long to find the outlines of the concealed sliding panel. It had been hidden very skilfully, with centuries-old craftsmanship, but the outlines all but jumped out at me now I knew what I was looking for. Opening the panel took longer, and I was almost ready to give up and kick it in when Penny's sensitive finger-tips found a concealed trigger. The panel slid back smoothly, revealing shadows and cobwebs and a dark space stretching away beyond. Penny started to stick her head in, then stopped to wrinkle her nose.

'This smells seriously foul! I don't think anyone's sent a cleaner in here for generations.'

'That would rather give the game away,' I said. 'But someone must have oiled the mechanism recently so we wouldn't hear it being used.'

Penny scowled into the dark opening. 'I'll bet there are rats and spiders, and horrible scuttling things. And all kinds of droppings.' She paused, as a thought struck her. 'Speaking of which, if Parker really is a walking dead man, shouldn't you be able to tell from the smell? All the decay and stuff? Couldn't you track where he's been with your amazing nostrils?'

'I may be specially gifted,' I said, 'but I'm not a bloodhound.'

Just to keep her happy, I took a good sniff at the stale air inside the wall.

'OK,' I said, 'I'm getting mould, rising damp, rotting wood, and dust from crumbling stone . . . But that's about it.'

'No rats?' said Penny.

'No,' I lied. Because otherwise I knew I'd end up having to push her into the tunnel ahead of me.

'It's very dark in there,' she said dubiously. 'I mean, I'm all for exploring but maybe we should go back downstairs and get some torches first?'

'If the killer has been using these tunnels, he must have some way of seeing where he's going . . .' I said.

I reached inside the panel and felt around the grimy stone wall, and sure enough there was a light switch. I hit it and leaned inside. A series of dull lights had come on, stretching away at intervals the whole length of the tunnel. The passageway was full of filth and cobwebs and the dust of centuries, and the floor dropped sharply down. I stepped inside the tunnel and waited patiently, until Penny had screwed her nerve up enough to join me.

'I thought you wanted to see the sights?' I said.

'The tunnels, yes,' she said. 'Rats and other small scurrying things, not so much.' She glared about her. 'Where are we exactly?'

'The outer wall of the Lodge must be hollow,' I said. 'But MacKay said there were tunnels leading off tunnels. This could take some time . . .'

'Then we'd better get moving,' said Penny. 'We have a killer to track down.'

She looked at me meaningfully, until I took the lead.

The tunnel dropped sharply away before us, rounded a corner, and then became a narrow stone chimney dropping a long way down. There was a series of steel rungs hammered into the wall to serve as steps. We descended for quite a while before we were able to step out into another tunnel, with a roof so low Penny and I had to stoop right over to avoid banging our heads. The rough stone walls were pitted with age and spotted with dark mould. Thick mats of spider webs hung down like ragged grey curtains. Great holes had been torn through them, where someone had forced their way through before. Puffy clumps of milk-white fungi blossomed where the walls met the floor. The air was stale, full of unpleasant odours, and so dry it irritated my throat. The various scents grew thicker and heavier; and I had a growing feeling there was something underneath them that I didn't like at all. I glanced back at Penny to make sure she was OK, and was surprised when she grinned cheerfully back at me.

'I don't care if there are rats,' she said defiantly. 'This is cool! Exploring centuries-old hidden tunnels . . . It's like walking back into history. What do you suppose this was all about originally? I mean, someone went to a lot of hard work to build all this. It's like a house within a house.'

'Could have started out as the support structure for a priest hole,' I said. 'Back in the days when a lot of the wealthier families were still Catholic, even after Henry VIII decided the whole country was going to be Protestant, no matter whether it liked it or not. Hanging on to their own private priest was just another way for old titled families to establish their independence from an overbearing monarch. Or this could all be down to smuggling. A very popular and profitable pastime, back in those days. You could hide a lot of illegal goods down here, and people.'

We kept passing openings in the walls, gaping stone mouths that led to more tunnels, and small dark rooms where the light couldn't reach. The passageways twisted and turned so often that I lost all track of where we were. Except we clearly weren't inside the Lodge any longer. We were deep down underneath it, and the smell was getting worse. As though we were getting close to something bad.

'No wonder our killer could appear and disappear so easily,' said Penny. 'He was literally running rings around us. Which is cheating, really.'

'A good way to avoid the surveillance cameras,' I said, 'when the damned things are working.'

'Pardon me for asking,' said Penny, 'but are we headed anywhere in particular? I'm starting to think I should be leaving a trail of breadcrumbs behind us. You seem very sure of which turnings we should take.'

'There's something up ahead,' I said. 'Something really bad.'

'So of course we're heading straight for it,' said Penny. 'At some point, we're going to have to sit down and have a serious talk about making better lifestyle decisions.'

I stopped so suddenly she bumped into me from behind. She started to say something, then broke off as I raised a hand and nodded at the way ahead.

'Someone's in here with us,' I said quietly.

Penny squeezed in beside me for a better look. Standing side by side we filled the narrow tunnel, our shoulders pressed against the rough stone walls. The bare light bulbs hanging from the ceiling at long intervals provided just enough light to show the tunnel ahead was empty. Penny put her mouth next to my ear.

'I don't see anyone . . . Are you smelling someone?'

'No,' I said. 'I heard them. I don't just rely on my nose.'

'Sorry,' said Penny. 'Who do you think it is?'

'The footsteps are heavy enough to suggest a man,' I said.

'A living man?' Penny said carefully.

I sighed, just a little. 'He's not dragging his feet and I'm not hearing any low moans, so yes, almost certainly.'

'What do we do?' said Penny. 'Chase him down?'

'He must have come into these tunnels for a reason,' I said. 'Either to look for us or to check on something. I say we sneak up on him and see where he's going. Unless he's just here to kill us, of course.'

'I've got my gun,' Penny said immediately.

'In such a confined space?' I said. 'I hate to think what a ricochet would do in here.'

'All right! I was just being prepared . . .'

'Listen,' I said.

We both stood perfectly still, breathing shallowly so we could concentrate on the quiet sounds up ahead. Footsteps, slow and steady, pausing now and again as though someone wasn't too sure where he was. Or where he was going. And always there was the smell, that bad smell, filling my head. Penny stirred at my side and put her mouth next to my ear again.

'I can't hear any footsteps, but I am quite definitely hearing small and nasty scurrying sounds behind me. We had better start moving soon, because if something furry runs over my foot I am going to make the kind of noise that will rattle around inside your head for days.'

'It's probably more frightened of you than you are of it,' I said.

'Daddy used to say that to me when I was small,' said Penny. 'But even then I had enough common sense to know complete and utter bullshit when I heard it. You're really not bothered by things like this, are you? You're the only man I ever met who didn't freak out at a spider in the bath.'

'Such things don't bother me,' I said.

I didn't say, 'Because I get glimpses of much worse things in my dreams – in brief glimpses of my old life.'

'Whoever this is, he's directly ahead of us,' I said. 'Definitely just the one person.'

'Then let's go grab him,' said Penny. 'I'm far less scared of confronting a murderer than I am of some great lumpy mutant rat. Are you ready, space boy?'

'Ready, spy girl,' I said.

I charged forward down the narrow corridor, not even trying to hide I was coming. Penny pounded along behind me. A dark figure emerged from an opening in one of the walls up ahead and ran for it. I chased after him, unable to make out more than just a dim shadowy figure that might have been anyone. I could have caught him easily enough, but I didn't want to run on and leave Penny behind on her own. So I just chased the man through tunnel after tunnel, sticking on his tail, following the sound of his feet when I lost sight of him. Until he stopped suddenly, and screamed. A harsh, lost, despairing sound.

The bad smell was very close now, and it was exactly what I'd thought it would be.

I rounded a corner, and stopped before an opening in the tunnel wall. Just a dark hole, where the smell was coming from. Dark enough to hide anything. I went in, and found myself in a small stone chamber. My eyes adjusted to the gloom almost immediately, and I saw why the man ahead of me had screamed. The room might have started out as a priest hole, but now someone was using it to dump bodies.

*   *   *

Penny caught up with me, breathing hard, and stepped into the room with me. I heard her shocked gasp, but I didn't look away. There was no light bulb in the room, only what dim illumination spilled in from the tunnel. Which was just as well. The scene was hard enough to look at, as it was.

The dark stone walls and filthy stone floor were splashed with blood. Some of it still drying. There were long bloody scuff marks, where the bodies had been dragged across the floor. This was a murderer's place, steeped in horror and the terrible weight of desires indulged. A storage room for victims. And yet not just a holding room, but somewhere the murderer could come to gloat and savour what he had done. Death hung heavily on the air, a presence in itself.

Baxter sat propped up against the opposite wall, his head hanging down over the bloody wound in his chest. His eyes stared helplessly back at me, as though trying to understand how he could have ended up in such a terrible place. Redd's headless corpse sat next to him, only recognizable by his bloodstained jacket. The two of them sat almost companionably close together. Not separated, even in death.

The headless body of Alice Hayley was sitting propped up against the left-hand wall, her smart suit soaked in gore. And sitting facing her, against the right-hand wall, Parker. Indisputably dead, with the single bloodstain high up on his chest. His eyes drooping and his mouth hanging open. He seemed such a small broken thing, too insignificant to have been the cause of so much blood and horror.

His being unkillable was just another story, after all.

There were beetles moving back and forth on the floor, and around the bodies. Along with clear signs that rats had been here too, gnawing at the bodies. Our arrival had scared them off, but they would be back.

Doyle was kneeling before Hayley's headless body. He was the one we'd been chasing through the tunnels. He was still breathing hard, though mostly from harsh emotions now. He knelt before the dead body of the woman who had changed his life for good and bad, but he wasn't crying. And when I stepped cautiously forward, he didn't look round. Penny moved with me, holding my arm tightly; as much to comfort herself as me.

'Dear God!' she murmured. 'Are you sure we're not dealing with a monster after all, Ishmael?'

'Men can be monsters,' I said. 'This is how the killer made the bodies disappear. This is why I couldn't detect any trace of them.'

'So it was him?' said Penny. 'It was Doyle?'

'Of course not,' I said. 'Look at him. Look at what finding this place has done to him.'

I moved across to stand before Parker's body, and placed two fingertips against the side of his neck.

'Judging by body temperature, he's been dead for some time,' I said, taking my hand away. 'So there's no way he could ever have been walking around the Lodge. He was murdered, and he stayed murdered.'

'Are you sure?' said Penny.

I prodded Parker's chest with one finger, and the body rocked stiffly back and forth for a moment.

'Pretty sure,' I said.

Penny looked at the headless bodies, her mouth a tight grimace of shock and outrage.

'Whoever did this . . . must have been soaked in blood. We'd have noticed.'

'Unless they were wearing protective clothing,' I said. I gestured at a discarded coat and heavy gloves, soaked in dried blood, piled up in a corner. There was a long knife too, caked with blood from hilt to tip.

'What kind of man could do this?' said Penny.

'A very determined one,' I said.

I moved over to Doyle and he stood up to face me. His eyes were dry, and his gaze was steady. He was back in control again. What he'd found in this room had forced shock and grief aside.

'Who did this?' he said. His voice was full of cold focused anger.

'Come outside into the tunnel and the light,' I said. 'This isn't a place for people to talk.'

He nodded briefly and shot Hayley's headless body one last look as though saying goodbye, before allowing me to lead him out of the room full of death. Penny was already outside in the corridor, one hand clapped over her mouth and nose so she could breathe through her fingers. Doyle met my gaze squarely. Ready to demand answers, if necessary.

'Who did this?'

'You don't think it was me?' I said.

'Of course not,' said Doyle. 'Now I'm thinking straight, I know it couldn't have been you. Sorry about the needle.'

'Sorry about the kick,' said Penny.

Doyle didn't even look at her.

'How did you end up here?' I said.

'I thought I'd better leave, after the sedative didn't work,' said Doyle. 'And before Miss Belcourt did something even worse to me. Once I was off on my own and thinking clearly again, Martin's voice came to me. He said he'd found a secret opening in one of the walls, and asked me to check it out.' He smiled briefly, humourlessly. 'I got lost and ended up here. Almost as though something, or someone, called me here . . . Do you know who's responsible for all of this?'

'Yes,' I said.

'You've finally got it all worked out, haven't you?' said Penny.

'Most of it,' I said. 'I've been putting the pieces together for a while now. But it's all rather obvious, when you think about it. The computers showed evidence of ghosts in Ringstone Lodge even though I never saw any. The computers showed Parker walking around even though he clearly wasn't. The computer screens kept breaking down every time they might have proved useful. And the computers said Martin never left his security centre. But who was in charge of the computers?'

'Martin!' said Penny. 'It was him!'

'Right from the beginning,' I said. 'He manufactured all those ghostly images, and used them to distract us. You heard him speak to us through the hidden microphones; it was just as easy for him to broadcast spooky sounds as well, such as footsteps and knockings. Which is why I never felt any physical vibrations accompanying them. They were all just distractions. To occupy our minds and keep us from thinking about the one thing that really mattered: how could Parker have been killed inside a cell that was never unlocked. Well, who said it hadn't been unlocked? The computers. Because that's what Martin told them to say. And it was Martin who unlocked the cell and went in to talk with Parker, who had no reason to fear a simple young techie.'

'The cameras only shut down because he shut them down!' said Penny. 'There's never been anything wrong with the systems!'

'When we thought he was safely locked up in the security centre, he was using the hidden tunnels to run around killing people,' I said. 'Then to hide the bodies. And because his victims never saw Martin as a threat, none of them ever defended themselves. Until it was too late.'

'What made you suspect him?' said Doyle.

'Parker's disappearance on the stairs. That was the clincher. It was just too much to accept. Martin said he saw Parker on his screens and sent me chasing back and forth after him. But I never saw Parker once. His disappearance, between the top and bottom of the stairs, was simply impossible.'

'I said that!' said Penny.

'So you did,' I said. 'And it started me thinking. If you ruled out the supernatural explanation, what did that leave?'

'Martin was lying to you . . .' said Penny.

'Exactly,' I said. 'If he was lying about that, what else might he be lying about?'

'And we trusted him to protect us,' said Penny. 'The little rat-shit!'

'I'll have his balls,' said Doyle. 'But why has he been doing all this?'

'I think I know,' I said. 'But I need to ask him a few questions to be certain.'

'Then let's go talk to the man,' said Doyle.

'Talk?' said Penny.

'Talk first,' said Doyle.

EIGHT
A Good Judge of Character

'First things first,' said Penny. 'How are we going to get out of these tunnels? We've twisted and turned so much I haven't a clue where I am inside the Lodge. Never mind how far we've come from the entrance.'

'We're not actually inside the Lodge any more,' I said. 'We're underneath it. There's no way you could fit all these tunnels and rooms inside the infrastructure of the house, hollow walls or not. When we climbed down that stone chimney, it took us down past the house and into a maze of connecting passageways carved out underneath.'

'I wonder which came first,' said Penny, 'the maze or the Lodge. Did someone create the tunnels first, for some reason, and then build a house over them to conceal them? Or did they start with the Lodge and excavate the cellars later, when they had a need for them?'

'Why are you looking to me for an answer?' I said. 'I read the same family history you did, and there was nothing in there about any of this.'

'I was just wondering!' said Penny.

'Right now,' I said, 'All we have to do is find another chimney to take us back up. Wherever it comes out, there's bound to be an exit nearby.'

'You have to love his optimism,' Penny said to Doyle. 'It's either that or scream a lot and tear your hair out.'

'It's like we're in the dark subconscious of the house,' said Doyle. 'Where all the really bad thoughts take place.'

'You can overthink these things,' I said. 'Follow me.'

I was sure I remembered passing a chimney earlier, and it didn't take me long to find it again. Just a ragged hole in the stone ceiling that became a dark and narrow shaft with more of the steel hoops hammered into the wall to serve as a ladder.

I had to boost Penny and Doyle up into the chimney, then jump up after them.

There were no electric lights anywhere in the chimney. The stone channel was claustrophobically tight, growing steadily darker the higher we climbed. The air was close and foul, and so thick with dust we were all coughing harshly. The steel hoops jerked unsteadily under my hands, and rocked under my feet as though they might tear themselves out of the old stone at any moment. I put my faith in a rapid ascent, and urged the others on with loud encouragement and harsh words.

We soon left the tunnel's light behind, and the dark of the chimney closed in around us. Trapped, confined, and almost suffocating on the rotten air, with no bearings left except up and down and no idea how far we'd climbed or how much further there was to go. At least there was a gleam of light at the top of the chimney, giving us something to head for.

Doyle suddenly panicked and froze in place. I hit his shoes with my head as I came up after him, and he almost screamed.

'I can't do this!' he said shrilly. 'The rungs are coming loose, I can feel it. If I keep climbing, I'll fall. I know it! We have to go back down!'

'We can't,' I said. 'Our only way out is to go up.'

'Come on, Doctor Doyle,' Penny called down. 'It can't be much further.'

'I'm not moving!' said Doyle. 'It's not safe!'

I looked up, but I could barely make him out. Just a darker patch in the general gloom. There was no way past him.

'You can do it,' I said. 'And you're going to start right now, because if you don't . . . I'm right beneath you and I will do something to your undercarriage that will make Penny's kick feel like a fond memory. So move!'

Doyle started climbing again. I stuck close behind him, making lots of noise as I climbed the steel rungs so he knew how close I was.

Not long after, I heard Penny cry out happily as she reached the top of the shaft. She hauled herself up and out. Doyle climbed out after her, and I hurried up after them. They helped pull me out, into a dimly lit stone tunnel. The relatively clear air was a relief after the foul atmosphere of the chimney, and we all took some time to cough and hack until our throats were clear again. Doyle looked at me reproachfully.

'There was no need for threats like that.'

'Yes there was,' I said. 'You'll thank me later.'

'I really doubt it,' said Doyle.

A concealed door in the wall opposite was easy enough to spot now I knew what I was looking for. I forced it open, and we stumbled out into the warm and comforting light of the entrance hall. We all breathed deeply, glad of some fresh air and a chance to shake the oppression of the tunnels out of our heads. It felt good to be out in a wide open space again.

We'd emerged halfway between the stairs and the security centre. There was no one else about. It was all very still and very quiet. As though someone was watching us, and waiting to see what we would do.

'I knew there had to be a door somewhere around here,' I said. 'So Martin could get to it easily from the centre.'

'I want to see Martin,' said Doyle. 'I have things to say to him.'

'I'm sure you do,' I said. 'But not yet. First, I need you to go upstairs and fetch MacKay. He's having a nice lie-down in my room, right at the end of the corridor. You'll need this to open the door.'

I fumbled in my pocket for MacKay's master key and handed it to Doyle. He looked dubiously at the plastic key card.

'You're sending me off on my own?'

'There's no one left in the house to threaten you,' I said. 'You'll be fine.'

'What do we need MacKay for?'

'Getting in to see Martin won't be easy,' I said. 'He's bound to have sealed himself inside the centre and disabled all the usual measures that would let us override the locks from outside. Hopefully MacKay will know how to get around that. So, off you go and wake him up. He might be sleeping a bit deeply, so don't be afraid to give him a good shake. Though you might want to step back quickly afterwards.'

Doyle nodded stiffly, started towards the stairs, and then stopped abruptly.

'I think . . . you'd better come and take a look at this.'

Something in his voice had me moving immediately, with Penny right there beside me. We joined Doyle at the foot of the stairs, and I saw immediately what had stopped him. The two severed heads were gone. Nothing left but bloody stains on the bottom step to show where Redd and Hayley's heads had rested. I quickly looked around the entrance hall, but there was no sign of them anywhere.

'He's taken them,' said Doyle. 'Why would he do that?'

'He's still playing tricks,' I said. 'Trying to scare us. He doesn't know what we know about him now.'

'You're sure this is all down to Martin?' Penny said quietly. 'There couldn't be . . . something else going on in the Lodge?'

'You saw the chamber down below,' I said. 'And what was in it. That's horror enough for any house. Doctor Doyle, go upstairs and wake MacKay. Penny and I will deal with this.'

'Don't kill Martin until I get back,' said Doyle. 'I want to be there when he dies. I need to see it happen.'

He set off up the stairs, not looking back. I watched until he was almost at the top and well out of earshot before I turned to Penny.

'He's changed.'

'He's been through a lot,' said Penny. 'Do we really need MacKay?'

'Maybe,' I said. 'But I don't think Doyle is in the right frame of mind to confront Martin. He might just kill him out of hand. Which is understandable, but not necessarily in everyone's best interests. By the time Doyle's got MacKay up on his feet and taking an interest again and got him back down here, hopefully the good doctor will have calmed down a little.'

'Would you be calm if Martin had killed me?' said Penny.

'No,' I said. 'But I wouldn't kill him. Not while there were still things I needed from him. I've learned self-control the hard way.'

'Would Martin's death really be such a bad thing?' said Penny. 'After everything he's done? After what we saw in that room?'

'We need information from him,' I said patiently. 'In particular, whatever Parker might have shared with him concerning traitors inside the Organization. I'd hate to think all those secrets were lost. And anyway, we're in the spy game, Penny, not the assassination game.'

'You've killed people,' said Penny. Not accusing, just making a point.

'It's not good to kill people just because we think they need killing,' I said. 'That's a hard road to start down. It leads to men like Parker. It's easy to find reasons to kill people, but the more often you do it the easier it becomes to find reasons to let you do what you want to do. It should never be easy to kill people.'

'This is experience talking, isn't it?' said Penny.

'I've had a lot of experience,' I said.

As we approached the security centre, I wasn't surprised to see the heavy steel door was closed. No welcome for us this time. I knocked on the door politely, but it stayed shut. I looked it over carefully.

'He must know we're out here,' said Penny.

'He always knows where we are,' I said. 'The cameras never shut down. He just said they did.'

'But he doesn't know what just happened down in the tunnels?'

'I don't see how,' I said. 'He didn't install the surveillance equipment in the Lodge, just made use of it. And since no one up here knew about the tunnels down there . . .'

'Someone must have put the lights in,' said Penny.

'Good point,' I said. I raised my voice and addressed the door. 'Martin! Let us in, please. We need to talk.'

'You honestly think that's going to work?' said Penny.

'I have to try,' I said. 'I really don't want this to end in violence. There's been too much already.'

'You can get reasonable at the strangest times, Ishmael,' said Penny. 'What about MacKay's master key? Would that get us in?'

'I doubt it,' I said. 'That's one of the first things Martin would have protected himself against. Which is why I gave the key to Doyle.'

'So what do we do?' said Penny. 'Wait for Doyle to bring MacKay down, and hope he's got some ideas?'

'I've done enough waiting,' I said. 'Stand back. I'm going to smash the lock's keypad and see if I can do something inventive with the wiring . . .'

'That won't work!' said Martin's voice. It seemed to come from somewhere overhead, rather than the other side of the door. 'I've isolated the door from the lock mechanisms. I'm the only one who can open it now. You can't get in, and I'm not coming out. I don't trust any of you. I'm staying right here, where I'm safe. How safe do you feel?'

And from behind us came the sound of heavy footsteps, approaching slowly and steadily across the entrance hall. When I turned to look, there was no one there. The hall was completely empty. The footsteps were slow and menacing, and coming straight for us. Penny glared about her.

'This is really starting to get on my nerves!'

'It's just Martin,' I said.

'I know!' said Penny. 'But are you sure, Ishmael? It does sound very convincing . . .'

'Sound is all it is,' I said. 'I'm not feeling any vibrations through the wooden floor, none of the physical side effects that should accompany impacts that heavy.'

I concentrated, listening carefully. Penny stood beside me, her hands clenched into fists. I turned my head back and forth, searching for the source of the sounds. Until finally my gaze fell on a vase of flowers standing on a side table. I strode over to it, pulled the flowers out of the vase and threw them aside, then smashed the vase to reveal the tiny speaker hidden inside. I held it up to show Penny and then closed my hand around it. And just like that, the footsteps now sounded muffled. I crushed the tech in my hand, and the sounds cut off. I opened my hand and let the tiny fragments fall away.

'Son of a bitch!' said Penny.

More footsteps started up, from another part of the hall. And then more, coming down the stairs. More and more footsteps, advancing on us from all sides at once until it sounded like an invisible army was tramping through the hall. And then they all stopped at the same moment, replaced by mocking laughter from Martin.

'Fooled you . . .'

'Not really,' I said.

I marched back to the security centre and considered the closed door. Penny looked at me expectantly.

'Could you smash it in?'

'Almost certainly not,' I said. 'It's too big and too heavy. If you drove a truck straight at it, you'd probably just write off the truck. This kind of door was designed to keep things out, to protect the sensitive information stored inside. Some heavy-duty explosives might do the job . . .'

'Have you got any?' said Penny.

'No,' I said. 'I'm not that sort of spy.'

'So how are we going to get in?' said Penny.

'Easy,' I said. 'I'll talk Martin into opening the door for us.'

Penny raised an elegant eyebrow. 'You really think you can get him to do that?'

'Of course,' I said. 'I am an excellent judge of character.'

'Best of luck,' said Penny. 'Maybe I should go see if there's a crowbar in the kitchen.'

I raised my voice again. 'Martin? You need to open this door.'

'Pretty sure I don't,' said Martin.

'But you do,' I said. 'Because I know something you don't. Something you need to know.'

'I really doubt that,' said Martin. 'From in here, I see all and hear all.'

'Then you know we found the sliding panel on the upper floor,' I said. 'And you know we went inside. But you don't know where we went or what we saw, and what we found.'

'What makes you think I care?' said Martin.

'Because you're the murderer, Martin,' I said. 'I know how you killed your victims, using the hidden tunnels to get around unnoticed. I've been inside the room where you dumped the bodies. I even know why you did it. And I've worked out the one thing you've forgotten. Which will mean all your hard work has been be for nothing. Can you really risk not knowing that?'

There was a long pause.

'All right,' said Martin. 'Let's talk about this.'

The door swung slowly open.

'You're damn good!' said Penny.

I gave her my best 'Told you so!' look, and we went inside.

Martin was sitting on his swivel chair, his keyboard on his lap, surrounded by brightly glowing monitor screens, all of them working perfectly. He had a gun in his hand, trained on Penny and me. We came to a halt a respectful distance short of him. Martin smiled and aimed the gun squarely at Penny.

'I saw how quick you were, Ishmael, when you jumped MacKay and took his gun. Very impressive. I'm still not sure how you did that. But while you'd undoubtedly be ready to risk your own life to take this gun away from me, like the good little secret agent you are . . . I don't think you're as ready to risk Penny's life. Because if you even look like making a move I don't like, I will shoot her.'

'You little shit!' said Penny. 'What did you do with the heads?'

'Oh, they're around somewhere,' said Martin, still smiling. 'Now hush. Grown-ups talking.'

'Stand very still, Penny,' I said. 'Don't move an inch from where you are.'

'Not a problem,' she said.

'Now, Penny,' said Martin. 'I know you've got MacKay's gun. I saw you stick it in the back of your belt. So take it out, slowly and carefully, and drop it on the floor.'

Penny reached back behind her, took out the gun, and let it fall. I flinched, just a little. Guns can go off when you drop them, but it seemed Penny had taken the time to engage the safety.

'Very good,' said Martin. 'Now kick it out of reach.'

Penny did so, not taking her eyes off Martin or his gun for a moment.

'Where did you get your gun, Martin?' I said.

'I took it off Redd's body,' Martin said casually. 'I already had the gun that I'd taken off Baxter, but I decided I preferred this one. It's bigger. Now let's talk about what you know, or think you know, Mister Big-time Secret Agent. Starting with how was I able to kill Parker without his cell ever being opened.'

'That was one of the first things I worked out,' I said steadily. 'You opened Parker's cell from here, then fixed the computer records afterwards to make it look as if the cell had never been unlocked.'

'Very good!' said Martin. 'Haven't I been a clever boy?'

'Then all you had to do was check your screens to make sure the way was clear and you could go down to talk to Parker. You knew he wouldn't be alarmed because, using your speakers, you had told him you were on your way.'

'You are good,' said Martin. 'But is this the information you thought I needed to know? Because I really don't . . . In fact, I'll feel a lot safer when both of you are dead. So stand very still, please. I'd hate to miss you and hit something important.'

'Are you sure you want to do this?' Penny said quickly. 'With help on the way? They could be here any time now.'

'But there aren't going to be any reinforcements, are there?' I said to Martin. 'Because no emergency call ever went out.'

'Very good again!' said Martin. 'The call for help and support is supposed to go out automatically, but I had no trouble countermanding it. And then amending the records to make it look like it had gone out, and been received and acknowledged. Not that anyone ever checked. Because everyone trusts the techie. Everyone believes everything he tells them. If he says the computers have done something or the systems have gone down, they just accept it. Because he understands these things and they don't. They never really think about what the man behind the curtain might really be up to.

'I'll contact Headquarters once you're all dead. And when the reinforcements finally get here they'll find me securely locked in the security centre, with computer records to confirm I never left and that all of the cameras have been down for some time. I'll be ever so upset when they tell me everyone else has been murdered, by some mysterious opposition agent who got in and out through the unguarded lounge window.'

While he was still talking, smiling, and showing off, I aimed carefully and lashed out with my elbow to exactly where Penny was standing. Driving my elbow into her side, under her ribs, so as not to damage her. She fell over backwards, and I jumped Martin. He pulled the trigger a moment after I moved, but it was already too late. The bullet shot through the air where Penny had been standing, but she was already sprawling on the floor. Martin tried to turn the gun on me, but I just snatched it out of his hand, stepped back, and turned it on him.

Martin stared at me in shock, then his mouth went all wobbly, like a child who's just had a treat taken away from him. I kept the gun trained on him as I heard Penny scramble back on to her feet behind me.

'Are you all right, Penny?'

'Yes,' she said, just a bit breathlessly. 'You might have given me a little warning, darling.'

'That might have given the game away,' I said.

Penny hunted around until she found the gun she'd dropped, and then she moved in beside me and aimed it at Martin. He sat slumped in his chair, scowling sullenly.

'You're not human!' he said to me. 'Nothing human could move that fast. What are you?'

'A trained field agent for the Organization,' I said.

Martin smiled suddenly. 'So was Parker, and it didn't save him. Not from someone who really wanted him dead.'

'He trusted you,' I said. 'I won't make that mistake. How did you find out about the secret tunnels, when even MacKay didn't know about them?'

'I spent a lot of time in the library here,' said Martin, 'because there wasn't much else to do. I found this other history of Ringstone Lodge, which did mention the tunnels and the hidden entrances. I took the book, so no one else would find out, and used it to open the sliding panel on the top floor. And then I went exploring. Just for the fun of it. Of course, later on tunnels and hidden entrances made life so much easier for me.'

'When you started murdering people!' said Penny. 'Are you sure we can't just shoot him, Ishmael?'

'Do you want to?'

'Yes. I really do.'

'That's why we can't,' I said.

'Well said, Mr Jones,' said MacKay.

He marched in through the open door, with Doyle right behind him. I'd heard the two of them approaching across the entrance hall for some time, but I needed to give all my attention to Martin. I risked a quick glance back. MacKay had an ugly bruise on his jaw, but he wasn't interested in me. He was staring at Martin as if he'd never seen him before. Doyle stood beside him, his gaze a very cold thing. There was only just enough room in the confined space for the two of them to crowd in beside Penny and me, so we could all glare at Martin. He snarled back at us, not looking even a little bit cowed or guilty.

'You lied to me, Mr Martin,' said MacKay. 'Over and over, you lied to me. You even persuaded me Mr Jones had to be the murderer. Why? Why did you do all this?'

Martin refused to answer, so I answered for him.

'Because Frank Parker was his father,' I said. 'When I first talked with Parker in his cell, he told me he left the country because he was forced to choose between his job and a woman he'd got pregnant. That was why he left the Organization – because they'd made him choose. But then he got old and decided he wanted to come home. To be with the family he'd never had, the only thing in his life he regretted. And when Martin told me he never knew his father, it seemed a bit of a coincidence. Even then.'

'You're so clever,' said Martin. 'But you don't understand everything. I knew that the infamous Frank Parker was my father. Mother told me when she started getting ill. She'd never approved of my being in this business, but would never say why. Once I knew the truth, it all became clear. I never made any attempt to contact Parker . . . He'd left us, and as long as he was gone and couldn't hurt my mother any more I didn't care. But when I was told he was coming here it was like a sign. A chance at last to make him pay for what he did. To her, and to me.'

'But why, man?' said MacKay. 'Why did you want to murder your own father?'

'Because he went away and left us,' said Martin. 'I had to

grow up without a father, and my mother had to work herself
to death to support us. All so he could run around the world
playing secret agent!'

'He came back for you,' I said.

'Too little, too late,' said Martin. 'My mother died still
waiting for him to come back to her.'

'Did it never occur to you,' I said, 'that he left in order to
protect you? No one knew your names, he made sure of that.
If he had stayed, word could have got out and his enemies
might have come after you, in order to get to him.'

'I did think that, for a while,' said Martin. 'I made myself
believe it, because cold comfort is better than none. But once
I had access to the computers here, I was able to get into his
files. And that's when I found out what a cold self-centred
bastard Frank Parker had always been. Oh, he tried to convince
me otherwise when we talked in his cell, but I knew better. I
stabbed him in the heart while he was still lying to me. He
looked so surprised . . .'

'He gave up so much, risked so much, to come home,' said
MacKay, 'and you killed him.'

Martin looked at me craftily. 'He did tell me things down
in the cell. The names of all the traitors inside the Organization,
and many other important things. Because he wanted to impress
me. I've got the whole conversation recorded, and protected
by my very best encryptions. If the Organization wants what's
on that recording, they're going to have to make a deal with
me. I want money and freedom from all charges . . . And a
whole bunch of other things I'll come up with later. My father's
information is going to buy me the kind of life I should have
had. You can all look as disapproving as you want! You can't
touch me, any of you.'

'Wrong,' said Doyle. Something in his voice made us all
turn to look at him. His smile was grim, and his eyes were
fierce. 'You forget who I am, and why I'm here. I will get
the information out of you one way or another, Mr Martin. I
am, after all, a professional interrogator and very highly
motivated . . .'

For the first time, Martin seemed shaken. He looked at all
of us, and found no comfort there.

'You'd let him do it, wouldn't you?' he said. 'You'd let him torture me!'

'Murderers don't get to take the moral high ground,' I said.

MacKay shook his head slowly. When he spoke, he sounded heartbroken. 'It never even occurred to me that you might be the killer. How could you, boy? Not just your own father, but all the others . . .'

'They were in the way,' said Martin. 'And once I started, there was no going back. Don't look at me like that, MacKay . . . How could I do it, after everything you'd done for me? Is that what you were going to say? Because you were like a father to me? Well, now you know how I feel about fathers.'

'All these deaths,' said Penny. 'Just because one little shit had Daddy issues . . .'

Martin sat up straight in his chair and fixed us all with a hard, confident smile. 'You really should have been paying more attention, people. You should have taken my keyboard away as well as my gun. Because in my hands a keyboard can be even more dangerous. All the time we've been talking I've been quietly entering commands, and now I have complete control over the Lodge's self-destruct system. I've also installed a dead man's switch. If I take my hands from the keyboard, the command goes out and the whole place goes up. Unless you let me walk out of here, I'll take you all with me.'

Penny looked to MacKay. 'Does the Lodge have a self-destruct system?'

'Unfortunately, yes,' said MacKay. 'To ensure that important information and people cannot fall into enemy hands. And it is controlled from here. Mr Martin should not be able to access the self-destruct system, but then he has been able to do a great many things I did not believe him capable of. If he has got past the safeguards and activated the device, he holds all our lives in his hands.'

'You could just let me walk out of here,' said Martin, 'and make my deal with the Organization from a safer location. You don't have to die.'

Penny looked at Doyle. 'You're the shrink. Would he do it?'

'Well . . .' said Doyle.

'No,' I said.

I lunged forward, punched Martin out, and snatched the keyboard from his hands. I broke it in two, just to be on the safe side, and threw the pieces away. Then I looked at the others, staring wide-eyed at me, and smiled.

'I was keeping an eye on him all the time we were in here. I never saw him enter any commands. And he took both his hands off the keyboard more than once without being aware of it. Besides, he wasn't the type to commit suicide. He wanted to live too much.'

'That's it?' said Doyle. 'You risked all our lives on a guess?'

'I'm an excellent judge of character,' I said. 'Mostly.'

Doyle and MacKay moved purposefully towards the unconscious Martin, sitting slumped in his chair. I led Penny out of the security centre.

'Why did it have to be him?' said Penny, after a while. 'I liked him.'

'Being likeable is a great disguise,' I said. 'You'd be amazed what you can get away with if you can just make people like you.'

'At least it's over now,' said Penny. She looked at me. 'It is all over now, isn't it?'

'I think so,' I said. 'MacKay will throw Martin into one of the basement cells, and Doyle will start the process of softening him up. While he's doing that, MacKay will regain control of the computers, reverse the lockdown, and contact Headquarters. Tell them everything that's happened.'

'The people at the top aren't going to be too happy that Frank Parker is dead,' said Penny.

'No. But at least we have Martin's recording of what he said – naming the traitors inside the Organization'

'Assuming there is a recording,' said Penny. 'He might have been lying. He did a lot of that.'

'I had noticed,' I said. 'Let's hope for the best. After so much blood and horror, I'd like to think something good could come out of this mess.'

'At least we saved some people, this time,' said Penny. 'Not like Belcourt Manor. Tell me, what was it you knew that Martin had forgotten?'

'Oh, that,' I said. 'I was lying. I knew he wouldn't be able to stand the idea that he'd forgotten something, that I knew something he didn't. In the end, it helped that Martin was a very bad judge of character.'

EPILOGUE

After Martin had been safely tucked away in the basement, and lockdown had been reversed, Penny and I went outside into the grounds for some fresh air. The sun had come up, and it was morning. Golden sunlight splashed across the lawns like a benediction, birds were singing like it was some great new idea they'd just had, and all seemed well with the world. Penny tucked her arm through mine and leaned in companionably close as we walked. Not going anywhere in particular, just walking. It felt good to be out among living things again, after so long in a house full of death.

'At least this time we have a live murderer to hand over,' said Penny. 'That should please the Colonel.'

'I'm not sure this new Colonel is ever pleased,' I said. 'I have a feeling it may be against his religion. Of course, he may not come out here. This was supposed to be an entirely unofficial case, after all. Officially, Frank Parker was never in this country, never mind in Organization hands. Unless they decide to say otherwise, to put the wind up the opposition. Just because he's dead, doesn't mean he couldn't have said things first.'

'How will they explain all the deaths here?' said Penny.

'No one ever knows the truth about what goes on in places like Ringstone Lodge,' I said.

'If we don't have to wait for the Colonel to turn up,' said Penny, 'could we leave? I'd really like to get away from this place.'

'I don't see why not,' I said. 'MacKay and Doyle can cope without us. And I'm really not too keen on answering any questions the reinforcements might have when they finally show up. I'll get MacKay to drive us back to the station.'

'What if he says he's too busy?'

I grinned. 'Then we'll just steal his car and go anyway.'

'You have the best ideas,' said Penny.

We walked on for a while, enjoying the morning. We rounded the side of the house, and looked out over the rows of tombstones. I wondered whether the recent dead would end up buried among the old graves. It seemed likely.

'It was a complicated case,' said Penny.

'Most of it was just distractions,' I said. 'But we got there in the end.'

'So there never was a supernatural element to the case?' said Penny. 'It was all just Martin, playing his tricks?'

Out of the corner of my eye, I caught a glimpse of a tall slender figure in a long black dress, perched crouching on one particular tombstone like a great dark gore-crow. But of course when I turned my head to look at her directly, there was nothing there. Just a trick of the light, or my imagination at work.

'No,' I said. 'Nothing supernatural at all.'